# Praise for Daryl Wood Gerber's Cookbook Nook Mysteries

"There's a feisty new amateur sleuth in town and her name is Jenna Hart. With a bodacious cast of characters, a wrenching murder, and a collection of cookbooks to die for, Daryl Wood Gerber's *Final Sentence* is a page-turning puzzler of a mystery that I could not put down."

—Jenn McKinlay, *New York Times* bestselling author of the Cupcake Mysteries and Library Lovers Mysteries

"In *Final Sentence*, the author smartly blends crime, recipes, and an array of cookbooks that all should covet in a witty, well-plotted whodunit."

—Kate Carlisle, *New York Times* bestselling author of the Bibliophile Mysteries

"Readers will relish the extensive cookbook suggestions, the cooking primer, and the whole foodie phenomenon. Gerber's perky tone with a multigenerational cast makes this series a good match for Lorna Barrett's Booktown Mystery series . . ."

—*Library Journal*

"So pull out your cowboy boots and settle in for a delightful read. *Grilling the Subject* is a delicious new mystery that will leave you hungry for more."

—Carstairs Considers Blog

D0879297

# Books by Daryl Wood Gerber

## The Cookbook Nook Mysteries

*Final Sentence*
*Inherit the Word*
*Stirring the Plot*
*Fudging the Books*
*Grilling the Subject*
*Pressing the Issue*

## The French Bistro Mysteries

*A Deadly Éclair*
*A Soufflé of Suspicion (coming soon!)*

## Writing as Avery Aames

*The Long Quiche Goodbye*
*Lost and Fondue*
*Clobbered by Camembert*
*To Brie or not To Brie*
*Days of Wine and Roquefort*
*As Gouda as Dead*
*For Cheddar or Worse*

## Stand-alone Suspense

*Girl on the Run*
*Day of Secrets*

# PRESSING THE ISSUE

## A Cookbook Nook Mystery

Daryl Wood Gerber

BEYOND THE PAGE
PUBLISHING

Pressing the Issue
Daryl Wood Gerber
Copyright © 2018 by Daryl Wood Gerber.

Beyond the Page Books
are published by
Beyond the Page Publishing
www.beyondthepagepub.com

ISBN: 978-1-946069-52-8

All rights reserved under International and Pan-American Copyright Conventions. By payment of required fees, you have been granted the non-exclusive, non-transferable right to access and read the text of this book. No part of this text may be reproduced, transmitted, downloaded, decompiled, reverse engineered, or stored in or introduced into any information storage and retrieval system, in any form or by any means, whether electronic or mechanical, now known or hereinafter invented without the express written permission of both the copyright holder and the publisher.

This is a work of fiction. Names, characters, places, and incidents either are the product of the author's imagination or are used fictitiously, and any resemblance to actual persons, living or dead, business establishments, events or locales is entirely coincidental. The publisher does not have any control over and does not assume any responsibility for author or third-party websites or their content.

The scanning, uploading, and distribution of this book via the Internet or via any other means without the permission of the publisher is illegal and punishable by law. Your support of the author's rights is appreciated.

# Acknowledgments

"One of the things I teach my children is that I have always invested in myself, and I have never stopped learning, never stopped growing."
~ Chesley Sullenberger, Aviator

Thank you to my family and friends for all your support. Thank you to my talented author friends, Krista Davis and Hannah Dennison, for your words of wisdom and calm. Thanks to my brainstormers at Plothatchers: Krista Davis, Janet Bolin (Ginger Bolton), Kaye George, Marilyn Levinson (Allison Brook), Peg Cochran, and Janet Koch (Laura Alden). It's hard to keep all the aliases straight, but you are wonderful friends with a wealth of talent and a font of terrific ideas! I adore you. Thanks to my blog mates on Mystery Lovers Kitchen: Cleo Coyle, Krista Davis, Leslie Budewitz, Mary Jane Maffini (Victoria Abbott), Roberta Isleib (Lucy Burdette), Peg Cochran, Linda Wiken (Erika Chase), Sheila Connolly, and Denise Swanson. Eight years and counting. Love you all! Thank you to my Delicious Mysteries and Cake and Dagger group mates: Roberta Isleib, Amanda Flower, Krista Davis, Jenn McKinlay, and Julie Hyzy. PR is not easy. You have made it much more fun!

Thanks to those who have helped make this sixth book in the *Cookbook Nook Mystery* series a reality. To Bill Harris and Beyond the Page for your insight and expertise. (My fans were really getting after me to publish a new title.) To my agent, John Talbot, for believing in every aspect of my work. To Sheridan Stancliff, an Internet wizard and creative marvel. To my sister Kimberley Greene for your endless support.

Thank you librarians, teachers, and readers for sharing the delicious world of a cookbook nook owner in a fictional coastal town in California with your friends. There is no better PR than word of mouth!

And last but not least, thanks to my cookbook shop consultant and former cookbook store owner, Christine Myskowski. I will never forget that first moment I walked into Salt and Pepper and felt like I was *home*. Please, if you see this note, reach out and tell me how you are doing. I hate losing touch. I hold you in my heart.

To all my sweet boys:
Eliijah, Miles, Chase, Desmond, Tyler, Beau, Kayden, and Sparky.
You are my light.
Thank you for making me smile every day
and for keeping me on my toes!

# Chapter 1

"Bailey Bird, stand still for a minute!" I said. Honestly, my best friend could drive me nuts when she was in a state, and today, on our one day off, she was in a state *beyond* a state. She was huffing and puffing while pacing between bookshelves at the Cookbook Nook. Her short hair was a mess, her flouncy white blouse askew. She hates to be *askew*.

Our current project was not causing her distress. It wasn't requiring any heavy lifting, just extra hours. We had both agreed to come in at seven a.m. to get a jump on it. We wanted the window display honoring the Crystal Cove Renaissance Fair, which officially kicked off tonight, to be perfect. When we were done, we would eat lunch. Afterward, we would primp for the evening's revelry.

I followed her to the sales counter. "Talk to me."

Bailey spun around, hands on hips, and exhaled hard enough to make her bangs fly up. "I'm worried, Jenna. Worried with a capital W."

Watch out. Whenever she spouts capital letters, she is ready to have a meltdown. A cute meltdown, but a meltdown nonetheless.

"About the display? Don't be. It's going to be great. With the muted colors, it goes nicely with our beach-themed color scheme." I'll never forget the first day I walked into the shop. It hadn't been open to the public since the 1980s, back when it was a used bookstore. The walls were a funky color and were the first things we painted. "We've already set out the marionettes and the backdrop of a forest, the beer stein tapestry, the shaft of wheat, and the bow and arrow." Researching the Renaissance Fair websites for inspiration had been a joy. "I still have a box of Celtic jewelry to unpack. After that, all we have left to do is position the cookbooks and the Renaissance-themed adult coloring books, and—"

Bailey leveled a searing glare at me.

"The chaotic display isn't what's bothering you?" I asked.

She shook her head.

"Then what is it? The sun is shining. The temperature is a perfect seventy degrees." April is always a good month weather-wise in Crystal Cove. I aimed a finger at my pal. "I know what you need . . . music." I slipped into the storage room and switched on a queue of medieval-style music that started with "Maids When You're Young" to lighten the mood. I reemerged and moved to the main display table to arrange copies of *The Medieval Kitchen: A Social History with Recipes.* I had plenty more unique books to add, with long exotic titles on a variety of topics, that I would sprinkle throughout the store. I hoped fairgoers would come and browse. Ours was the sole bookstore in town, let alone at the fair. "Are you concerned about your wedding plans?"

"Why would you say that? What have you heard?" Bailey's voice skated up an octave. "Should I be —"

"No, you should not." I gripped her arm. Being a whole head taller and a ton stronger, I held sway. "I haven't heard anything. I was worried that Tito —"

"What about Tito?" Bailey wriggled out of my grasp.

Bailey and her beloved Tito Martinez, a reporter for the *Crystal Cove Crier*, are getting married two weeks from now at Baldini Vineyards, a beautiful spread in the hills that boasts an incredible view of the Pacific Ocean. Bailey had her heart set on saying *I do* at a vineyard, and when the one she had secured slipped up — CC Vineyards had double-booked and had no other dates available for two years — I contacted Nick Baldini, who is a regular customer of ours and the main person responsible for putting on the annual Crystal Cove Renaissance Fair. Baldini Vineyards doesn't do a lot of weddings, but when it does, the event is top-notch. For Bailey's gig, Nick had engaged the catering services of a local hotshot chef.

I said, "I was worried that Tito might be changing things up, or —"

"It's Mom!" Bailey stomped toward the storage room.

My anxiety kicked up a notch. "What about your mother?" I zipped after her, my flip-flops flapping. I'm a sandals girl unless tennis shoes are required. Occasionally I'll stuff my feet into heels. *Occasionally.* When I'm dressed up. Today, however, I was wearing an aqua spring sweater and matching capris. "Bailey, talk to me! Is she okay? Is it her health?"

"She's as strong as an ox."

"Phew!" I whistled. Long story short, two years after my mom died, my father and Bailey's mother hooked up. They are now engaged. Lola has always been like a second mother to me. I would be devastated to lose her. "So what's the problem?"

"She's got" — Bailey wiggled her hands next to her head — "vibes."

"Vibes as in *V-I-B-E-S*?"

"I can spell it."

"Don't snip. Vibes about what? The wedding? Relax." I fanned the air and shifted to another display table to set the books upright. Presentation is everything at a bookstore. Covers need to be visible and appealing. "It will go off without a hitch." As of Nick's latest update, everything at the vineyard was going swimmingly.

"That's not it."

"Is she miffed that she isn't in charge of the catering?" I asked. Lola owns the Pelican Brief Diner, which is known for its scrumptious seafood. We sell her cookbooks in the shop. "Is she getting vibes that something about the food will go haywire?"

Bailey growled. "No. She's got" — more hand twirling . . . *vibes* — "that something *bad* is going to happen. Heck, she's so crazy, she even has Hershey and me feeling vibes, and we don't feel vibes."

"Um, cats *do* feel them," I said. Hershey is Bailey and Tito's cat. Bailey has never owned a cat before. "Is Hershey acting oddly?"

My rescue ginger cat Tigger mewed from beneath the children's table at the rear of the shop and lifted his chin as if to signal that he was being a model cat. He's not always, especially of late. I waved for him to go back to sleep.

"Whatever." Bailey swatted the air.

"Has your mother been more specific? Does she foresee what bad thing might happen?"

"No, but I'm warning you, the next thing you know she'll claim she has ESP and want to start giving palm readings like your aunt Vera."

"Are you talking about me?" My aunt, who owned the Cookbook Nook as well as Fisherman's Village, the mini-shopping mecca in which the shop is located, pushed through the storage room curtains, her arms filled with an assortment of cookbooks. "Because if you are, I want to be able to defend myself." She headed toward the sales counter, the folds of her shimmery amethyst caftan rustling. My aunt loves wearing caftans and turbans and a phoenix amulet that she swears has saved her life a time or two. She is the reason why I gave up my job as an advertising executive in San Francisco and moved home to Crystal Cove. She lured me with the enticing offer of managing the bookshop and a new life filled with the unexpected. "I have a right to—"

"Holy smoke!" Bailey shouted.

"C'mon, pal, chill."

"No, I mean it. Smoke! Smell it?" Bailey raced toward the breezeway that connected the bookstore to the Nook Café, which my aunt also owns and I oversee.

*Uh-oh.* I detected smoke, too.

"Heavens," my aunt exclaimed. "Is Katie all right?"

Katie, our illustrious chef and one of my best friends, had closed the place for the morning so she could test recipes for the fair. During the next week, the Nook, as many like to refer to it, planned to feature all sorts of medieval foods: hawker's mush, ginger cheesecake, mead, and more. Had something gone amiss?

"I'll check," I said. "Tina!"

Tina Gump, a twenty-year-old we'd hired a few months ago to help her earn enough to go to night school—she was taking culinary classes; she dreamed of becoming a chef like Katie—bolted from the storage room, her arms filled with cookbooks. The yellow play dress with flounce hem that she was wearing, um, *flounced*. Man, she had long legs. "What's wrong?" she asked as, one-handed, she tried to rearrange her dark hair, which was tied into a knot. Strands were sticking out of the knot every which way.

"Smoke! In the café."

"Your aunt and I will make sure everything is fine here. Go!" Tina had been a real find for the store. She was the epitome of calm.

I tore after Bailey. She made it to the all-white and stainless steel kitchen first. I skidded in after her. I didn't see fire, but smoke wafted toward the ceiling. The smell of burnt something saturated the air.

Katie, taller than me and more substantial in a Julia Child way, was stationed at the kitchen exit, working the door to the outside like a gigantic fan. Open, shut, open, shut. What was going on? She never burned anything. Ever.

I rushed to her. Her eyes and nose were red. Tears streaked her usually cheery cheeks. "Are you all right?" Katie, Bailey, and I have been friends for years, although during high school none of us had hung with the same crowd. Bailey was one of the popular girls; I was in the arty clique; Katie was in the foodie group. Amazing how, after a dozen years, all of those labels didn't matter anymore. "Are you hurt?"

"My ego's bruised."

"What happened?"

"I . . . I . . ." She shook her head. Her white toque bobbled to and fro. Her corkscrew curls bounced. "I destroyed the scones."

"You sure did." Bailey donned a pair of oven mitts and grabbed the tray of blackened scones. She is as confident as Katie in the kitchen. Me, not so much. I am a work in progress when it comes to cooking. I'm a foodie, and I adore delicious meals, but whipping up a gourmet meal is a challenge. "They're charred inside and out," Bailey said as she scooted past Katie and darted through the door leading to the alley.

I heard the utility garbage can open, then a flurry of *thuds* — dead scones falling — and the lid clacked shut.

Bailey returned and tossed the mitts on the counter. "What did I miss?"

"Nothing," I said, wondering if this was the *bad* thing her mother had foreseen. If so, no big deal. *Phew.* "Katie, what happened?"

"I lost track of time."

"How is that possible?" I asked. "You are a devout timekeeper."

Katie wears a timer pinned to her chef's coat, and she always sets two or three timers per item so that nothing overcooks.

"From the beginning," I coaxed.

"Keller stopped by." Her boyfriend, Keller, is a charming entrepreneur who pedals around town selling homemade ice cream. "He said he missed me, but then he . . . he . . ." She slurped back a sob and pointed.

Through the prevailing smoke, it was difficult to make out what she was indicating, but then I saw it. A small box sat on the marble pastry counter. It was propped open. Inside was a pretty, single-diamond ring.

"He proposed?" I chirped with glee.

She nodded.

"And you said *yes*?" I asked.

"I was so astounded that I didn't say anything, but I must have done something that made him think I said *yes* because he whooped and kissed me and left. I was so distracted that I—" She gestured to the mess.

Bailey said, "I'm distracted, too. Getting engaged is a big deal. It uses lots of tiny gray cells."

Katie laughed.

I hugged her. "Don't worry. We don't have anyone coming in for a couple of hours. We'll clear the air and neither Bailey nor I will spill the beans. We wouldn't want your reputation of being ultra cool in a crisis to be tarnished." I winked. "As if it could be."

A half hour later, after ridding the kitchen of any telltale odor, Bailey and I returned to the shop.

"Whew, that was something," I said. "Katie never loses it. What if—"

"*Shh.*" Bailey grasped my arm and jutted her chin.

Aunt Vera was seated at the vintage table where we typically set out foodie-themed jigsaw puzzles, but this week's puzzle featured a Renaissance theme with medieval spirit minstrels complete with flying dragons. Very cool and exceedingly difficult. Tigger was roaming beneath the table chasing a spool of ribbon.

Sitting in the chair opposite my aunt was Dolly Ledoux, a forty-year-old blond Louisianan whom some might call Rubenesque. Fifteen years ago she relocated to Crystal Cove and opened Dolly's Duds, a dress shop that featured fun, colorful clothing. Over the past year, however, the shop had morphed into a Renaissance Fair–themed store that she had renamed Thistle Thy Fancy. Never wrong and occasionally loud, Dolly is one of the main reasons the Renaissance Fair has become an annual occurrence. She adores every aspect of the event. Her shop features costumes and garlands and crafts with which to make an assortment of goods for the fair.

My aunt appeared deep in thought. So did Dolly, whose eyes were shut. Deep furrows lined her forehead as she absently ran a finger along the décolletage of her emerald green wench costume.

Quietly, so as not to disturb Dolly's session with my aunt, I picked up the box of Celtic jewelry that was sitting on the checkout counter and tiptoed to the display window.

Bailey gripped a cookbook and followed me. "I love the artwork on this one." She held up a copy of *Seven Centuries of English Cooking: A Collection of Recipes*, an amusing book with clever pen-and-ink drawings and a wealth of recipes. A largish woman in colorful garb graced the cover. "Is it okay to set it out?"

"Sure."

She fanned the pages so the book stood upright. "What were you going to say before?"

"When?"

"Before we spotted your aunt and Dolly, you said *what if*."

"What if" — I set an ornate silver-and-green stone necklace on a white lace handkerchief between the bow and arrow and shaft of wheat — "Katie's mishap was what your mother was picking up on?"

"I don't think so." Bailey tweaked a few other items in the display window. "She didn't mention smoke. She didn't mention fire. She — " My pal shuddered.

"What?"

"She said she had visions of blood."

"Whoa, not good."

Call me nuts, but suddenly I was experiencing vibes like I'd never felt before. I glanced at Dolly, who lived and breathed by vibes. All good Louisianans did, she'd once told me. Her eyes fluttered open. She pulled free of my aunt's grasp and cut a look at me. Her mouth dropped open; her green eyes glistened with fear.

Nope. Definitely not good.

• • •

Around two in the afternoon, Pepper Pritchett entered the shop and sang, "Good morning, Jenna. Happy day off!" Pepper, who was somewhere north of sixty-five and owned Beaders of Paradise, a shop kitty-corner from ours, usually wore drab-colored dresses that were adorned with beads. Today she looked colorful and almost youthful in a long rose pink dress, the hem hovering above a pair of Birkenstock leather sandals. She'd added a cream-colored smock and wore multiple strings of exotic beads. "Mind if I come in?" She didn't wait for an invitation. She never does.

"Please do." I continued to sweep the floor by the children's table. After tussling with the ribbon beneath the vintage table, Tigger had decided that shredding paper every which way from Sunday was a wonderful pastime. Now, he watched the bristles of the broom with rapt attention as I made quick flicking movements to gather up the mess. Whatever was up with him was driving me batty, but I adored him and didn't chastise him.

"Pepper," Bailey said from the sales counter, where she was counting cash, "you're already dressed for the fair."

"Do you like it? I'm a milkmaid." She did a twirl, then faced us while fidgeting with her short gray bangs. "I've been out and about, getting set up for the opening. I bought this at Dolly's shop on Buena Vista." Buena Vista Boulevard is our main drag and runs parallel to the seashore. "Dressing the part is appropriate, even if a day early. There are others, like me, already in the mood." In girlie fashion—highly unusual for Pepper—she gripped the seam of her skirt and swung it to and fro, then she stopped short and held her breath, as if she were ready to crow about something.

I bit back a laugh; so did Bailey. Pepper is pretty readable. Her mouth purses; her nose draws down. She loves lording something over anybody. Not that she is a bad person. She isn't. She simply needs reassurance that her life has *meaning*.

"Got gossip?" Bailey asked.

"It's not gossip." Pepper swept the door closed and bustled to the counter. "My, that's a lot of money, Bailey."

"Sure is." I swept the paper into a dustpan and dumped it into the trash. "Aunt Vera said fairgoers like to pay in cash, in keeping with the feel of the era."

Pepper's eyes widened. "I'd better get to the bank then."

"Not until you tell us why you popped in," I said.

"Yes, do tell." Bailey stopped counting and leaned forward on her elbows. Her mouth was twitching, which meant she couldn't care less.

"We-ell . . ." Pepper dragged the word out. "You won't believe it, but I've set up my house as an Airbnb rental."

I've heard of Airbnb. They find hosts in a variety of cities with extra rooms or entire homes to let. They even drum up unique accommodations like igloos, prairie tents, and castles. Pepper's ranch-style house in the hills was fairly typical for Crystal Cove.

"Is that safe?" I asked.

Pepper clucked her tongue. "It's regulated."

"It is?" Bailey raised an eyebrow.

"Absolutely. It's a worldwide company now. Quick as a wink, the moment I put the house on the market a couple—a very lovely couple from San Francisco—took me up on the offer. They've already settled in."

"Are you staying in the house?" I asked, worried that she might be a little too eager and, therefore, an easy mark for a hustler.

"Of course not," Pepper said. "I'm rooming with my daughter."

"Does she know that you've rented out your place?"

"Yes, and she said she's delighted to spend some quality time with me."

I stifled another laugh. I'm sure that was *not* how her daughter had phrased it. Cinnamon Pritchett, the town's chief of police, is an extremely private person. She and I are friends, but even our friendship borders on the cool side because she doesn't like to reveal much about her work or her life. I've asked her numerous times about her budding relationship with a hunky fireman, only to get shot down.

"The couple I've rented to are so excited that I have a garden," Pepper went on, undaunted. "They're health nuts and eat only organic. Did I mention they make pottery? Well, she does. Beautiful long-necked pottery. He runs the business."

"How did you find them?"

"They found me, silly. Through Airbnb." Pepper exuded positive energy. "There are lots of folks in town renting their places these days."

That was news to me. "What else do you know about your tenants?" I asked and resumed sweeping.

"They're called *guests*, and FYI," she went on, using the abbreviated term for *for your information*, "he has stayed with me before."

I gawped. "He has?"

"Yes. The first time I let him a room, it was for a weekend. He wanted to scope out the area."

"What's his name?"

"Sean Beaufort. He and his wife plan to develop a chain of pottery stores in California. Melody — that's his wife — teaches pottery classes in addition to making her own. They have a booth on the Pier. You'll see it."

Crystal Cove is set on the coast of California, south of Santa Cruz and north of Monterey. To the west is a beautiful crescent of sandy beaches and shops. To the east are the Santa Cruz Mountains. An age-old lighthouse marks the border at the north end of town, and the Pier marks the south end. It features a carousel, a number of shops, a theater, carney games, and restaurants. In addition, tourists can hire boats for sunset or sightseeing cruises and fishing expeditions. The Crystal Cove Renaissance Fair, which was smaller and more in keeping with our town's size than the typical fair, would take place on the Pier.

"Sean is a darling. So is Melody. The two seem perfectly matched. They're the same height and they have the same winsome smiles." Pepper used her hands to describe them. "Did I mention that they're both athletic? He's a long-distance runner. She loves to hike. Sean says exercise is good for the heart. Those hills in San Francisco can be quite tasking." Obviously, her guests had impressed her. "He's very protective of Melody, making sure she has sunblock and such. It's quite sweet." Pepper started to leave and turned back. "I almost forgot. For Ren Fair—that's how fairgoers shorten the name, by the way—they're going to dress as two of Shakespeare's famous lovers."

"Really? Which two?" I asked. My boyfriend, Rhett Jackson, and I were dressing as a well-known medieval couple.

"Petruchio and Kate."

"From *Taming of the Shrew*?"

"Exactly." Pepper chuckled, an endearing sort of *snort-sniff*. Cinnamon had a similar laugh. "I would cast them as Romeo and Juliet, but what do I know? Maybe they felt they were too old for that. They're close to forty." She chuckled again and gathered the seams of her skirt. "Well, that's all the news that's fit to print. Too-ra-loo," she crooned—a saying she'd picked up from my aunt—and departed.

As if on cue, Aunt Vera entered the shop from the breezeway that led to the café. She was carrying an armload of boxed tarot cards. Lola Bird, who was almost the spitting image of her daughter, Bailey, other than the silver hair and a few more well-earned wrinkles, traipsed behind my aunt. Her royal blue skirt and white blouse with its royal blue corset waist cincher made her look quite regal. It didn't hurt that she was wearing a sparkling silver tiara.

"What are you two up to?" I asked.

Lola pecked her daughter on the cheek.

"We had tea"—Aunt Vera set the boxes of cards on the vintage kitchen table—"and chatted about our respective offerings at the fair." My aunt had rented a stall so she could give palm readings or tarot card readings. She was also selling tarot cards; hence, the boxed sets. She claimed people who asked to hear their fortunes were often curious how to pursue the art on their own. I particularly liked the whimsical Tarots of the Renaissance decks she had found, which vividly captured the feel of Renaissance art while evoking the diversity of an age when courtiers dominated the palace halls and farmers worked the fields.

Lola flapped a recipe card. "I am hawking Katie's famous chicken kebabs. Of course, I'll call them meat on a stick." In a big, boisterous voice, she chanted, "Come fair maidens and gentlemen. Prithee, quench thy hunger here!"

I applauded. "I love fair-speak. Good job."

"Why are you selling Katie's kebabs, Mother?" Bailey asked. "Yours are to die for."

"I'm selling both, but mine are made with soy sauce, and there might be too many who can't eat it, like the soy-free or the gluten-free people. Why have a product half the population can't or *won't* buy? Katie's are made with olive oil and a secret blend of spices." Lola spread her arms to include everyone in the shop. "What better way to show the world that a competing diner and café can work hand in hand? We're all family, right?"

"What did Pepper want?" Aunt Vera jutted her chin toward the front door. "She rarely comes in to visit."

"She came to boast," Bailey said.

I swatted her. "She wasn't boasting. She's excited because she has rented her home as an Airbnb for the week."

"My word," Aunt Vera said. "Isn't that dangerous? I've heard some horror stories."

Lola blanched. "Me, too."

"It's perfectly safe," I assured them, though I was skeptical.

I peered out the display window. Was Pepper's new venture the reason we were experiencing worrisome vibes? Were there scam artists or drifters coming to town to take advantage of our gracious locals?

A shiver skittered down my spine as I made a mental note to chat with Cinnamon about her mother's new *business*.

# Chapter 2

That evening, after a crazy afternoon unpacking a boatload of Renaissance-themed cookbooks, which included *Cooking and Eating in Renaissance Italy: From Kitchen to Table*, as well as *Medieval Celebrations: Your Guide to Planning and Hosting Spectacular Feasts, Parties, Weddings, and Renaissance*, Bailey and I donned our costumes and drove to the Pier for a night of fun.

The parking lot for the Pier was packed with cars and campers. A large white tent stood off at a distance. I wasn't quite sure what it was for. No one was making a beeline in that direction. Perhaps it was a staging area. The majority of fairgoers were filing toward the admission booth. Others, if they'd already purchased their fair passes, as we had, strode to the entrance, an archway that was elaborately swathed with gold and burgundy fabric.

A bagpiper in a green-and-red kilt greeted everyone who passed beneath the arch with a cheery drone. Barkers in tan peasant shirts, trousers, and bold burgundy sashes stood on either side of the entrance calling "Hi-ho" or "Good morrow" to all who entered. At the booth to the right of the entrance, a sign was posted stating that all sites accepted cash, and vendors could elect whether to accept the ethereal plastic kind of payment. The instructions on the sign added that if one desired, one could purchase *farthings*, which were coinlike tokens.

Once we passed through the archway, I drew to a stop and studied the fair's layout. To the left, between Bait and Switch Fishing and Sport Supply Store and the other year-round establishments along the Pier, stood a stage as well as a variety of stalls—many were plain white tents; others were designed with a distinctive flair. To the right, which was usually wide open and provided a view of the beach and ocean, stood another string of tents and venues. Down the center of the boardwalk there were smaller stalls. The lanes created by the divider were aptly named North Street and South Street. As we proceeded, I noticed a few cut-throughs in the center aisle, each marked with a wooden, hand-carved sign. Overall, the layout gave the Pier a small-town feel.

I caught the aroma of everything from roasted meat to sweet desserts and my stomach grumbled. "Yum."

"Double yum!" Bailey said. "I'm starved."

"Fine maiden!" Rhett hailed me from the front of Bait and Switch, the store he'd purchased after his career as a chef ended. My heart did a happy dance when I saw him. In his Robin Hood costume, complete with a brown hat lined in green velvet and a green feather accent, he was as handsome as any movie star. My darling Tigger, who I'd left at home, would be dressed in a similar costume tomorrow. "Stop a while and pass the time, my lady!" He doffed his hat, offered his typically roguish grin, and did a courtly bow.

I hurried to him, the skirt of my Maid Marian costume fluting up and revealing my medieval leather sandals. I had ordered them online. They were as comfortable as moccasins.

Rhett drew me into a warm embrace and kissed me tenderly. "You look beauteous."

"So do you," I murmured. And he did. That dark hair. That strong square jaw. I melted nearly every time I saw him. Now that my deceased husband was really dead—sad story that was better told on a rainy day, not on a star-filled night like tonight—I was emotionally free to give my love to Rhett, and I was thrilled to do so. He deserved every ounce of my affection.

He eyed Bailey, who had opted for a dark blue tavern wench's costume, complete with apron. "Good e'en, young lass. You look pretty, as well."

"Good e'en to you, sir."

*E'en* means evening in fair-speak. For the past few days, Bailey and I had been practicing words we were to use throughout the week. *Good morrow* means good day, *verily* means truthfully, and so on. Thanks to Nick Baldini, I'd learned there are tons of Internet sites to help fairgoers through the process.

Rhett pressed a scroll of parchment tied with ribbon into my hand. "For you."

"What is it?"

His ocean blue eyes twinkled with delight. "Open and you'll see."

I unfurled the paper and read in beautiful, handwritten script:

*A woman's face with nature's own hand painted,*
*Hast thou, the master mistress of my passion;*
*A woman's gentle heart, but not acquainted*

*With shifting change, as is false women's fashion:*
*An eye more bright than theirs, less false in rolling,*
*Gilding the object whereupon it gazeth;*
*A man in hue all hues in his controlling,*
*Which steals men's eyes and women's souls amazeth.*

My eyes welled up. I gazed at Rhett and blinked. "Did you write this?"

"Ha! Are you kidding?" His eyes twinkled with humor. "That's Shakespeare's sonnet number twenty. I am *no* poet." He hitched a thumb over his shoulder. "I bought it at Shakespeare's Poetic Inspirations. It's the tent beyond the theater, near the games."

At the far end of the Pier regularly stood a series of carney games. Many of the vendors had switched out typical games with fair-style pastimes. Darts was for everyone; the ax toss was for adults.

"It's the thought that counts, isn't it?" Rhett asked.

"I love it. And I love—"

"Me?" he asked.

"Don't get cocky." I winked as I tucked the poetry into the pocket of my skirt.

Rhett and I are an official couple and have been for a few months. We have taken a number of mini trips, including a delicious jaunt to the wine country and an exhilarating outing to Santa Barbara for a hot air balloon ride.

"Come with me." He clasped my hand and led me along North Street. Bailey followed, keeping a sharp eye out for Tito. He was somewhere in the vicinity doing interviews for the newspaper. Because of the crush of fun-loving people and Bailey being so short, she had to pop up and down to catch a glimpse.

When she leaped for the fifth time, I said, "Cool your heels. I'll keep a lookout." At my height, I had an advantage. "What is he wearing?"

"He's a town crier, what else?"

A man dressed like Friar Tuck pulled alongside Rhett and said, "Prithee, sir, which way to the, um, outhouse?"

Rhett gestured.

The man hustled in that direction. An elderly woman with winter-white hair and knobby cane chased after him. Apparently, the cane was a prop.

A younger woman, an archer who had slung a fake dead bird over her shoulder, strode by.

"Hello, fellow hunter," she said to Rhett in passing.

"Hello, to thee," Rhett said.

"Do you know her?" I asked.

"Nope. Hunters always greet other hunters. It's a fair custom." He gestured to a pottery stall on our right with the placard *Beaufort's Beautiful Pottery*. Beneath that was a handwritten sign that read *Lessons within*. Rhett said, "Hey, remember our trip to Taos?"

Our two-day excursion had been heavenly. We visited art galleries, went on long walks, and attended a pottery class.

Bailey said, "Hey, Jenna, isn't this the stall for the couple that's staying at Pepper's place?"

"I believe you're right."

We stepped inside.

"Aren't those beautiful?" Bailey gestured to the assortment of long-necked pottery displayed on two narrow tables, which were front and center in the tent. Each piece of pottery was a color of the sea: aqua, azure, cerulean, and navy.

I nodded. "My favorite colors."

Rhett said to me, "They're offering lessons. I think we should throw a pot."

"If I could learn to make something like those, I'm in."

"Ha! I'll be lucky if I can throw something that doesn't look like a glob of mud," he quipped.

In Taos I'd struggled; Rhett had given up.

"Yoo-hoo, Sean, I need help." An elderly woman in a nun's habit, who was sitting on a stool by one of the five pottery wheel stations at the rear of the tent, waved to a handsome dark-haired man stationed at the sales desk.

Sean Beaufort, I assumed. He was wearing an elaborate gold-and-royal-blue Elizabethan costume—Petruchio from Shakespeare's *Taming of the Shrew*, if Pepper was correct. He didn't seem to hear the woman. He was too busy blowing his nose while reading something on his cell phone. *So much for total authenticity at the fair*, I mused, though I had to admit, my cell phone was nestled in the left-hand pocket of my skirt. Just in case.

"Sean, please," the woman pleaded. She twisted the pottery

wheel. The cube of clay sitting on top wobbled.

To the left of the woman stood a cafeteria rack installed with trays. Works of art sat on the trays. Apparently, Beaufort's Beautiful Pottery had done well on the first night of the fair. Beside the rack, a table covered with a pale blue tablecloth held a variety of pottery tools, including a clay hammer, a mallet, a wire cutter, and a variety of scrapers. I didn't see a kiln. Most likely the Beauforts took the finished works to wherever they had stowed their kiln—Pepper's perhaps?— and would fire the art there.

"Sean." The woman blew out an exasperated breath.

"What? Oh, sure. Sorry, Mrs. D." Sean pocketed his cell phone and snatched a fresh tissue from a box on the sales desk. He skirted around a steamer trunk fitted with antique brass inlays to get to her and apologized further, adding that he was helpless when it came to making pottery and his wife would return momentarily. "Why don't you take a piece of clay and roll it between your hands so you can get the feel of it?"

"Wonderful idea," she murmured, now beaming at him. All she had wanted was attention.

"Jenna!" a woman hollered.

Recognizing my chef's throaty voice, I pivoted. Katie hailed me from our stall, the Nook's Pasties, which was located in the center aisle, kitty-corner from the Beauforts' stall. Katie's sous chef was running the café for the evening. They would alternate days operating the booth at the fair.

I waved to her.

"Go," Rhett said. "I'll set up our lesson."

"Forget it. We'll do it later. Come with me." I yelled to Katie, "Be there in a sec."

Cutting a path through the swarm of revelers was challenging, but I managed. Bailey and Rhett trailed me. When I arrived at the stall, I hugged Katie. To the left of our bentwood booth—Katie had been adamant about designing our stall with a true medieval flair—stood a bold, red-striped stall. No one was manning it yet.

"What's going to go in there?" I asked.

"Tankards and Mead," Katie said. "It'll make for a lively location, don't you think? Do you like my costume?" She plucked the puffy sleeves. Like Bailey, she had dressed in a common tavern wench's outfit. Hers was rust and cream with a cream apron. The colors went well with her skin tone.

"Love it."

"Very unique," Bailey teased.

"Hi-ho, Jenna." Hannah Storm, a tall, athletic woman with black spiky hair, paced in front of Ye Olde Wine Shoppe, the neighboring white canvas booth. Inside her stall, she featured wines from Hurricane Vineyards—which she owned—as well as antique winepresses, corkscrews, wineglasses, and wine racks. Aged wine barrels and a burlap carpet gave the stall a rustic look. A wine-tasting setup was laid out on the petite oak bar.

"Hi-ho, Hannah," I said. "Pray tell, what is that you're holding?"

In her hands she wielded a tool consisting of a copper foot welded to a copper pole. "It's a . . . a . . ." Hannah sneezed. The black ribbons on her garland of flowers kicked up. She plucked a tissue from beneath the sleeve of her smoky black gown.

"Bless you," Katie, Bailey, Rhett, and I said in unison.

"Thanks." Hannah dabbed her nose. Dropping the fair accent, she hissed, "How I loathe pollen season."

"What are you dressed as?" Bailey asked. "A Renaissance widow?"

"Don't be silly." Hannah giggled. "You know me. I always wear black. I'm a lowly saleswoman." She nodded at her foot-pole thing. "As for this, my dear friends, it is a winepress tool. Isn't it great?" She offered a sassy smile. "I had a few made specifically for the fair. Back in the day, they didn't have all the new-fangled equipment we have now." She waggled the tool in my face and pointed to the stash of other similarly shaped tools slotted into a white oak wine barrel. "I've sold three already."

Rhett lifted one and, like a baton twirler, wove it through his fingers. "Clever."

"Oho!" Katie raised a finger. "Hannah might have sold three of those, but I've peddled over thirty of our pasties." On a long table, she had assembled trays with a variety of Cornish pasties. The warm brown color of the pastry was beautiful. The aroma of meat, cinnamon, and something else—rosemary?—was downright sinful. Copies of *How to Make Cornish Pasties: The Official Recipe* cookbook were featured on a nearby table. Whoever purchased one of the books would need to know how to convert from metric to U.S. measurements, so Katie had printed up a few freebie reference cards.

Hannah said, "Right before you showed up, I was begging Katie for the recipe for the pork pasty, but she refused." She pronounced the word properly — *pass-tee*. "Can you believe the gall?"

I bopped Hannah on the shoulder. "Didn't she tell you that you'd find it in the cookbook?"

Hannah growled. "You sneak."

Katie coyly played with the apron of her costume. "You never asked."

"Sold!" Hannah lifted a cookbook from the stack and thrust it at Katie. "Hold this for me, my dearie, and watch and weep." She beckoned a redheaded woman in a purple gown who was approaching. "Fair lady, how now? Come hither. See what I have to offer. Me-thinks you could do well with an antique winepress."

Bailey knuckled Hannah on the arm. "Wow. Listen to you. You're a hawker now."

"Verily, I am."

Clearly intrigued, the woman in purple moseyed to Hannah. Bailey, Rhett, and I bid Katie and Hannah adieu and moved on.

"I like Hannah," Bailey said. "She's got spirit."

Rhett agreed. "Her older brother, Hugh, and I were good friends until he left the country."

"I didn't know she had a brother." I'd recently met Hannah when she'd become fascinated with five-ingredient recipes. Being an aficionado myself, we had instantly bonded. "Why did he leave?"

"He hated the family business and wanted to work in the food industry. That's how we got to know each other. He took a few cooking classes from me at the Grotto before . . ." Rhett didn't finish. The memory still galled him. The Grotto was where he had worked as a chef until the owner burned it down on purpose. The incident had left a bitter taste, which was why he'd switched careers. "It didn't help that Hugh was allergic to grapes."

I tittered. "I'm sorry. Allergies aren't funny, but the likelihood of being allergic to the very thing your family did for a business seems ironic. Can you imagine a wheat farmer being allergic to gluten?" I clasped Rhett's hand. "Do you think Hannah misses him?"

"I know she does. She could probably use help tending to their aging grandmother, but I'm not sure she'd let on. When Hugh finally found the courage to quit town, she was ecstatic for him."

"Where is he now?"

"Paris. Living the dream. He has his own bistro. He's earned one Michelin star and striving for the second. By the way, he and Cinnamon dated back in high school."

"Re-e-eally?" I said, dragging out the word. I love getting insider information on our chief of police.

We neared Thistle Thy Fancy crafts booth, which was situated next to Pepper's beadery. Dolly Ledoux was standing at the entrance. "Hark! If it please thee" — she waved a bouquet of thistles at us — "come inside and make yourself a strand of beads or a wreath for thy hair." She was dressed in the same emerald green wench costume she'd worn to the shop earlier, her blonde hair twisted messily with curly tresses spilling out, and she spoke with an English accent instead of her Southern one.

Inside her tent stood numerous wooden-doweled racks upon which hung selections of ribbons, beads, silk flowers, and floral wire. A wide, easel-style pegboard filled with finished wreaths stood at the rear of the tent. A do-it-yourself table crowded with other supplies was situated in the middle of the tent. Two teenagers, a little girl with her mother, and a craggy-faced man occupied the various craft stations. Each worked intently on a project.

"Dolly, what pretty trims," I said, admiring the ribbons. "Did Hannah make her wreath here?"

"Aye. Indeed, she did."

"I will return to make one for me," I told her. "Perhaps tomorrow."

"Bless thee."

Bailey, Rhett, and I continued along the wharf.

"I love this fair," I said. "Everyone is so merry."

"It's a wonder that Dolly is," Bailey said.

"Why?"

Bailey glanced over her shoulder. "Didn't you hear?" She leaned in close. "Nick dumped her. I think that's why she was visiting your aunt this morning. She wants a magic spell that will help her keep him."

Rhett guffawed. "Vera doesn't do magic spells."

"Dolly thinks she can."

For the second time I wondered whether Dolly's anxiety was what was causing the negative vibes that Lola, Bailey, and I were picking up.

Bailey said, "I heard she was so distraught over losing Nick that she destroyed a shelf in the stockroom at her shop with a baseball bat."

I gasped. "You're kidding. A bat?"

"Makes sense," Rhett said.

"Why?" I asked.

"In high school she was a softball star, and in college she set the NCAA career home run record. A baseball bat would be the first thing she'd reach for."

"You know this because . . ."

"She comes into my store. She likes to fish. We talk." Rhett spread his hands. "She said her temper kept her from going pro."

Bailey said, "Huh. I was wondering what all those trophies in her shop were for."

I hadn't paid attention to the trophies because whenever I visited Dolly's place for items to use in our displays, I was so in awe of her sense of color that I didn't look beyond her wares. Plus, entering the shop reminded me of time spent with my mother, which made me a tad emotional. Mom and I had often created craft projects. She could paint like a dream, knit like a professional, and her beading handiwork was almost as good as Pepper's. How I missed her.

Bailey punched my arm. "Have you seen Tito yet?" She started popping up and down again, trying to peer over the crowd.

"Nope. I've been keeping my eyes peeled. Rhett, do you see him?"

"Not even a glimpse."

Bailey huffed. "He said he was meeting the mayor by the *Punch and Judy* puppet show."

"That's located on South Street. Follow me." I cut through the center aisle and exited between Mum's the Word Diner and a tent filled with toys. The Word, as the locals call it, serves some of the best comfort food in town. Its cheery and retro turquoise-and-yellow theme always gives me a boost. "There." I pointed. "I spy a horde of poppets yonder."

"Cut out the fair-speak," Bailey snipped. "Lead me in that direction."

Teasingly, I wagged a finger. "Temper, temper, speaking of temper."

"I'm feeling a little claustrophobic. I need air."

In her defense, if I were as height-challenged as she was, I'd be gulping in breaths of air.

"This way," Rhett said. "Jenna, help me out."

He took hold of one of Bailey's arms. I hooked my hand around the other. Together we steered her to the Theater on the Pier, a modest playhouse that offered a variety of performances throughout the year.

In front of the theater stood a charming red-and-gold puppet show booth with illuminated signboards that featured a city view and stars in the sky. Children sat in a semicircle in front of the setup. Adults were huddled behind them. The puppet show was under way. Traditionally, *Punch and Judy* is an over-the-top and aggressive display. I caught snippets of parents criticizing the violence. Nervous laughter abounded.

"There's Tito," Rhett said. "Standing next to Nick Baldini."

"Where?" Bailey pleaded. "I still can't see him. Why is he talking to Nick? Does Tito look worried? Please don't tell me Nick is canceling the wedding venue. He wouldn't do that to me, would he? I mean, we're friends now and—"

"Relax," I said. "Everything's fine." I urged my pal to climb the diner's steps for a better view. "Tito isn't talking to Nick at all. He's interviewing the mayor, as promised."

Bailey peered in the direction I was pointing and exhaled. "Whew! Got it. Bye." She pressed through the throng and dashed to Tito. When she reached him, she acted like she hadn't seen him in months. A big kiss on the cheek. An arm around his back. It tickled me to see my friend so happily in love.

"Speaking of Nick," Rhett said, "who's that woman with him?"

# Chapter 3

"I have no clue who she is," I said to Rhett.

Nick, a sizeable man in his early forties and clad in a lavish red-and-black King Henry VIII costume—very apropos since he was the lynchpin of the fair—was stroking his black goatee while chatting with a willowy blonde with dark roots and alluring eyes. She was dressed in one of the prettiest gold gowns I'd ever seen, with narrow burgundy inserts in the skirt and a hint of burgundy lace peeking above the low-cut bodice.

"I don't think she's a local," Rhett said.

"Me, either."

The glittery ribbons on the wreath that graced the woman's hair fluttered in the breeze. A ribbon twined itself beneath her turned-up nose. Nick freed it with his pinky and slipped it back where it belonged. She smiled tentatively. Was she the reason Nick had ended it with Dolly?

Nick said something. The woman shook her head and dabbed her nose with a handkerchief. As she did, she caught me looking her way. Her eyes narrowed. Quickly, she ended the conversation and fled by skirting the crowd.

A roar from the fairgoers drew my attention. *Punch and Judy* was at that critical point where Judy made her entrance carrying a club.

"Look out, Punch!" a few children shrieked.

Nick flinched at the violence. Was he wondering whether he should beware of Dolly Ledoux and her baseball bat? He didn't hang around to watch the outcome. He hightailed it the same way the woman in gold had gone.

"Jenna! Rhett!" Mayor Zeller, a squat woman with more energy than the Energizer Bunny, came rushing toward us. The folds of her brown innkeeper's skirt whisked to and fro. A brown jacket buttoned to the neck completed the ensemble. "Did you see which way Nick Baldini went?"

"Toward the carney games." I pointed. I could see the rise and fall of his crown.

"Ooh, that man is quick on his feet. I was coming to nab him when Tito Martinez waylaid me."

"Why do you need Nick?" I asked.

"We're shooting an instructional video so the newbies at the fair can learn the language and see how to build a character. Would you and Rhett catch him, please, and remind him? I have to rally the other players. We're meeting in the big tent in the parking lot."

Aha. That was what the tent was for.

"Whatever you do, don't let him wriggle away. Nick's a sly dog."

The mayor was right. Nabbing Nick wasn't easy. As if he knew we were in pursuit, he slipped into one booth, out the other side, and into another. Before we could draw near enough to chat, he eluded us again by circumventing the crowd. When we were in range to yell to him—me, gasping for air; Rhett, laughing out loud—I noticed Nick was holding a wine tool as well as a piece of cerulean long-necked pottery. Apparently, in his escape, he'd done some shopping.

"Nick!" Rhett bellowed over the roar of the swelling throng. "The mayor needs you for the video."

He acknowledged us with a wave and detoured toward the entrance to the Pier. Within seconds he slipped through the draped entry and disappeared.

"C'mon, Rhett." I tugged him forward. "Let's watch them make a movie."

Giving up my job in advertising was one of the best decisions I'd ever made, but I missed being around cameras and actors and hearing the word *Action*. Granted, the fair's instructional movie would probably not be up to the same professional standards that I was used to, but it would be fun to observe.

We sprinted across the parking lot to the huge white tent and entered on Nick's coattails.

The mayor applauded. "At last. The king has arrived."

The tent was dressed up to look like a street at the fair with a few stalls and wooden signs. Carpet that resembled the boardwalk lined the floor. Well-placed klieg lights helped give the area ambience.

"Okay, everyone, listen up, please." The mayor gestured to a group of more than a dozen players. "Bow to the king and let's get cracking."

The entire group, except an outlier who was manning a handheld video camera, made courtly bows.

"Don't you mean bow to the bombastic king?" the outlier said.

Nick held a hand over his forehead and searched for the offender.

The outlier removed the video camera from his eye, and I realized he was none other than Nick's younger brother, Alan. The two were as different as night and day. Whereas Nick was brown-eyed and tan and looked like a man who worked the earth, Alan was green-eyed, pale, and not in the least muscular.

"Very funny." Nick saluted Alan, who in turn mimed tipping the brim of an imaginary hat. Neither was smiling.

Those bowing to Nick rose and burst into laughter. The men in the group huddled around him and whacked him heartily on the back.

"Let's get this show on the road." Mayor Zeller, or Z.Z., as many call her—short for Zoey Zeller—clapped her hands. "Grab what you need over there." She gestured to a table filled with bottles of water and props. "Jenna and Rhett, good to see you here. Want to act?"

"Uh-uh," Rhett said. "I'm camera shy."

"Don't kid a kidder." Z.Z. knuckled his shoulder. "I'll bet you're as much of a ham as Nick."

"I'm content to watch."

I said, "Z.Z., I recognize most of the players but not the lady in gold." I indicated the willowy blonde that we'd seen speaking with Nick near the *Punch and Judy* show.

"You don't know Melody?" Z.Z.'s brow puckered. "No, I don't suppose you would, come to think of it. This is her first fair in Crystal Cove. She and her husband are renting Pepper's house."

Though Melody was tall, she appeared as delicate as Pepper had described.

"She makes pottery in San Francisco," the mayor continued. "She has quite the knack. Nick is holding something she made. Do you see it?"

"I do." It was one of the pieces I had admired in the Beauforts' stall.

Nick sidled up to Melody and said something. Her mouth formed the word *no*. Dabbing her nose with her handkerchief, she moved on to a frizzy-haired older woman in a lavender gown with split sleeves.

"Okay, folks!" Z.Z. signaled to Nick's brother. "For now, Alan, roam through them without running the camera. Give them a feel of what it's like to have you among them. In a minute, turn it on."

Alan shot her a thumbs-up gesture.

Z.Z. said, "Remember, people, use the words *aye*, *anon*, and *prithee*. Don't forget that the Internet is the *ether*, and if you see a cell phone, act as though it is a strange novelty from another world. Ask about it. Make fun. Tease. Fantasy is what matters, even to those who will be dressed in shorts and crazy T-shirts."

Not everyone who attends the fair comes dressed for the occasion.

"Ready . . . and action."

Nick pursued Melody, who had separated from the woman in lavender. He said something. Melody shook her head and coyly lowered her chin. Nick spoke again. Melody responded briefly and then sashayed to a couple of women dressed as wenches.

Moving on, Nick strutted to a man in a brown tavern owner's outfit and loudly said, "Good morrow!"

"Good morrow, sire," the man replied.

"Wherefore willst I find ale for my parched tankard?"

"I shall fetch yon ale mistress." The tavern owner bowed gallantly and swaggered away.

At the same time, the woman in lavender approached Nick. "Varlet! Fie on thee. How dare ye slander my daughter."

"What ho?" Nick planted his hands imposingly against his hips.

Melody hurried up to the woman and gripped her arm. "Nay, Mother, do not assail him. Verily, he is not the scoundrel."

The woman in lavender shot a finger at Nick. "By my faith, should I learn otherwise . . ." Letting her threat hang in the air, she made a U-turn and pranced away.

Nick clasped Melody's elbow and said something under his breath and then gently swept a loose strand of her hair to one side. In keeping with her character, Melody swatted his hand away and traipsed after her mother.

The players continued interacting for a good ten minutes. I hadn't attended a Renaissance Fair in a long time, but watching them all having such fun and relishing their roles made me eager to participate during the rest of the week. Tomorrow I would encourage Bailey, Tina, and my aunt to use fair-speak language nonstop in the shop. The more fun we had, the more fun our customers would have.

"Let's take a break," Z.Z. announced. "Great job!"

As the group disbanded, Sean Beaufort entered the tent. He was carrying a lady's white knit shawl. Melody caught sight of him and waved. He hustled to her, pecked her on the cheek, and draped the shawl over her shoulders.

"Everyone, this is Sean," Melody announced. "My husband."

The players greeted him in unison.

Sean responded cheerfully and sauntered to the edge of the tent, obviously not intending to take part.

Playacting resumed and Melody weaved through the crowd, speaking to everyone with an easy grace.

A few minutes into the scene, a gawky young man in a royal blue messenger's costume, his tunic trimmed with gold braid, raced into the tent. "I have a missive." His strident voice could have carried halfway across the ocean. He cut through the knot of players. When he came upon Melody, he dropped to one knee. "My lady. For a beautiful lady of song."

How cute, I thought. A lady of song—Melody.

He offered her a tube of parchment tied with ribbon, like the gift Rhett had presented to me.

Rhett nudged me. "Looks like someone is receiving a love note."

"Looks like." I pecked him on the cheek. "I adore mine."

Melody accepted the note and started to open it, but Sean strode to her and held out his hand. Had he decided to join the playacting after all? He didn't say a word. He gazed into her eyes. Melody's face flushed. Without reading the note, she handed it to him, took his hand, and allowed him to usher her toward the exit.

The mayor yelled, "Sean, what ho! Wherefore goest thou? Do not make haste." Apparently, his interruption wasn't part of the scenario.

"We have to leave," he said without an accent—definitely not part of the scene.

"No, you don't, young man." Z.Z. hustled to him and clasped his arm. "Melody promised to star in our production, so now you're taking part. Come on, ye yellow-livered, moneygrubbing rascal, buck up. Act the merchant that ye are. Or at the very least pretend to be bellicose Petruchio, come to dominate your Kate."

I elbowed Rhett. "Whoa! Aren't you glad you didn't try to remove me from the building? Z.Z. would've taken you to task."

Sadly, the mayor's magic didn't work on Sean. He wrested free of her and murmured something to Melody.

"Apologies, everyone," Melody said, addressing the group. "I must take my leave. I shall be with you in spirit. Until the morrow." She waved like royalty and followed Sean out of the tent.

Z.Z. hurried to Nick and held a quiet conversation. Then she darted to Alan and did the same. He cut a look at Nick and splayed his arms, as if asking what could he do. Obviously miffed, the mayor circled a finger to continue. "Again, fine ladies and gentlemen. Anew! We may have lost a precious lass, but we are a force."

She retreated to us and said, "Come on. Join in the fun. For a few minutes. You'll get a videotape for your troubles. Two more players would really help us out."

Rhett shrugged. "Sure, why not." He charged into the group and began interacting with the others.

I did the same. My fair-speak wasn't very good, but the others were kind enough to help me with it.

Alan, who must have picked up on my unease, slipped up beside me and said, "Go for it. The newbies at the fair will love your courage."

Emboldened, I took up with the frizzy-haired woman in lavender and led with the story about Melody. "Good mother, you seem to have lost your daughter."

The woman glowered at me. "Wretched varlet ran off with her."

"Didst thou not know him?"

"I have never spied him before."

"Verily, he is a long-distance runner," I said, stating what Pepper had told me about Sean.

"Forsooth, he is a fool." Enjoying her slur, she slapped her thigh. "My daughter shall return, and when she does, I shall chain her to the bed for her disobedience."

Rhett joined us. "Thou art a vengeful soul, woman."

"Aye, I am, sir." She clenched a fistful of skirt and did an about-face.

Alan left us to keep pace with her.

I slipped my hand around Rhett's elbow. "Having fun?"

"Absolutely."

"Do you think Melody is okay?"

"Why wouldn't she be?"

"Her husband seemed angry."

Rhett shook his head. "Alas, I think you missed the signals, my love. I believe he has other plans for the two of them tonight." With a wink, he added, "Me-thinks the love letter was an invitation to go home and play footsie."

"You . . ." I swatted his arm.

Nick approached us. "What ho, Maid Marian. You have a secret. Share it with the king."

I peeked at Rhett.

"Out with it," Nick demanded. "The secret hast made you blush."

"Do I blush, sire?" I put a hand to my cheek.

Rhett wrapped an arm around me. "We were discussing the sweet Melody, who needed to leave so quickly."

"Fie on her husband," Nick cried. "A pox on his house. Her departure didst not please the king." He hailed his brother. "Alan, come hither." He waved for Alan to join us. "Make sure these two are part of the fun."

Alan looked miffed. Under his breath, he said, "I already have."

"Make sure," Nick said.

Alan pivoted and said to Rhett and me, "Go ahead, you two. Make another pass. Ready. Action."

He followed us for a few minutes. Rhett asked a tavern owner for a pint of ale. I begged for directions to the theater. It was challenging.

When Z.Z. announced a break, Rhett and I said goodbye and exited, ready to taste the wares on the Pier. For some reason, as we neared the exit, I felt compelled to turn back. I caught sight of Nick genially wielding the foot-shaped wine tool he'd purchased from Ye Olde Wine Shoppe like a baseball bat. He was making everyone in the tent laugh.

Everyone, except his brother.

# Chapter 4

The next day, Bailey bustled from the storage room to where I was tidying a display table and set down a stack of books bound with raffia ribbon. She heaved a sigh. "Jenna." A world of woe filled that single word.

"What's up?" I asked.

"I have to check on things at the vineyard. Nick made me promise I would meet the chef today and go over the menu. Come with me."

"I can't. We're slammed."

We had been hopping for six straight hours. Customers, in fair costumes and normal dress, had been arriving in waves since we'd opened. Many were browsing the main attraction, a table I'd packed with Shakespearean-themed books including *The Shakespeare Cookbook*, which included recipes for a feast, and *Shakespeare's Kitchen: Renaissance Recipes for the Contemporary Cook*, which featured lovely recipes and annotations from seventeenth-century cookbooks. Others were flipping through baking-themed cookbooks while enjoying the assortment of bite-sized scones Katie had set on the table in the breezeway.

"Please, Jenna," Bailey pleaded. "I need moral support. I'm so nervous that I'll screw everything up. I am not a hostess. Tina"—she caught the attention of our darling assistant—"these are for Gran." Gran is our best customer; she buys at least ten items each week. "She'll be here in a half hour." She carried the books to the checkout counter and slipped a note under the raffia ribbon. "Got that?"

Tina, who was clad in an apple-red wench costume that she had sewn herself, nodded. She didn't miss much.

Bailey returned to me and grabbed my hands. "Pretty please. An hour. Tina has this place under control. And your aunt is here."

"For a nanosecond. She's heading back to the fair in minutes."

Bailey's eyes glistened with apprehension. She pressed a hand to her chest. "Prithee, have mercy on this wretched soul."

I laughed. How could I refuse? "Okay, fine, but no more than an hour."

We drove through town, a breeze cutting through the opened windows of my VW. Renaissance Fair people were out in droves. At most Renaissance Fairs, the main event is held within the confines of one location, but in Crystal Cove the entire town was serving as the setting. City regulations didn't allow booths or tents along Buena Vista Boulevard, but there were plenty of fairgoers carrying turkey legs or meat on a stick. I saw a couple of people toting our shopping bags and joy zinged through me. Business was good. Free advertising was priceless.

Baldini Vineyards is located near the top of the Santa Cruz Mountains and boasts a spectacular view of the ocean. The slope below the vineyard's main buildings is packed with pinot noir grapevines.

I maneuvered my VW Beetle up the winding road and pulled to a stop in front of the Baldinis' stately Italianate house. Bailey hustled out of the car and slammed the door. I paused on the gravel driveway and took a moment to admire the trellises of red bougainvillea that flanked the grand windows and the flower beds overflowing with gorgeous red roses.

A diminutive Hispanic housekeeper met us at the door and led us through the expansive foyer and living room. As I had on previous occasions, I enjoyed taking in the lavish white furniture and hand-carved white mantel around the marble fireplace, as well as the dozens of portraits that decorated the walnut-lined walls, all of whom were Baldini ancestors. They had arrived in Crystal Cove in the early 1900s. Their family history was rich.

"Over my dead body!" a man yelled. Nick. I recognized his distinctively gravelly voice.

"You can't make me do anything," a second man shouted. His brother, Alan, I was pretty sure. "I run my life."

"I'll tell the history. Everyone will know."

"I don't care."

"I'll cut you off."

"You wouldn't dare."

"Try me."

Through the opened doors leading to the expansive verandah where the vineyard often hosted lavish tasting parties, I saw Nick pacing the light gray travertine tile. His face was hard, his eyes as dark as his shirt and trousers. Alan, also clad in black on black, was wielding the winepress that Nick had purchased at Hannah's stall and jabbing it toward Nick like he was an animal in a cage.

"Put it down," Nick ordered.

Alan didn't.

"Do it. Now."

"Fine." Alan flung the tool to one side. It crashed against the railing. "I quit!" He threw up his hands.

"You can't quit."

"Sure I can. I'm an employee, not a partner." Chuffing like a tiger — a very meek tiger — Alan stormed into the house, flew past Bailey and me, and exited through the front door. He slammed it so hard that the walls shook.

"Mr. Nick?" the housekeeper said.

Nick whirled around, caught sight of us, and rubbed his jaw. "Geez, ladies, I'm sorry you had to witness that. Alan can be a hothead." He twirled a hand. *"C'è la vita,* as we say in Italian. Such is life."

"Alan quit?" Bailey stammered. "But he's the wedding photographer."

"Don't worry. He'll chill and come crawling back. He likes to quit once a week. He's very opinionated and hates that I am, too." Nick picked up the winepress and waved it nonchalantly. "Promise. It was a typical brother go-round. Brothers fight. Nothing to it. Come with me."

He gestured for us to follow him into his kitchen, which also served as his office. The granite counter was cluttered with plates and glasses, typical countertop items like flour and sugar containers, a bowl of fresh fruits and vegetables, a desktop computer, and a mess of folders. The long-necked cerulean piece of pottery Nick had bought yesterday stood on the sill by the kitchen window. Inspirational magnets clung to his refrigerator. Post-it notes adhered to his computer. The computer screen displayed an impressive photograph of the view of the ocean from the verandah.

Nick crossed to the adjacent utility room and stowed the winepress by its "toes" on the hat-and-coat rack that stood next to the exit door. In addition to sunhats and raincoats, a huge leather glove dangled from one of the rack's pegs. Piles of laundry cluttered the floor.

"Josefina, please set up a beverage tray," Nick said, "and take care of the dishes, would you? Tomorrow you can tackle the dirty clothes."

31

The housekeeper opened cupboards and fetched three colorful goblets.

"What'll it be, ladies?" Nick asked. "White wine, red wine, iced tea, water?"

"Water for me," I said. "I've got to have a steady head the rest of the day." Back when I worked at Taylor & Squibb, I drank liquor once during the middle of the day and I was a basket case for the rest of it. All I'd wanted to do was curl up in a corner and take a nap.

Bailey opted for water, as well.

The housekeeper set a pitcher of ice water beside the goblets and exited the kitchen.

Nick filled three glasses and handed one to each of us. "Follow me. We'll sit outside and breathe in the fresh air as we deliberate."

On his way out the door, he snatched a binder from a wall filled with an array of cookbooks and colorfully bound albums.

"Are all of the albums filled with family photographs?" I asked.

"Most of them. History means a lot to us. However, the one I'm holding contains a series of wedding menus. The topmost one is yours, Bailey. This way."

A soft breeze wafted across the verandah. Pots of colorful geraniums stood in clusters. A seagull squawked overhead. Seconds later, a crow cawed and swooped toward us. Leather tethers hung from the bird's ankles.

Nick scowled. "Cut it out, Alan!"

I scanned the area but didn't see his brother. "Alan?" I asked.

"That's his bird." Nick jammed a finger in the direction of the crow. "Alan's an amateur falconer. Those leather things . . . they're called jesses."

"Ah," I said. "I was wondering who owned the glove hanging in the utility room."

"That's his backup gauntlet," Nick grumbled. "Heaven forbid he loses one. FYI, you'll see my brother with that idiot crow at the fair. He likes to show off how many tricks the bird can do. Right now, he's sending it up here to irk me. I don't want it pooping on the tile."

*Or on our heads,* I prayed.

The bird made another pass.

Nick bolted to the cement railing decorated with ornate balusters. "Alan, I mean it!" he yelled, slapping the top rail for effect. He sighed and returned to us. "Sorry about that. Ever since the accident, he can be so infantile. He was a pretty good lacrosse player in college. We all believed he would go pro until he got whacked in the head with a lacrosse stick."

"I heard about that," I said. My aunt had shared the story. "What a fluke."

"Alan drew into himself after that. Our mother was beside herself with grief."

"I'll bet she was."

"Sit. Please."

We sat at an oversized stone table and set down our water glasses.

"Let's review your menu again." Nick placed the photo album in front of Bailey. "If you've changed your mind about anything, you can swap it out at this juncture. Chef Guy is a whiz and can prepare whatever your heart desires. You know Guy, don't you? He works at Nature's Retreat."

Bailey nodded. "He's got a reputation for making some of the finest food in the area."

"And a reputation for having a huge ego." Nick's eyes sparkled, the spat with his brother a thing of the past.

Bailey rose. "Before we peruse the menu, do you mind if I take some photographs, Nick?"

"Be my guest."

She whipped her iPhone from her purse and began roaming the patio while snapping shots of the view, the gardens, and the vineyard slope. When she aimed the camera at Nick, she said, "Something's different."

"About the place? It's the same as it's always been."

"No. About you." She twirled a finger, as if trying to pinpoint what she sensed. "Your eyes are brighter."

"Because Alan is out of my hair."

"Uh-uh. It's more than that. Are you in love?"

Nick roared with delight. "Why would you think—"

"I'm right, aren't I, Jenna?" Bailey eyed me. "There's this glow about him." She refocused on Nick. "Brides can tell these things. We have a sixth sense, Vera says. I believe her. I feel tuned in." She wriggled her fingertips, begging for the scoop. "C'mon, admit it."

He swung an arm over the back of his chair and chuckled. "Okay, you got me. I'm hopelessly in love."

"He's kidding," I said.

"No, he's not. He's deadly serious."

"Deadly." The corners of Nick's mouth twitched.

"With Dolly?" I asked. Maybe they had patched things up. "I heard you were, um, on the outs."

Nick's eyebrows knitted together. "Did Dolly tell you that?"

"No, I—"

"Yes, she and I have officially ended it. It's amicable."

*Amicable?* Dolly demolishing shelves in her shop with a baseball bat wasn't amicable. What planet was he living on?

"Do we know the lucky woman?" Bailey asked. "Is it Hannah Storm?"

"Are you kidding?" Nick shook his head.

"Jenna, I think the man doth protest too much," Bailey teased. "Hannah is quite a catch, and you're both in the same business. It's a win-win."

Nick wagged a finger and in fair-speak said, "I canst tell you who the fine maiden be."

"Hannah is pretty darned fine," Bailey said, unrelenting.

"My lips are sealed."

Bailey slapped the table. "You rogue."

"I canst tell because I needs wait until she loves me in return."

"You're full of it, Nick." I laughed at his phrasing. "There's no one, Bailey. He's toying with you."

"Aye, there is," Nick said earnestly. "And I wish to make her my queen."

"You're the king," I said. "You can have whomever you wish."

"True, but isn't it better if she comes willingly? Wouldst thou want Rhett to grab you by the hair and drag you to his cave?"

I tapped the tabletop. "You're pulling our legs."

"Perhaps. Perhaps not." He rose to his feet. "Enough about my love life. Let's talk about yours, Bailey." He motioned us to follow him as he roamed the verandah. "You've heard my vision for the wedding many times, but let's make sure we're on the same page. We've discussed your color scheme—burgundy and moss green with a splash of white."

"Check," she said.

"We'll drape moss green chiffon banners between the columns." He swept a hand toward the horizon. "They'll look beautiful against the ocean backdrop, don't you think?"

"Absolutely."

He drew in a deep breath and let it out. "How I love our little town. I adore the view, and the weather is divine year-round."

"Don't kid a kidder," Bailey said. "We get rain and fog."

"But not now. Not on my watch. Ren Fair will be blessed with sunshine. So will your wedding. I am the king." He shot a finger into the air. "The king has decreed."

Bailey applauded.

For some reason, I shivered. I peered over the railing, down the incline, and searched for Alan and his crow, hoping the bird wouldn't soar up and ruin Nick's rosy forecast. I didn't spot either. However, I flinched when I spied a dark-haired woman at the fence beyond the bottommost step. She was studying us through binoculars.

"Is that the border between Baldini Vineyards and Hurricane Vineyards, Nick?" I pointed.

"It is." He didn't follow my motion. Instead, he strolled to the center of the verandah. "Continuing on. Bailey, there will be plenty of flowers. I see red roses and white gerbera daisies. Your bouquet should contain a smattering of thistle for texture."

"Love it." Bailey followed him, lapping up his vision.

"What do you think of a spray of balloons by the cake table?" He gestured to the imaginary spread.

"You don't think they're too childish?"

"Balloons? Never. They imply that you're carefree. I'm also thinking of serving appetizers and wine prior to the wedding, to put guests in the celebratory mood."

Each word Nick uttered earned a murmur of approval from my pal.

I, on the other hand, couldn't stop staring at Hannah. Why was she spying on Nick? That's what it felt like—*spying*. Choosing to defuse the situation, I waved at her.

Hannah released the binoculars and let them dangle on the strap around her neck. With venomous force, she seized a long-handled tool—a shovel, by the glint of it—and began digging.

Turning, I said, "Nick, what's up with—"
But he and Bailey had exited the verandah.

• • •

On the way back to the shop, Bailey and I dropped Nick's housekeeper at the bus stop. When she exited the VW, Bailey launched into boisterous praise of Nick's taste and vision. I considered attaching cement boots to her ankles for the next few days or weeks. That might be the only way to keep her glued to planet Earth. Unwilling to spoil her mood, I chose not to mention seeing Hannah having a snit at the property line. Whatever was bothering her was between her and Nick and would have no affect on Bailey's wedding. None.

When we arrived at the Cookbook Nook at half past four, I was surprised to see Sean Beaufort browsing the kitchenware items. He was admiring a pair of swan salt and pepper shakers, their necks intertwined. He looked quite stylish in a navy blue doublet and trunk hose. I didn't see his wife anywhere. A dozen other shoppers roamed the aisles. Tina was tending to a line of three purchasers at the register.

Bailey handed me her purse and said, "Would you mind stowing this for me? I need to think."

"About?"

"Tito and me and the wedding and . . . you understand." She moved to the vintage kitchen table, perched on a chair, and immediately started to connect the dragon-related pieces of the jigsaw puzzle.

"Have fun," I said. In my book, there is nothing like creative concentration to help a person sort through life's issues.

I placed our purses beneath the cash register, told Tina that I'd help her in a second, and sauntered to the children's corner to give Tigger a scratch. He was beneath the crafts table, clawing the carpet near the feet of three children who were icing mini scones. His festive Robin Hood hat and green vest lay discarded in the corner.

"Are you okay, pal?" I asked. He threw me a mischievous look and continued his attack. Soon I would have to address his uncharacteristically bad behavior—or replace the carpet.

I rose, brushed off my hands, and approached Sean. "Hi, there. We didn't meet the other day at your pottery stall, or later at the taping of the fair-speak video. I'm—"

"Jenna!" Dolly entered at a pace, the skirt of her lime green fair ensemble swishing to and fro. Her arms were loaded with garlands and accessories. "Where do you want me to set up?"

*Oops.* Due to the hoopla about helping Bailey, I'd lost track of time and had forgotten about Dolly's headwear decorating clinic.

"There." I pointed to the children's table. "Bailey will help you." I refocused on Sean. "I apologize. As I was saying, I'm Jenna Hart. I run the Cookbook Nook."

"Nice to meet you." His nose was tinged red, as if he'd been sneezing, but his eyes were bright and his gaze direct. "What a great place. My wife would love everything in it, especially the dessert cookbooks. She's a cookie fiend."

As slim as Melody was, I doubted she ate sweets of any kind. "Where is she?" I asked.

"At the fair teaching a class. I'm"—he jiggled the set of swans—"buying her a surprise. She collects swan things. One of our customers told me you carried these in the shop. I'm so glad you hadn't sold out of them."

"I've heard of all sorts of collections but never swans. Is that what inspires her to make long-necked pottery?"

"It is. She has a Swarovski swan, a Murano swan, a Lladro black swan." He ticked the names off on his fingertips. "She's picked them up everywhere we've lived."

"Her pottery is beautiful, by the way."

"Thanks."

"I'm thinking of taking a class."

"I hope you will." Holding on to the swans, he navigated through the aisles to the dessert cookbooks.

I followed. "How long have you two been married?"

"A while."

"You live in San Francisco, I heard."

"We do now."

"Where did you move from?"

"We've been all over the map."

"Tell me something, Sean. I've never used Airbnb. How do you like staying in Pepper Pritchett's place?"

"We love it. Melody especially likes the backyard with its fresh herbs and vegetables. She enjoys cooking." He pointed at the cookbooks. "Which one should I get her?"

"If she's a dessert nut, how about *The Cookies & Cups Cookbook: 125+ sweet & savory recipes reminding you to Always Eat Dessert First.*"

"That's a mouthful."

I smiled. "Most cookbooks have extraordinarily long titles. The pictures in this book are worth the purchase." I pulled a copy from the shelf and handed it to him. "Pepper told me you stayed at her place before. By yourself."

"I did. To check out Crystal Cove. Melody wanted to come, but she couldn't. She had scheduled classes in the city. She didn't want to let her students down, you know?" He flipped through the pages of the cookbook and stopped at a photograph of chocolate chip cookies, one half eaten. "Nice," he said, showing it to me, and then continued browsing. "I came to do some recon. I wanted to know what we were getting into. We hadn't attended a Renaissance Fair in a while, but Melody really wanted to do this one."

"Did she enjoy making the fair-speak video?"

"Mm-hm," he mumbled.

"A couple of customers who came in this morning watched it at the venue on the Pier and loved it."

"Good to know." He glanced at his watch. "Gee, I've got to get going. Could you ring me up?"

"Sure." I slipped behind the sales counter and took control of the register. Tina had finished with her three customers. "It was lovely that you sent Melody that scroll of poetry last night. My boyfriend Rhett gave me one. It brought tears to my eyes. Are they all Shakespearean sonnets?"

"No."

"Really? You were able to make up your own? What did you say?"

He cocked his head. "That's sort of private."

"Of course." I felt my cheeks flush. "I'm sorry. I didn't mean to pry. I—"

"No worries. I apologize for being abrupt. I'm in a rush to get back." He thrust the swans and cookbook at me. "Ring these up, please." He pulled cash from his wallet and set it on the counter.

I enfolded the swans in tissue, sealed the package with a store sticker, and set them and the cookbook into a pretty gift bag. I tied the handles with blue raffia ribbon and handed the bag to Sean. "Here you go. If there's anything else . . ."

"I almost forgot. Melody wanted a vegetarian cookbook. No need to help me. I'll find something." He walked to the natural foods section to peruse the shelves.

I joined Dolly and Bailey at the kitchen table. Bailey had abandoned the jigsaw puzzle and was helping Dolly smooth the ribbons. I sorted beads. A few spilled into the wrong slots in the Plexiglas containers. "Dolly, lots of people have told me they're coming to your workshop."

"I'm glad to hear that." Her eyes said otherwise. They were blinking rapidly, as if she was doing her best not to cry.

"Bailey!" Tina cried. "Telephone. Nick Baldini needs to talk to you."

Bailey grimaced. "Please don't let it be bad news. Please, please, please don't—"

I swatted her arm. "Will you stop that? We were just there. Everything is fine. He probably wants to pin you down on wine selections. We neglected to do that."

Bailey hurried to answer.

"Nick," Dolly sighed as she continued to sort beads.

"Is everything okay between you two?" I asked, not revealing that I'd already heard.

"He and I broke it off. I was afraid he would. That's why I met with your aunt yesterday. He's been pulling away, you know? I hoped it was because he was busy with the fair." She set a stack of bare garlands on one of the chairs. "He's been doing them since he was a kid. He loves dressing up and doing the fair-speak thing. I love it, too." She started to weave ribbon around one of the garlands. "Alas, our love 'twas not to be. If it were possible to win him back, I would. But I cannot. Woe is me." Melodramatically, she waved a hand. "Got any ideas how to do it?" she asked, dropping the fair-speak.

"No." I didn't have the heart to say that he'd found someone else. He and the woman hadn't hooked up yet—he'd made that clear—but I didn't want to give Dolly false hope.

Bailey returned and sat down. "Phew. Cheese platter or no cheese platter. That is the question."

"It's a no-brainer," I said. "Cheese platter."

Bailey smirked. "That's what I told him."

"*Psst.*" Dolly hitched her chin in the direction of Sean. "I don't mean to gossip, but that guy and his wife are a little odd, don't you think?"

I said, "Pepper says they're darling."

Dolly *tsk*ed. "Pepper has had her head in the clouds ever since she started dating the haberdashery guy."

"She's dating the hat guy?" I asked.

"With the Einstein hair?" Bailey hooted. "What a pair. He preens over his wares like they're priceless jewels."

"Yes, he does. As for Sean and Melody, take it from me" — Dolly crossed her heart — "they are different. He treats her like she's a porcelain doll, which is funny seeing as she makes delicate pottery." She tapped my wrist. "By the way, I heard him say his wife was at the fair teaching, but I didn't see her there as I was leaving."

A shadow loomed over Dolly and her wares. I glanced up. Sean was standing behind her. I gulped. Was he upset to hear his wife wasn't where he expected her to be? He was holding a *Medieval Tapestries Coloring Book* as well as a copy of *The Good Cook's Book of Tomatoes: A New World Discovery and Its Old World Impact.*

"I'm ready to check out again," he said. "Melody has become obsessed with Mrs. Pritchett's ugly tomatoes as well as this coloring for adults fad." He waved the tapestries book. "Honestly? Like she has extra time."

I breathed easier. If he had overheard Dolly's account, he didn't seem in the least perturbed. In fact, his face was one hundred percent neutral.

# Chapter 5

It never ceases to amaze me how quickly the night turns dark after Daylight Savings ends. As Bailey, Tito, and I were walking to the Pier, the sky turned as black as ink. If not for a smattering of stars and the glow of torches and lanterns lighting our path, the evening would feel eerie. The walk didn't take long, but I was thankful to be wearing my comfortable fair sandals. I was equally thankful to have my dainty crocheted purse. It was the perfect size to hold the basics: comb, cell phone, tube of lip gloss, and keys.

At the entrance to the boardwalk, a band of minstrels in green fitted jackets, green-and-red doublets, and red hose greeted us with a sprightly tune on their lutes. Along North Street, a group of female madrigals in matching honey-toned, long-sleeved gowns sang "Greensleeves" in three-part harmony. They were competing with a noisy bagpiper who merrily danced about them. Cinderella's stepsisters couldn't have looked more peeved by his presence.

I spotted Rhett and shouted, "Hi-ho, Rhett!"

He escaped a swarm of jovial fairgoers and strolled toward me looking dashing in his Robin Hood outfit. Even better, he was carrying chicken kebabs. I was starved. He offered one to me. "For you, my lady."

"Thankee." I pecked his cheek and took my dinner from him. "Lola's?"

"None other." He handed me a napkin.

I bit into the kebab and wiped juice off my face. "Scrumptious." The blend of ginger and soy sauce was perfect.

"Rhett, where did you buy those?" Tito asked.

"Lola's Lusciousness is on South Street, near the Word."

"Babe, can you hold this for me?" Tito asked Bailey. "I'll be right back with dinner." He handed her the large bell he carried to complement his town crier outfit and dashed off.

"My mother is a riot." Bailey snickered. "Honestly? *Lola's Lusciousness?* Hey, there's Dolly. Yoo-hoo, Dolly." She waved. "Join us."

Dolly, who had changed since her clinic at the shop, was wearing yet another green gown, this one a rich loden green with a beaded bodice and puffy sleeves. She strolled in our direction carrying a staff illed with garlands. The ribbons on the garlands fluttered in the air. Colorful beads strung together on silk ropes clacked together. Dolly's face was a tad flushed and her hair was bedraggled, as though she'd rushed through a wind tunnel. Otherwise, she seemed in good spirits.

"Your clinic was amazing," Bailey said when Dolly drew near. "Everyone was ecstatic. I bet you'll see many of your students sporting their artwork tonight."

"Bailey's right," I said. "It was awesome."

The workshop had lasted forty-five minutes and had gone off without a hitch. Twenty adults and children had shown up to learn how to make a garland. A few had chosen to make caps with feathers. Around five p.m., Dolly remembered an important appointment and apologized profusely for not being able to stick around to see her students' finished products.

"Where did you run off to?" I asked.

"An errand," she said curtly. No elaboration.

"Off with your head!" a woman bellowed.

We all turned to see who was making the disturbance.

A woman dressed like the Queen of Hearts in a gorgeous red-and-black gown with three red hearts down the center of her skirt paraded along North Street swinging a croquet mallet. Behind her trooped a battalion of men dressed as playing cards.

A dimple-cheeked man in a simple brown frock preceded her and chanted, "The queen is playing croquet. Come see the queen play croquet. Challenge her if you dare."

The group, as a unit, continued to plow toward the far end of the Pier.

Rhett said, "If you haven't seen this spectacle, you should."

"When did you see it?" I asked.

"On my break. They held a match this afternoon. Near the petting zoo, they've laid out a large square of green grass and installed croquet wickets. Vendors closed up shops. Everyone was there. The guy selling the poetry scrolls and Dolly and . . ."

Dolly clapped her hands. "It was so much fun. It took place right before I came to the Cookbook Nook."

Bailey said, "When we were meeting with Nick."

"The queen is a hoot, as you can plainly see," Dolly continued.

"She's an actress from Los Angeles and travels all over California to do these fairs." She tapped my arm. "By the way, Jenna, I saw Melody Beaufort a minute ago. She's at her booth. No cause for alarm."

"Alarm?" I raised an eyebrow.

"I saw the way you reacted at the shop, like you were worried her husband might have . . ." She leaned in close. "I told you he was overly protective, and you freaked."

"Did not."

"Did too. You worried that he might hurt her when he caught up with her. Did a guy abuse a woman you knew?"

"Years ago." When I'd worked at Taylor & Squibb. The woman who had come up with the campaign for Poppi's Spicy bite-sized Poppers was delicate and sweet. Her boyfriend had mistreated her for years, but she had kept quiet. When she showed up in the emergency room with a busted arm and jaw, she caved and came clean.

"Well, Melody is fine," Dolly said. "She told me business was light so she'd gone for a stroll. P.S., given your, um, *concern*, I did a quick assessment. I didn't see any signs of abuse. Not even the telltale bruises from someone pinching her arms." Reassuringly, she petted my shoulder. "My college roommate was abused, as well."

"I don't know why I was worried. I barely know the woman."

"Because you are female and you care. In my humble opinion, I think Sean is madly in love with her and wishes he could put her in a bubble." She hoisted her staff of goods. "And now, lo, I must bid you leave and hawk my wares. Garlands! Garlands for sale. Prithee, who shall be my next taker?"

"Hey, everybody" — Tito raced up with two kebabs and clasped Bailey's arm — "you've got to see this. Rhett, Jenna, follow me."

He darted into a cut-through. We followed him out the other side to the railing. He pointed toward the beach, where klieg lights highlighted a man in a black troubadour costume who was kneeling on one knee, facing a young woman in a baby blue gown. A half dozen similarly aged women stood in a semicircle behind the girl in blue. A child in a Little Boy Blue costume, complete with a plumed hat, stood beside the man. He was holding a pillow. On top of the pillow — a jewel case.

"Tara-tara!" an angular man standing along the railing sang through a long antler-style horn. "Behold, the engagement!"

"That's a Savernake horn," Tito said. "It's from the Middle Ages."

"Or a replica," Bailey joked.

"The decorative bands near the horn's mouth are carved with creatures that include hawks, unicorns, and lions," Tito added.

"Is this a put-on?" I asked.

Tito shook his head. "Nope. They're really getting engaged. You can sign up to get engaged or renew your vows at the admission booth."

"Aw. How romantic." Bailey wrapped her arm around her fiancé, his town crier bell still clutched in her hand.

"Let's do it, babe." Tito thrust the kebabs at Rhett. "Hold these, will you? Eat them if you must. I'll go fill out the paperwork. There's an opening in an hour."

Bailey batted his shoulder. "Stop."

"I mean it." Tito took her free hand in his. "I love you so much. I want to renew our vows."

"We haven't said our vows yet, dufus. We aren't married. Speaking of which, I met with Nick Baldini today. We went over the menus, and I took photos of the venue." She pulled her cell phone from her silk clutch.

"Put that away," I said. "It's bad luck to have it out."

Bailey scoffed. "Get out of here. Bad luck?"

"You're the one who was worried about *vibes*." I wiggled my fingers.

She gazed at the cell phone screen. "I'm over that. I—" Her mouth pulled down in a frown. "Speak of the devil, I missed a message from Nick." She entered her password and pressed the Phone icon. She listened to her message and tears sprang to her eyes.

"What's wrong?" I asked.

Bailey shoved her cell phone at me and pressed Play.

"Bailey? Bail—" It was Nick. He sounded panicked. The time stamp showed the message came in about an hour ago.

I clicked Redial. Nick's voice mail engaged. Calmly, he asked the caller to leave a message.

"Something has happened," Bailey said, snatching her phone from me. "I'm sure of it."

"What's going on?" Rhett asked.

I recapped the cryptic message.

"Did you hear something else, Jenna?" Bailey asked. "It sounded like Nick was struggling with someone."

"I'm not sure. I heard a bird caw. In the background."

"I heard that, too." Bailey nodded. "It had to be Alan's crow. We've got to get over there."

"Hold it," Rhett said. "Why?"

"Nick and his brother had a fight earlier," Bailey said. "What if Alan hurt Nick this time, and Nick needs help?"

"C'mon, babe." Tito opened his hands. "Aren't you overreacting?"

"No!" Bailey shouted.

The *vibes* premonition was definitely fueling her worry. Mine, too.

Minutes later, all of us piled into Rhett's Ford F-250. I took the passenger seat. Bailey and Tito scrambled into the Super Cab's rear seat. As we drove, I reflected on how calm Rhett and Tito were acting. I hoped they were right. Maybe Nick had called Bailey, but Alan showed up so Nick ended the call mid-stream. *Brothers fight*, he'd said. Nick needed to have it out with Alan one more time. That was all. Nothing to be alarmed about.

However, when we arrived at Nick's house and I saw the front door was wide open, my stomach flip-flopped.

Bailey bolted out of the truck. "Tito and I are going in."

"We are?" His voice cracked.

"Nick might need our help." She tore into the house.

"Wait!" I called.

"Better to forge ahead as a group," Tito said and hurried after her.

I darted past him into the foyer. The lights were on in the kitchen but nowhere else. I gripped Bailey by the wrist. "Hold up. You don't know if—"

Something went *clack*. I snapped to attention.

"That was the ice maker," Bailey hissed and wriggled free. She rushed to the kitchen but paused in the archway and gasped. "Nick!" She charged forward.

I trailed her and skidded on my heels when I saw Nick lying facedown, motionless on the floor, his head in the direction of the computer, his feet toward the door leading to the verandah. Blood oozed from the back of Nick's head. I shoved a fist into my mouth to keep from screaming. Tears pressed at the corners of my eyes.

Tito and Rhett entered the kitchen and moaned.

Bailey bent and clasped Nick's wrist. "He's dead." She peeped over her shoulder at us. "Alan must have killed him."

"Don't jump to conclusions," I warned.

"You heard them earlier. Nick yelled, 'Over my dead body.' I'll bet Alan inherits everything. Look at this place. He'll be wealthy beyond his dreams, and Nick—" She sucked back a sob. "Poor Nick."

Tito lifted Bailey to her feet and hugged her. "Shh, *mi amor.*"

"The wedding," she stammered.

"Shh, it'll work out. Shh."

The horror of the scene cut through me. I began to shiver. Rhett threw his arms around me. Gazing over his shoulder, I scanned the kitchen. I didn't see anything that appeared out of the ordinary. The plates and glasses had been washed and put away. The bowl of vegetables, which now included more tomatoes, sat on the windowsill. The long-necked piece of pottery stood beside a companion piece—a vase with a rose. The computer was in sleep mode. Had Nick been researching something? If so, his back would have been toward the door. Did Alan—or whoever killed him— steal in and bash his head? Or had Nick spun away from his assailant? What weapon had been used? The gash looked irregular and gnarly.

"I'm fine," I assured Rhett and pressed apart. I inched closer to the computer and reviewed the Post-it notes. One read: *Fix it.* Another read: *Get MEDS.* Nick had drawn a heart symbol beside that. Another note contained his to-do list: *lunch, grocery store, pepper, p/u napkin rings, art supplies, dry cleaning.* Normal stuff. He was supposed to rise tomorrow and do errands. Live a normal life. Tears trickled down my cheeks. I mopped them with my fingertips.

"We should call 911," Rhett said.

"Forget 911," I muttered. "I'm calling Cinnamon." I have her on direct dial.

After I told her where I was and what had happened, she said, "You've got to be kidding. You found another dead body? Again?" She said she would arrive shortly and ended the call.

Bailey broke free from Tito and gripped my arm. "This must have been the bad vibes my mother was picking up."

Another sob caught in my throat. "Why did Nick have to die? He was such a good guy."

"Bad things happen to good guys." Rhett ran his hand along my back to comfort me. Sad to say, his caress didn't help.

I slogged to the verandah and gazed over the railing, scanning the dark horizon for Alan. Had he killed his brother? Was he lurking in the vineyard below?

Rhett, Bailey, and Tito followed me.

"Do you see Alan?" Bailey asked. "Or his bird?"

"No."

"Hey." Bailey lunged to pick up a cell phone lying on the tile beside the stone table, its face smashed to smithereens.

I said, "Don't touch—"

Too late. She scooped it up and, despite its decimated condition, swiped the screen. "Darn. It won't open."

"No surprise," I said.

Out of nowhere a black bird soared over our heads. It had to be Alan's crow. Was Alan nearby? The bird cawed shrilly and dive-bombed us. We all ducked. It landed on the tile and pecked at something shiny lodged against the railing.

"What is it after?" I whispered.

The bird cut a quick look at us. I whipped my cell phone from my purse, opened the camera app, and snapped a photograph of whatever it was trying to retrieve with its beak. The flash went off. The crow squawked, clearly agitated by the distraction.

"That's the sound I heard on the voice mail," I blurted.

Bailey nodded. "Me, too."

The bird nabbed its shiny reward and took to the sky, its jesses flapping like streamers.

• • •

Chief of Police Cinnamon Pritchett, clad in her brown-on-brown uniform, no hat, her bobbed haircut looking recently trimmed, banned us from the house but not from the premises. She wanted to question us after she was certain the investigation was properly under way. The four of us sat in the bed of Nick's truck, Bailey softly bemoaning that her wedding was *cursed*. Tito whispered sweet nothings in Spanish, but no words could console her.

Around ten p.m. Cinnamon exited the house and tramped toward us. At times, she could be perky and approachable; when she was on the job, however, she was as sober as a judge. She was carrying something long and irregular, a towel wrapped around its handle.

I leaped from the truck and met her halfway. "Is that—"

"The murder weapon."

It was a foot-shaped winepress like the one Nick had purchased.

"Hannah Storm is selling those at the fair," I said and stiffened as I recalled Hannah standing at the juncture of the neighboring vineyards, spying on Nick. When I had acknowledged her, she'd dug the ground angrily with what I assumed was a shovel. What was her beef with Nick? "Where did you find it?"

"In a bush down the slope."

Bailey joined us. "His brother must have thrown it there."

Cinnamon regarded my grief-stricken friend. "Alan?"

"He killed him." Bailey rehashed the afternoon conflict, what little we had heard.

Cinnamon repeated a segment. "Nick said, 'Over my dead body'? That's not much to go on."

"A bird cawed when Nick telephoned me," Bailey added. "We saw a bird on the verandah. A crow. Alan's—"

"Nick called you?" Cinnamon asked, cutting her off.

Bailey pulled her cell phone from her silk clutch, swiped the screen, entered her pass code, and clicked the Phone icon. She handed it to Cinnamon. "Listen."

The call was so short that Cinnamon replayed it twice. "Why did he call you?"

"Maybe it was accidental, you know, a pocket call."

"Except he said your name."

I said, "What if during the struggle, he pressed the number of the last person he'd dialed, and knowing it was Bailey, he cried for help."

Cinnamon nodded. "Possibly."

Bailey said, "Were your tech guys able to open Nick's phone? The screen was smashed, but—"

Cinnamon sprinted to the front door and yelled, "Appleby! Bring me Baldini's cell phone."

Although Deputy Marlon Appleby was a massive guy and in his fifties, he jogged out the door like a teenager. "Here you go." He thrust the smashed cell phone at his boss.

She didn't take it. She wasn't wearing Latex gloves like he was. "Did you find anything on it, or was it impossible to open?"

"As a matter of fact . . ." He whispered something in Cinnamon's ear then scratched his moose-shaped jaw, which was all the more prominent because of his new buzz cut.

Cinnamon scrunched her nose with distaste. "Yeah, okay. Let's hear it for fingerprints."

*Ugh.* I shuddered. They must have needed to use Nick's finger to decode the password.

"Show me the telephone records," Cinnamon said.

Appleby swiped the screen, pressed a button or two, and displayed it to her.

"Huh," she muttered.

"What's wrong?" I asked.

"The call records have been erased."

# Chapter 6

When Cinnamon released us, Rhett took me to the shop so I could fetch my VW — my aunt had brought Tigger home earlier. Afterward, he followed me to my place. My cottage isn't big, but I am thankful that my aunt, who lives in the main house on the beachfront property, lets me live here. I love waking to the sound of surf. I adore going for a walk or run to clear the cobwebs. The cottage is one expansive room with a bay window, a red brick fireplace, a wall of books, and a niche for my art supplies. The bachelorette kitchen is barely big enough for one person to move around in, let alone two.

Since we'd abandoned our kebabs at the Pier, I allowed Rhett to throw a meal together for us. He was a former chef; I was a foodie. I could have made something simple, like melted cheese and avocado on English muffins. I am quite adept at *simple*. But he wanted something more substantial. Luckily I'd purchased fresh vegetables and herbs at the farmer's market the day before yesterday. Rhett chose to stir-fry shrimp, tomatoes, zucchini, garlic, and basil. I boiled angel hair pasta. We didn't speak. I think we were too busy mulling over what had happened to Nick. Tigger orbited our feet questioning the quiet.

A half hour later, we ate at the kitchen table. The flavors were sensational, the textures divine. Even so, the food sat like a lump in my stomach. A small glass of chianti helped, but not much.

While washing the dishes, I said, "Bailey isn't going to be in good shape tomorrow."

Rhett took a plate from me and dried it with a towel. "We'll find her a new venue."

"She'll want to cancel the whole thing. She believes in curses."

"Your aunt can hypnotize her."

"Maybe if we could figure out who killed Nick — and it's not Alan — then she could still hold the wedding there."

He caressed the back of my hair with his fingertips. "Would you want to have a wedding where a murder occurred?"

"No." I swung around and placed my hands on his chest. "Oh, Rhett, I can't get the image of Nick out of my mind and that to-do list on his computer. He was supposed to wake up tomorrow and live his life. Not die."

Rhett cupped my chin and gazed into my eyes. "Cinnamon will solve this."

"Promise?"

"I do." He kissed me softly on my forehead. "Want me to stay?"

I nodded.

• • •

Thursday morning, I trudged into the Cookbook Nook feeling like I'd been hit by a Mack truck. "Whiskey in the Jar," a traditional and lively song by the Dubliners, was playing in the queue, but it did nothing to lighten my mood.

I set Tigger on the floor, and he instantly started attacking the carpet beneath the children's table. What was up with him? Were there kitty obedience trainers I could hire to squelch bad behavior? I'd probably done his emotions no favor by tossing and turning all night. I'd dreamed of Nick lying dead in his kitchen. And Post-it notes whipping through the air. And Alan yelling at his brother. I'd even had nightmares about Alan's crow keening and aiming for us on the verandah, which reminded me that I hadn't looked at the photograph I'd taken to see what the crow had made off with.

The moment I situated myself behind the sales counter, I opened my camera app. A close-up revealed that the bird had nabbed an ornate gold-and-green bead. I'd heard shiny objects could fixate birds. Had it seen the object in the dark of night, or had there been more beads at another time, and the bird had come back for the last one? Did the killer lose the bead?

*No, Jenna,* I chided. *The bead could have been lying on the tile for a long time.*

Where was Alan? Had Cinnamon tracked him down? Did he have an alibi?

"Good morning, Jenna." Tina emerged from the storage room. Beaming, she did a twirl in front of the sales counter. Tendrils from her updo hairstyle fanned out as she pirouetted. "Like my getup?" She was wearing yet another red wench's costume, featuring frothy sleeves and a white apron.

"It's lovely. Did you sew this one, too?"

"I did. Why the long face? You can't frown today." She clucked her tongue. "Chef will have a fit. It's Thursday—pasties demonstration day."

Discreetly, she pointed a finger at her palm, directing my attention to Katie, who had donned her chef's coat over a simple peasant dress, but instead of her toque she wore an old-fashioned cook's hat with a fluted brim. How had I missed her when I'd entered? She was standing near the cookware items, setting up a mobile cooking cart with the makings for pasties. She did so many demonstrations nowadays that we had invested in high-end carts.

"We have to be up, up, up," Tina said to me. "You know how Chef needs positive energy when she's giving a chat."

I clutched Tina's arm and steered her into the storage room. I drew the curtain closed. The cramped area was filled with shelves of books, unpacked boxes, foldable chairs, a small office desk, a file cabinet, a water cooler, and cleaning supplies. "Someone we know died."

"Who?"

"Nick Baldini."

"How horrible. Was he ill?"

"No, he—"

"What can I do?" Tina asked. "Is that why Bailey called in sick?"

"She's sick?"

"Don't worry. Her mother's with her. Nick Baldini is dead." Her voice caught. "Man, that stinks."

"He was murdered."

"Holy moly." She clapped a hand over her mouth. Then her eyes went wide. "He was king of Ren Fair. Who will take his place?" Tears pressed at the corners of her eyes. "Poor Bailey. She must feel horrible that she'll have to cancel her wedding."

"She won't cancel. She'll secure another venue."

"Well, she'll have to postpone it, at least. No one can arrange a site quickly these days. You need at least a year in advance." She snapped her fingers. "I know what we need. Fairy dust."

"Fairy dust?"

"To sprinkle on her. Flora Fairchild says it's potent stuff."

"Why does Flora know anything about fairies?"

Flora is the owner of Home Sweet Home, a place that features candles and tablecloths and such. Not fairies.

"Because she's the Mistress of Fairies at the fair. Haven't you seen her garden creations? They are something to behold. So pretty. So whimsical." Tina flitted her fingers as if sprinkling fairy dust. "She has a booth near Pepper's. What Flora can do with moss and miniature lights is astounding." She toyed with a tendril of her hair. "Did you know that fairies—"

"Enough about fairies. Neither they nor their dust will cure Bailey today."

"Maybe flipping through the fairy books you ordered would help you believe. I'm particularly fond of *Fairy House: How to Make Amazing Fairy Furniture, Miniatures, and More from Natural Materials.* You know the one I mean, with the darling cottage door and teensy mailbox on the cover. I love how the authors point out how to use different leaves and such."

I'd added a few fairy-themed books to the store because fairgoers often believed in the mystical. "Let Bailey be," I said. "Her mother will keep her grounded during this difficult time."

"Yoo-hoo, Jenna," Katie called from her mobile cooking cart. "Help me set up chairs. Twelve have signed up for the demo."

I joined her and eyed the makings for pasties: flour, eggs, butter, rolling pin, parchment paper, chopped meats, vegetables, and spices. "Nice array."

We unlocked the wheels on our portable bookshelves and glided them to the sides, then we fetched a dozen folding chairs from the storage room.

"You look glum, chum," Katie said as we positioned the chairs in two rows. "Did someone die?"

"Yes. Nick Baldini."

Katie blanched. "Golly. I was kidding. What happened?"

"He was murdered."

"What is up with your karma, Jenna?"

"Not *my* karma," I protested. "*Nick's!* Bailey, Rhett, Tito, and I found him. I still can't believe it. He was a real bastion of our town."

"I hate when someone nice dies." Katie slumped into one of the opened chairs. "And Nick was nicer than nice. He came into the café often and was always cordial. Why, he was in last week and asked me to make sure I made Scotch eggs during the fair. They were his favorite. I promised I would." She rubbed her finger beneath her nose. "Do the police know who did it?"

"Not yet. They're looking into Nick's brother."

"Hoo-boy. Not a chance. Not Alan." Katie shook her head. "He's as sweet as they come. We've chatted a number of times. There's something special about the way he stares intently at you, hanging on your every word."

"He and Nick argued." I told her how Bailey and I had come upon the two of them having it out. "Bailey thinks Alan might inherit a ton of money."

"That's always a good motive." Katie rose and resumed positioning chairs.

I opened the last chair; it squeaked loudly and didn't unfold completely. I pounded the seat to bend it to my will.

"How did Nick, um, die?" Katie asked.

"The killer hit him in the head with one of those foot-shaped winepresses that Hannah is selling."

Her mouth opened in astonishment. "The killer used an antique winepress? On a vintner? Is that significant?"

"I don't know."

"*Hmph,*" she muttered and returned to the cooking cart and rearranged the items on top.

While mulling over her query, I straightened the bookshelves. Was the murderer, by using a winepress, making a statement about Nick or his vineyard? I thought of Hannah, a fellow vintner, digging into his ground with venomous fury. Did she kill him? No, I didn't believe her capable of murder. She, like Nick, was one of the nicest people I knew. She donated time to the library and read books to kids at a children's hospital. According to Aunt Vera, she was a saint when it came to taking care of her elderly grandmother. I erased the possibility from my mind and tended to the book tables.

An hour later, customers showed up for Katie's demonstration. So many additional people had shown up that a few were forced to stand behind those who were seated.

Once the hubbub diminished, Katie carried in a tray from the café that she'd covered with a white cloth. A surprise lay underneath, she whispered to me. After setting it on the lowest shelf of the mobile cart, she clapped her hands and addressed the crowd. "Welcome, one and all." She went into her spiel with fervor, starting as she often did with the history of the food she was highlighting.

"How many know what a pasty is?"

Hands rose.

"For those who don't, it's a small pie usually filled with meat or vegetables. They are tasty with a capital *T*." She let loose with a hearty laugh. "The origin of the pasty is unclear, though a version of *Le Viandier of Taillevent*, the earliest recipe collection, which dates to around 1300, contains a number of pasty recipes. In 1393, *Le Menagier de Paris*, better known to us as *The Parisian Household Book*, shared more recipes." She held up a finger to make a point. "Now, here's an interesting tidbit. Because the pasty is attributed to Cornwall, England, some say it's not a pasty if it's not made there. Do you think that matters?"

A few in the crowd murmured, "No."

One young man in a courtier's costume cried, "Enough history, Chef. Show us how to make one."

In a matter of minutes, Katie demonstrated how to combine the flour and salt and cut in the butter. She added water and shaped the pastry into a ball.

Next, she lined a baking sheet with parchment paper. In a large bowl, she combined some shredded beef, diced potatoes, minced onions, and chopped carrots. She seasoned liberally with salt and pepper.

Following that step, Katie expertly divided the dough into six pieces and rolled one out on a floured surface. "Six-inch rounds. That's what you're going for." She lifted the round into the air, even though the audience could see what she was doing via the angled mirror attached to the top of the demonstration cart.

"Place a half-cup portion of filling on the round, leaving the edges free. Carefully draw the other half of the pastry over the filling and crimp the edges. I moisten my fingers to do this. Then, using a fork"—she demonstrated each step—"make tine marks and prick the top to let steam escape. Place the pastry on the prepared baking sheet." She held up the tray. "Now bake in a preheated oven for forty to forty-five minutes, until golden brown."

She bent down, set the tray on the bottommost shelf and retrieved the tray she'd covered with a white cloth. "Voilà. Behold! Finished pasties. Still warm from the oven. Try one. On your feet. Don't be shy."

The visitors formed a line. Each plucked a pasty from the tray. A chorus of *oohs* and *aahs* filled the shop. I could tell by the way Katie was primping the front of her chef's jacket that she was pleased.

"And now, you varlets," she went on, "this demonstration has come to an end."

The attendees burst into applause. Katie's cheeks flushed with pride.

"Remember to stop by my booth on the Pier and"—she hollered like a seasoned hawker—"pay the tender for another of me tasty pasties. I've made a vegetarian one featuring rutabaga."

As the crowd dispersed, many attendees who were regulars at Katie's demonstrations knew what to do. They folded their chairs and set them against the wall by the storage room, making our cleanup chore a tad easier.

"Thank you," I said to each.

"Hey, Jenna." Tina waved to me from the children's table, where she was setting up Middle Ages paper dolls for a children's afternoon workshop. I'd found a terrific educational Internet site through Pinterest that featured all sorts of free printouts. "There's Flora." She pointed outside. "See her coming out of Beaders of Paradise? She's walking really fast. Go catch her. Ask her about the fairy dust."

"You do it."

"Uh-uh. You're the curious one."

We were both resisting because Flora could be a nonstop talker. It depended on the day and her mood just how long she might bend one's ear.

"Fine." I exited the shop. Sunlight beamed down. I shaded my eyes and said, "Hello, Flora."

"Hi, Jenna." While adjusting the glittery garland that matched her mint green chiffon dress, she kept looking over her shoulder.

"Pretty wreath."

"Thank you." She repositioned the garland's ribbons, pulled her thick braid forward over one shoulder, and shifted the shopping bag from Pepper's place into her other hand.

"Is everything okay? You seem distracted."

"It's nothing. It's—" She flitted a hand and attempted a smile. Her apple cheeks did their best to lift the corners of her mouth but failed. "A slew of craft supplies, mainly beads, disappeared at the fair."

"How?"

"They were stolen. By a teenager, I would imagine."

"I'm sorry to hear that."

"I absolutely had to replace them." Flora is a serious beader. She regularly joins Pepper's classes, and she adds beading to nearly every piece of her clothing.

I beckoned her inside the Cookbook Nook. "Before you return to the fair, would you like a freshly made pasty to salve your loss?"

"Don't mind if I do. I'm starved."

I guided her inside to the breezeway, where Katie had set out the remaining pasties on a three-tiered cake plate.

Flora drew a paper napkin from the medieval-themed set and plunked a pasty on top. She nibbled the corner and hummed her appreciation. "Yummy."

"I hear you're the Mistress of Fairy Gardens."

Flora bobbed her head and nibbled the other corner. "'Tis so. I summon the darling creatures when the sun is arisen."

"Is that why you sort of look like a fairy today?"

"'Tis true. Verily."

"Okay, cut the fair-speak."

Flora giggled. "For you, anything." She shuffled in her purse, pulled out a set of photographs, and handed them to me. "Here are a few of the gardens I've created."

"Wow." I whistled, swept away by her artistry. One featured a little blue cottage, its roof made out of stained popsicle sticks. It was set in a forest paved with miniature blue stones and teeming with polka-dotted mushrooms. She'd created another inside a large clay pot, its front side carved off. Teensy steps wound up a hill within the pot to a castle. Petite succulent plants decorated the landscape. "These are gorgeous, Flora, but I don't see any fairies."

"Each fairy must match the needs of the buyer, so I make them individually upon request. And I never photograph them. They're quite personal. One mother wanted two fairies that resembled her little girls."

"How sweet. And the fairy dust?" I asked, getting to my point. "Do you sell it in your store?"

She winked. "Fairy dust is magical. It can only be sold at the fair where the magic is alive."

"I need some for Bailey—"

"Jenna!" Aunt Vera rushed into the shop, her bangles clacking and the myriad strands of her beads jangling. She extended her arms and dragged me away from Flora. Quietly she said, "Marlon phoned me and told me about Nick. You found him? How horrible. I can't believe it. Nick was one of the sweetest men I knew. His family and I—"

"Go way back," I finished.

"It's such a shock." She released me and covered her mouth with her hand. The sleeves of her royal purple caftan rustled as she did. "How are you? How is Bailey?"

"She feels her wedding is cursed."

"Nonsense." Aunt Vera rubbed the phoenix amulet she wore around her neck. "We'll do some cleansing spells, and she'll be right as rain."

"Ha!" I arched an eyebrow. "You don't believe that or you wouldn't be stroking your charm."

She let her hands drop to her sides. "White light. Think white light." She made sure I nodded in agreement before heading for the storage room. "I won't be staying long. Are you and Tina managing? I must return to the fair. Alas, there will be so many who need my guidance today. Everyone loved Nick."

*Not everyone,* I mused.

"Too-ra-loo," she crooned as she disappeared through the break in the curtains, although there wasn't much joy in her typically cheery trill.

Flora joined me in the shop and blotted her fingers on a cocktail napkin. "Why is she so upset? Why will people need her help?"

"There was a murder last night."

"Not another." Flora wadded the cocktail napkin. "Pepper didn't mention a thing when I was in Beaders of Paradise."

"She might not know."

"Surely her daughter would keep her informed."

"Not necessarily."

"Who was killed?" Flora crumpled the napkin.

"Nick Baldini."

"Mercy." Flora grimaced. "He was so engaging and funny." She paused, a little hum escaping her mouth.

"What?"

"Come to think of it, I saw him arguing with a woman yesterday. The one who makes the long-necked pottery."

"Melody Beaufort?"

"That's the one. Such a pretty thing. As delicate as a lily. She's fascinated by my fairy gardens. She wanders over whenever there's a lull. Our stalls aren't far from one another." She tossed the used napkin into the trash by the sales counter. "I know Z.Z. wants all the vendors to get involved in authentic playacting, but this quarrel between Nick and Melody seemed real. It was filled with emotion. Nick's face was red. Melody's tone was biting."

"What did they say to each other?"

"I have no idea. I blotted the incident from my mind. Fairies don't take kindly to negativity. They need peaceful environments filled with beautiful flowers like gardenias and heather and honeysuckle. Did you know fairies adore shiny objects?"

*Like a crow,* I reflected.

"Flora," I said, trying to keep her on track. "The argument?"

"As I said, it might have been in jest. They both used fair-speak. Melody said, 'Let go of me, rogue.'"

"Nick was holding on to her?"

"Yes. By the wrist. He said, 'Verily, you are a strong wench. Dost thee not recognize me?'"

"You claimed you didn't hear what they said."

"What I meant was that I didn't comprehend it. Melody responded by saying, 'Me-thinks thee art madder than a hatter.'" Flora gestured dramatically with each portrayal. "If they were pretending, they were doing a good job. You don't think she could have had anything to do with his death, do you?"

"I won't rule anyone out right now."

"Yes, of course. You can't." She sucked back a sob. "If you want some fairy dust for Bailey, stop by my booth. I'll give it to you for free. We must keep our spirits positive and call upon all who can restore sanity. Fairies are delighted to help heal." Falling into fair-speak, she said, "I shall take my leave to meditate." She bustled out of the shop and veered right toward Home Sweet Home, which was located less than half a block away.

As I glided the bookshelves into position and anchored their wheels, I recalled how tenderly Nick had acted toward Melody the night before the fair started, removing a ribbon that had clung to her face. I also remembered how they had interacted during the fair-speak video. Had they met that day, or had they known each other previously? She lived in San Francisco.

I halted, realizing that wasn't exactly true. Sean mentioned they had moved *all over the map*. Where had they resided before? Nick was a local. He was born here. I doubted Melody was from around here, or else Pepper—also a local—would have mentioned something.

Could Melody be the woman Nick had fallen for? He said that the lady in question wasn't in love with him yet. Was he trying to woo her away from her husband? Maybe that was what their altercation had been about. Had he overstepped his bounds? Did she warn him to stop his advances? When he didn't, did she lash out? Did her husband?

"Dear"—Aunt Vera exited the storage room, having donned a royal blue turban decorated with a fashionable gem—"call Bailey, please, and tell her I'll be over soon. A positive tarot card reading should bring her comfort. I'm going to fetch a cup of tea before I leave."

I dialed my pal, but she didn't answer. Lola didn't answer her cell phone, either. I resorted to texting both of them, and received a quick response: *I'm okay. Don't worry. Your aunt doesn't need to come.* I replied: *As if that will stop her* and added a slew of *OXOXOX*.

After returning my cell phone to my purse, I nestled on the stool by the cash register and initiated an Internet search on the desktop computer. Melody's relationship to Nick was bothering me.

Aunt Vera appeared with a to-go cup stuffed into a corrugated paper sleeve. "What are you up to?"

"I wanted to see if Melody Beaufort and Nick might have met before the fair." I told her about the argument Flora had witnessed.

"Nick was very active on Facebook," my aunt said. "He posted tons of photos about the fair. You could start there. See if a picture of her shows up."

I brought up Nick's profile and was astounded by how many digital albums he had catalogued in his photographs: family and friends and Renaissance Fairs dating back to the 1990s.

I clicked on the Renaissance Fair 2015 album. There were tons of pictures. Nick's Henry VIII costume that year was a forbidding black emblazoned with gold. For Renaissance Fair 2016, the king's costume was forest green with red trim. For Renaissance Fair 2017, he had worn a gold getup trimmed with blue. I didn't see any photos of Melody but hadn't expected to. Sean said they hadn't attended a Renaissance Fair in a long time.

"Click that album." My aunt pointed to one titled Ren Camp, 1992. "Let me see him when he was a young man." She sucked back a sob.

Over the years, Nick had taught lots of children how to playact for the Renaissance Fair. There were pictures of him teaching swordplay as well as the art of juggling. In every shot, children's faces were lit with delight.

Aunt Vera laid a hand on her chest. "That man. What a gem he was. Last year he expanded camps to eight weeks instead of four. He did them all for free. He never asked for a dime of reimbursement. How he loved this event!"

I typed *Melody Beaufort* into the Facebook search bar and found profiles for Melody Toomey, who went to Beaufort High in North Carolina, and Melody Gonzo, who worked at the Beaufort Medical Clinic, but no profile for Melody Beaufort. I typed in *M. Beaufort* and repeated the search. Nothing.

Using Google, I typed in *Beaufort's Beautiful Pottery* and landed on their website. Scanning the site, I discovered myriad pictures of Melody's pottery work, but there wasn't a single picture of her or her husband. That didn't surprise me. The art was what they were selling, not themselves. The *About Melody* page was brief and gave no indication of where she was born or had lived:

> *Based in San Francisco, California, Melody Beaufort believes that the best handmade pottery — art — encourages communication between people. While training to be a potter, she learned about many styles of ceramics. She developed a keen interest in crystalline glaze because it was different from any other type of pottery. She loves to experiment with contemporary-shaped vases. She is always trying to produce more exciting combinations. The colors of the sea call to her.*

Surprisingly, there was no mention of Melody Beaufort anywhere else on the Internet. I didn't find a lawyer, hairdresser, or even soccer mom with the name. The Melody Makers Band was quite popular at old folks' homes. Melody Martini was a noted psychologist specializing in autism. The Merry Little Melody Trio played ukuleles at children's parties. But no Melody Beaufort. *Odd.*

I tapped the countertop. "She's a ghost."

"Honestly, Jenna." My aunt clucked her tongue. "Simply because she doesn't engage in social media doesn't mean there's anything amiss. I'm not on the Internet." Aunt Vera didn't think it served a purpose. She admitted she was a bit of a fuddy-duddy about it, but she treasured her privacy. She had no interest in reading anyone's tweets or viewing their adorable photographs. Apparently, the man who died a year after jilting her at the altar to marry another woman had felt the same. Months ago, I'd conducted an Internet search trying to learn something — *anything* — about him and had come up as empty for him as I had for Melody.

"Ahem," a man said from behind me.

I pivoted and blanched.

Deputy Marlon Appleby, clad in a handsome green-on-brown hunter's costume complete with bow and quiver of arrows, leaned forward on his elbows and eyeballed the computer. His smile twisted into a frown. "What are you doing, Jenna?"

I stabbed the F4 key. The screen defaulted to the Launchpad view. "Ordering supplies," I lied.

He raised an eyebrow. "Vera, are you ready for me to escort you to the Pier?"

"Let me fetch my purse," she replied. "First, we have a stop to make on the way. All right?"

He nodded. Anything my aunt wanted to do was fine by him.

"Taking the day off, Deputy?" I asked.

"Indeed."

"Don't you have a murder to solve?"

"The rest of the force is working on it. Don't you worry."

"Have you or your cohorts questioned Alan Baldini?"

"Like I said, we're on it." He pointed to the computer screen. "And a word to the wise, Jenna, my boss won't be pleased that you are investigating. In fact, it would upset her greatly."

I offered a sly wink. "Then let's keep it our secret."

# Chapter 7

By midmorning, Nick Baldini's murder was no longer a secret. Reporters from as far north as San Jose and as far south as Monterey, having caught wind of my presence at the crime scene, showed up at the shop requesting — *demanding* — an interview. As a group, the reporters trapped me behind the sales counter. For ten straight minutes, they pummeled me with questions, like how I felt about finding yet another body and how well I knew Nick. I repeatedly stated *No comment.* When Tina came to my rescue and shooed them out of the store — she could be fearsome with a ginger cat in one arm and a broom in the other — I was grateful beyond compare. I hoped word would get to Cinnamon and her deputies about how tight-lipped I had been. I could use a few brownie points.

Soon after they departed, Rhett surprised me by showing up in his Robin Hood costume to escort me to the fair for lunch.

"But I'm driving myself," I said. Rhett had texted earlier to tell me that Bait and Switch was two salespeople short today, so he only had an hour to spare. I would need to drive myself back to the shop.

"Truth?" he said. "I wanted a kiss."

"How can I refuse?"

We exchanged a lovely one and talked briefly about reporters waylaying him like they had me. Afterward, I asked him if he'd mind if I completed a few tasks before we left because I'd fallen behind. He didn't.

I suggested he help himself to a buttery scone that Katie had set out, and then I finished arranging copies of *Medieval Celebrations: Your Guide to Planning and Hosting Spectacular Feasts, Parties, Weddings, and Renaissance*, which was a fascinating book filled with historical references and a calendar of medieval holidays. I added sets of gothic dragon salt and pepper holders made of gray cold-cast resin to the display. I knew they would draw our customers' attention.

When I finished my chores, I changed into my Maid Marian costume and followed Rhett in my VW to the Pier. Yet again, the parking lot was filled to the gills. I parked on the main road, as many other fairgoers had opted to do, and met him in the lot where he, being a shop owner, had a permanent spot.

We strolled past Bait and Switch and paused to watch a

swordfight that was in progress on the open-air event stage. One swordsman, a noble knight in a black uniform bearing the king's emblem on his chest, was hurling insults at his opponent.

"Ye artless, baseless cutpurse. Ye shall pay for thy transgression."

The opponent, clad in dark pantaloons and purple chemise with an impressive leather baldric to hold his sword, retorted: "Fie on thee, ye craven, dog-hearted coxcomb. I'll have none of it."

"Zounds," the noble knight bellowed. "Ye are besotted by my wife, thou fawning, fat-kidneyed tosspot."

"Verily, I've never met the wench, ye errant, earth-vexing varlet."

Indeed, the opponent *had* met the wife, and the audience knew it because she was comically shadowing every move he made as if to hide from her husband. One little girl in the crowd pointed and screamed at the top of her lungs for the opponent to *take heed*. The knight lunged; the opponent swiveled and dove at him. When the two connected, I shuddered because an image of Nick facing his opponent sailed through my mind—except he hadn't faced him; his assailant had struck him in the back of the head.

Rhett pressed me at the small of my back. "Let's move on."

A few yards later, when I spotted the tent bearing a sign that read *Enter Ye for an Instructional Fair-Speak Demonstration*, my breath caught in my chest. That had to be where fairgoers could view the movie.

"Are you okay?" Rhett asked.

I pointed. "I can't imagine the mayor will keep the venue open, can you? People will see Nick alive and be distraught."

"Maybe seeing him having fun will be a good thing," Rhett murmured. "A fitting tribute."

I spotted Mayor Zeller on the steps of Mum's the Word. She was talking into a cell phone. I waved to her.

When she caught sight of us, she ended the call and trotted down the steps, the folds of her innkeeper costume flapping in the breeze. She clutched my hand. "Jenna, it's so horrible. Nick. Dead. I can't believe it. He was the spirit of these fairs. He gave them life."

"I'm so sorry for your loss," I said.

"Our loss." She flailed an arm. "The whole town's loss."

"About the video . . ." I hooked my thumb over my shoulder.

Her eyes grew misty. "I considered closing the venue, but I couldn't. Everyone is viewing the film. I think many are paying their respects in this way. It's an homage."

Rhett elbowed me. "Like I said."

"Who killed him?" Z.Z. asked. "Somebody diabolical, to be sure."

"To be sure," I repeated. "The police are investigating. I think they're looking into Nick's brother."

"There's no way Alan would do such a thing." She spanked a hand against her palm. "He is a docile young man without an ounce of guile in him. He and Nick were very close."

"You and Nick were close, as well."

"As close as two people who were often at odds can be."

"Often at odds?"

Her eyes lit up, though tears pooled in the corners. "That man was as feisty and stubborn as a mule. He had so many opinions about how this affair was to be run. We locked horns many times."

I licked my lips. "Z.Z., speaking of locking horns, do you happen to know much about Melody Beaufort?"

"Melody? Why?"

"Flora saw Nick and her exchanging words yesterday. I can't find out anything about her on the Internet."

Rhett gave me a sidelong glance.

"I was wondering if Melody and Nick might have known each other before. Is she from California, or did she reside in Crystal Cove at one point? Her husband told me they've lived in lots of places."

Z.Z. screwed up her mouth. Her forehead creased. "I believe she relocated from the Midwest, but don't quote me on that. Melody made a reference to taking classes at an art school in Ohio. We were chatting about the benefits of higher education and how she wished she'd earned her college degree. She dropped out after two years. I told her artists don't necessarily fit into a mold. My son didn't." Mayor Zeller had lost her daughter at the age of two. The onus fell on her son to follow in Z.Z.'s footsteps and pursue law. He wound up dropping out of UC Santa Cruz in his sophomore year and now lives in an artists' commune in Idaho. The mayor's cell phone jangled. She scanned the readout and said, "Sorry, we've got a crisis. I must run. A goat from the petting zoo is on the loose. Oy. These festivals are going to be the death of me." She balked when she realized what she'd said. "I didn't mean . . . I . . ."

I squeezed her hand. "Go."

"Yoo-hoo, Jenna!" Pepper hailed us from the end of the cut-through leading to North Street. "Come see my wares."

I said to Rhett, "Do you mind?"

"Of course not."

Pepper's beadery shop was situated next to Thistle Thy Fancy. Upon entering the stall, I was astounded by how many beads she had toted to the venue. Were there any left at Beaders of Paradise? Each of the four antique tables held countless trays. Racks filled with colorful twine, wire, and string lined the enclosure's walls.

"Come, see." Pepper, looking almost fetching in a cream smock over a flamingo pink dress, gestured to us to enter further. "These are beads for a French hood." She motioned to strings of fake pearls hanging on a bent hook stand. She added that a French hood was characterized by a rounded shape rather than a gabled hood, and was worn over a coif. "This assortment" — she showed me display boxes with sixty-four divisions filled with sparkling crystal beads and charms, as well as metal spacers, eye pins, and ear hooks to construct earrings — "are for jewelry makers. Don't you love the silver lutes?"

"Everything is beautiful, Pepper."

"Take a look at this." She continued on, pointing out chains and silk ropes. "I'm not giving any classes, like the others. I have to split my time between here and the shop, but I've done quite well with sales."

I glanced over my shoulder at Rhett. He grinned. Pepper was certainly chatty. Maybe spending time at her daughter's house was doing her a world of good in the interaction department. At times she could be terse, bordering on rude.

"I've taken photos on my iPhone that I can share on a couple of Internet sites." Clandestinely, she removed her phone from the pocket of her costume and surveyed the area — to make sure the fair "authenticity police" weren't hovering nearby, I imagined. "I must keep it low. Z.Z. doesn't like it if I enter the present."

As she swiped the screen and showed me her photographs, I recalled the picture on my cell phone of the bead that the crow plucked off Nick's verandah.

Acting as furtively as she, I fetched my cell phone from my purse and opened up my camera app. I chose the photograph that I wanted and dragged my fingers along the screen to zoom in on the bead. I displayed the result to her. "Pepper, I don't see this gold-and-green bead among your items. Do you carry something like this in your shop?"

She shook her head. "I've never seen that before. I mean, I've seen the type—in sales magazines—but I've never purchased any. They're quite expensive. Maybe it's one of Dolly's. She goes overboard around Ren Fair time." She let out a dismissive cough. "Truth be told, she wants to outdo me at every turn. She's the sole vendor that makes wreaths and garlands, and yet her competitive spirit rises up whenever it comes to crafts. Where did you see it?"

Rhett flicked me with his finger to keep the secret.

I threw him a look indicating I understood and said, "On the floor at a friend's house."

"It's very pretty. You know . . ." She didn't continue.

"What?"

"Nothing." Pepper fidgeted, like she wanted to say something else, but she didn't.

Rhett wrapped an arm around me. "Hate to cut this short, ladies, but Jenna, we have to eat if I'm going to return to work on time."

"Fie on your shorthanded staffing issues," I jibed.

"I heard the food at Mum's the Word is scrumptious this week," Pepper offered. "They're serving shepherd's pie."

Thanks to her suggestion, Rhett and I popped into the Word for a quick bite. The fair-themed menu didn't disappoint. In addition to shepherd's pie, they were offering beef stew in a bread bowl, Scotch eggs, and more. We ate at the counter—all the booths were occupied—and opted for the shepherd's pie and glasses of sparkling water.

As we waited for our meals, Rhett said, "Jenna, I hate that you're dealing with this again."

"What do you mean?"

"A friend dying. Seeing another body. Knowing you as I do"—he traced a fingertip along my knuckles—"you're going to get involved, aren't you?"

"No, I—"

"You asked the mayor about Melody."

"Yes, but—"

"And you showed that photograph to Pepper. You saw the bead on Nick's verandah, didn't you? Alan's crow picked it up."

I nodded.

"You're curious. I get it. But, sweetheart—"

"I'm heartbroken and Bailey is suffering, too. She bonded with Nick over the last month while making wedding plans. She needs closure. And don't even talk about my aunt. She's distraught. She's known the Baldinis for years."

"Cinnamon will get closure. For all of you. She's the best there is." Rhett and Cinnamon had been involved years ago. Their relationship ended when she began investigating the arson at the Grotto. Once Rhett was proven innocent, they became friends again. "All I'm saying is don't put yourself in harm's way. I couldn't bear to lose you. I..." He hesitated. "I love you."

My heart skipped a beat. In a good way. I treasured hearing him say the words. "Do you really?" I tipped my head coyly to one side and batted my eyelashes.

"Indeed, I do, lass."

"Well, I love you, *lad*." It was the first time I'd said the words aloud, too, but that didn't mean I couldn't say them playfully. "And I promise I'll be mindful."

He kissed my cheek, his lips lingering a few extra seconds. "Thank you."

We ate our meal in silent companionship. After paying, he said, "I'm sorry I've got to run."

He rose and held out a hand. I grasped it and clambered to my feet. Outside Mum's the Word, he kissed me purposefully on the lips and sped away.

Because I still had a few minutes before I needed to get back to the Cookbook Nook, I decided that Maid Marian should have a wreath for her hair. I hadn't purchased one yet, and I had promised Dolly that I would.

I entered Thistle Thy Fancy and said, "Hi-ho, Dolly."

Dolly was hunched over the do-it-yourself table giving tips to three avid customers. She glimpsed me, and I noticed her eyes were puffy, as if she'd had a good cry. She held up a finger to signify she'd be a minute. I gave her the don't-worry-about-me sign and sauntered to a pegged wall that displayed at least two dozen wreaths. I fingered one made with multicolored silk daisies, baby's breath, and fake ivy.

"It's nice, isn't it?" a man with a melodious voice said.

I glanced over my shoulder. Sean Beaufort was standing behind me.

"What are you doing here?" I peeked past him for Melody but didn't see her.

"Buying a wreath for my wife. She refuses to spend money on herself. But with her features and hair . . ."

"She's quite pretty."

"The fairest maiden of them all."

"Sean" — Dolly inserted herself between us, the satin folds of her forest green gown swishing noisily — "you're biased beyond belief." She plucked the wreath I was interested in from its peg.

"And why not? I'm madly in love."

"She is indeed the fairest of them all," Dolly said. "Even I'll admit that."

He returned to browsing the wares, and Dolly handed me the wreath. "Try it, Jenna. It suits you."

I positioned the wreath on my head. As she adjusted it, I said gently, "I'm sure you've heard about Nick."

"Mm-hm." Her voice quavered.

"How are you holding up?"

"You know me." Her eyes glistened with moisture. "All grit and spit. The show must go on, right? Nick would want it that way."

Sean brandished a green crystal wreath made of vines and sea-green beads, one that would be perfect for a woodlands bride. "I like this one."

"Not for me." I shook my head. "I prefer flowers."

"No, I meant for my wife. She loves sea-green."

"I love anything green, too," Dolly chimed. "Green eyes, green gown." She dragged her hand along the bodice of her dress and performed a slight curtsy. "That wreath is one of my favorites, Sean. The beading is so delicate. I nearly went blind completing it."

Dolly's quip about the beading made me recall my conversation with Pepper. She had suggested that Dolly might sell the kind of bead the crow had stolen. "Dolly, I don't see a lot of beads around." I swiveled to take in the entire stock. "I spy some on the do-it-yourself table. Where are you keeping the rest?"

"They're hidden. They're the first things the varmints around here steal. Want to see my stash?"

I pressed my lips together, remembering what Rhett had said to me—I should let the police do their job—but I truly believed the bead had some significance. Granted, it was a long shot, but if I learned something, I could share my findings with Cinnamon. I clicked the photograph icon on my cell phone and showed the snapshot to Dolly. "Do you sell this one?"

"I used to. They're very expensive. I sold my last set to Hannah Storm. Is that Nick's patio?"

I nodded.

Sean sniffed. "Hannah."

"You don't like her?" I asked.

"I didn't say that. I . . ." He worked his tongue inside his cheek.

"Go on," Dolly encouraged him. "It's not healthy to keep negative feelings inside. Believe me, I know."

"It has nothing to do with me, but"—Sean folded his arms across his chest—"I saw her arguing with that guy that was killed. Nick Baldini."

"Where were they?" Dolly inclined her head.

"Between booths. Out of sight of the mainstream crowds. I'd gone to buy a coffee and was taking a cut-through to our stall."

"What were they fighting about?" I asked.

"I'm not sure. I heard Hannah say, 'Leave me alone.' Her tone was sharp. I peeked around the booth. Baldini was gripping her shoulder." Sean aimed a finger at me. "Come to think of it, she was wearing a necklace of those beads. She knocked his hand away and said, 'Stop.'"

"Was Nick making a pass at her?"

"No . . . I don't know. She said, 'You owe me,' and he said, 'Do not.' She said something else that I couldn't make out, about water. They separated, so I didn't think anything more about it." Sean rubbed his chin. "Gee, you don't think she had something to do with his death, do you? If you found the bead on his patio . . ."

Honestly, I wasn't sure what to think. How many people had Nick argued with over the last few days? Had pretending to be the king gone to his head? An off-the-wall notion struck me. Bailey had teased Nick about Hannah being the woman he loved. Except Nick said the woman wasn't *free*. Was Hannah in a committed relationship? I didn't think so, but I could be mistaken. I didn't know everyone's comings and goings. Had she fallen for Nick, too? *You owe me*, she said. Were they quarreling over how long it was taking him to break it off with

Dolly and how he owed her resolution? No, he had ended that relationship days ago. Maybe *You owe me* meant Hannah had refused his advances and she deserved his respect.

Sean resumed his search for a wreath.

"Dolly." I spun around to question her, but she had drifted away and was straightening ribbons on a rack.

She glanced furtively at me over her shoulder. What was up with that? A horrible notion flew into my head. Maybe she went to Nick's place, enraged that he had ended it, and hit him with the winepress, and then she planted the bead to throw suspicion on Hannah. She just said to Sean that it wasn't healthy to keep negative feelings inside. Had she let hers goad her into action? No, that didn't make sense. Dolly had been in love with Nick; Hannah would have been her target.

*Pummel the competition,* my boss at Taylor & Squibb used to say. I didn't agree, but he had made it his mantra.

"Dolly," I repeated.

She didn't glance my way.

I plucked the wreath from my head and strode toward her. "Dolly, I'd like to purchase this."

In an overly theatrical way, she clapped a hand to her chest and said, "Were you calling me?"

*Hmph.* She knew I had been.

She took the wreath from me and sashayed to the cash register. "You've made a good choice. This will look lovely on you." She rang up the purchase.

I handed her cash. "May I ask you something?"

"What?"

"Following your workshop yesterday—"

"Jenna, I can't believe Nick is dead," she blurted, tears spilling uncontrollably down her cheeks. "What will I do without him?" She whisked a tissue from a Kleenex box beside the register and dabbed her eyes. "It's so unreal. So unfair."

"Yes, it is."

"We could have patched things up. I know we could have. Deep down, he loved me."

"I'm sure he did." I reached across the sales counter and petted her shoulder. "Um, after you left the shop yesterday, did you—"

"Kill him? You can't possibly believe I had anything to do with his murder."

I shook my head, unwilling to say the theory had flitted through my mind. "I was going to ask if you reached out to him or talked to him after you left your workshop. You ran off in such haste."

"I went straight home to make some wreaths."

I cocked my head as I replayed the event in my mind. She had abandoned the workshop simply to do more crafts? Why didn't I believe her?

As if reading my mind, she hastened to add, "I'd completely sold out."

"You should tell the police."

"Why? Do they think that I could have . . . that I would have . . . ?" She chewed her lower lip.

"They might."

"I didn't kill him, Jenna. I loved him with all my heart." She slammed the cash register drawer and handed me my change along with the wreath and three lethal-looking hairpins. With a bite, she added, "Stick those in tight."

# Chapter 8

As I left Thistle Thy Fancy, my mind was reeling about my encounter with Dolly. I glanced at the hatpins in my hand. Luckily, she hadn't had a voodoo doll available. What was she hiding? I couldn't imagine her hurting Nick. On the other hand, if the story about her taking a baseball bat to a shelf in her shop was true, she had a serious anger issue.

To ease my anxiety, I headed toward the end of the Pier, where Aunt Vera's tarot reading stall was located. I didn't need a reading, but I could sure use a pep talk. Outside her purple tent hung a sign that said it all: *Palm Reader/Tarot Reader*. Two red palm prints flanked the words. Silk purple bearded iris festooned the signpost. She required a farthing for a reading.

I stole a look inside. A round table covered with a lavender-colored cloth stood in the center of the room. My aunt sat on one side. A humped-back woman who was dressed like a witch, complete with a bulbous nose and a wart on her chin, sat opposite her. Gracing the rear of the stall were two smaller round tables, each set with lit lavender-scented candles. A battery-operated tea set sat on a narrow rectangular oak table. The aroma of lavender tea was enticing.

My aunt ended the session and handed the witch a deck of tarot cards.

The witch gave my aunt a few coins and swept past me. "She'll do right by you, dearie. Mark my words. My gingerbread cottage will be graced by tasty visitors very soon." Cackling, she whisked her black cape across her body and scurried out.

"What a character," I said as I slipped inside.

"Indeed she is."

"Got a sec?"

"For you, I have hours." She met me halfway and clutched my arm. "What's wrong? If it's Bailey, I visited with her. She's going to be fine. She'll be back at the shop by the time you return."

"It's not Bailey."

"Sit. Would you like tea?"

"No, thanks." I perched on the antique three-legged stool the witch had vacated. "I went to Thistle Thy Fancy—"

"I like the wreath. It suits you. Would you like me to put it on you?"

73

I handed it and the hatpins to her. "Sure. I don't have a clue how to do it."

She deftly anchored it to my head. "There. Lovely. Now, what ails you, besides the obvious?" She sat opposite me and clasped my hands, her spirit radiating warmth and calm.

I replayed my conversation with Dolly and shared the feeling that Dolly was hiding something of importance.

"Don't read into things."

"She's lying about her alibi. I'm sure of it."

"Alibi?" Aunt Vera *tsk*ed. "Marlon warned me that you were revved up. He could see it in your eyes."

"I'm not revved up. I'm attentive."

"Give Dolly time to report to Cinnamon. If she doesn't, you can tell Cinnamon what you sense. Okay?"

I nodded and then filled her in on Sean overhearing Nick and Hannah going at it. "How many people did Nick fight with this week? Even the mayor said she and he quarreled."

"Nick was a passionate man, dear. Everyone knew that about him. As for Hannah, I'm sure the police will be speaking to her. She's a neighbor of the Baldinis. The police will want to know whether she heard or saw anything." She patted my hand. "You take care of Bailey. The rest will work itself out."

"Is that your official reading?" I shook free of her grasp.

"Don't mock me."

"Never." I kissed her on the cheek and left.

• • •

When I returned to the shop, it was overrun with customers. We apparently were having a sale that I hadn't planned. A sign sitting atop the bestsellers' table read *Buy 2, get 1 free*. I approached the sales counter, where Tina was assisting a customer. Her cheeks were as red as her dress. A tinge of perspiration lined her upper lip. Due to the excess of customers, it was hotter than an oven in the shop. I considered kicking on the air-conditioning unit. We rarely used it. Instead, I propped open the front door using a doorstop. A cool breeze wafted in.

Tina handed the customer one of our pretty bags and turned to me. "Bless you for letting in air, Jenna. I am roasting."

"What's up with the twofer sign?"

"Your aunt gave me the order. She said it had slipped her mind earlier with all the . . . you know." Tina swooped a tendril of hair into her bun and secured it with a bobby pin. "She suggested we have some item on sale every day this week to lure customers. Guess it worked. Some folks are tweeting the sale while they stand in line. And take a look at how many are holding the castle cookie jars."

In addition to salt and pepper shakers and aprons and puzzles, we stocked lots of cookie jars. For this week's specialty, I'd made sure to find the cutest castles I could. My particular favorite was the glazed brown-and-white one with family crests on either side of the drawbridge.

I said, "If Aunt Vera authorized it, okey doke." I was the merchandizing whiz. I knew how to decorate the shop and lay out books. My aunt juggled the accounts and knew what we could afford to discount. Our business relationship was a match made in heaven.

"Bailey's here, by the way. She's not in costume, but that's okay, isn't it? She's wearing a really pretty silver dress, espadrilles, and earrings." Tina wiggled her fingers. "You know how jingly earrings boost her spirits."

"It's fine. Where is she?"

"She went to the café, but she'll be right back."

I made my way toward the breezeway and ran smack into Bailey exiting. She didn't see me because she was devouring a delicious-looking morsel.

"What is that?" I begged. My stomach grumbled.

"Frozen chocolate cheesecake bites. There's a raspberry in the middle. Katie is calling them sin-in-a-cup."

I licked my lips. "I must have one, but first . . ." I gave Bailey a hug and held her at arm's length. "How are you?"

"Okay. Not bad. So-so." She sighed. "Tito is worried. He's afraid I'll cut bait and run."

"You won't, will you?"

She shook her head. "Are you nuts? I adore that man. Plus, your aunt convinced me to hang tight. I haven't contacted Tito to let him know that I'm rebounding, but I will after I have two or three more of these." She brandished the sweet treat and grinned, which thrilled me. Her humor was returning. "Have you heard anything from Cinnamon about Nick's murder?"

"Like she'd call me."

"She might."

"When the ocean freezes over." I didn't mention my suspicions about Dolly or Hannah to my pal. I wanted her to remain as upbeat and worry-free as possible. "Do you want me to put in a call to another winery to see if we can relocate the wedding?"

"Who would say yes?" She shook her head, her sadness sneaking back in. "I can't see it happening on short notice, can you? I think Tito and I will have to postpone until next year."

"But you can't! Tito will have a conniption fit."

"I'll buy him a scratching post. Go! Get sustenance." She flaunted the remaining bite of her goodie in my face. "Wait, I'm coming with you." She poked her head into the shop. "Tina, can you manage? When I get back, you can take your break."

Tina waved. "Sure."

"I love that girl," Bailey said to me as we hurried to the Nook and veered left into the kitchen. "She told me her private cooking classes with Katie are going great. You know, if Katie had the wherewithal, she would open up her own culinary institute."

"I hope she doesn't. What would I do without her?" I cut my friend a sideways look. "That was selfish of me, wasn't it?"

"Yes, but understandable."

We entered the café's kitchen and halted by the rectangular oak table fitted with an L-shaped bench, more commonly known as the chef's table. Occasionally Katie would serve private dinners for four to six people there.

"Okay to enter, Chef?" I asked.

Katie beckoned us inside. She was making more sin-in-a-cup goodies and working alongside her sous chef, a handsome thirty-year-old with a distinctive silver streak in his dark hair, who was whipping together batches of meat-based pasties.

"Must have chocolate," I said to Katie. She handed me a mini dessert set in a red-striped paper candy cup. I bit into it and moaned my delight.

"Glad you like it." Katie rested her palms on the countertop and blew a loose strand of hair off her forehead. "I'm only serving them here at the café. It's too hard to keep them frozen at the fair. They're selling like crazy. Three to a dessert plate. Keller came up with the idea." Her voice caught. "Aw, heck. Keller . . ."

"What about him?"

"He hinted . . ." She didn't finish.

"Go on."

"He was talking about Nick. He hinted he might not have been such a great guy."

"What do you mean?" Bailey asked. "He was as nice as they come."

I slid onto the bench at the chef's table.

Bailey joined me. "What did Keller say exactly?"

"Reynaldo, take ten," Katie ordered her sous chef.

"Sure, boss."

Katie placed two more sin-in-a-cup goodies and a pair of napkins on the chef's table and sat down with us. She folded her hands on the table and leaned forward. "Keller stopped by this morning, hence the new creation"—she motioned to our delicious desserts—"and he let on that he heard Nick arguing with Hannah Storm the other day."

I gawked. "They had another clash?"

Katie's eyes widened. "They had a first?"

I nodded. "Where did this one take place?"

"Right near Keller's mother's shop."

Keller's mom owned Taste of Heaven Ice Cream Parlor, a charming place on Buena Vista Boulevard. That was where Keller, as a teen, became an ice cream maker.

"Did he hear what they were quarreling about?" I asked.

"How could he not? It was a full-blown row. Hannah was claiming a problem with water rights. Nick was denying any hanky-panky. When the shouting settled to a dull roar, she asked if she could buy Nick out. He would have none of it, so they went at it again. Tooth and nail—Keller's words."

I wondered if water rights were the essence of the spat Sean had listened in on. He mentioned hearing the word *water*. Hannah had said *You owe me*. Why? Had Nick reneged on a deal to sell his property or water rights to her?

"Keller didn't want to mention it to anyone because he likes Hannah a lot, and so do I, but I told him he had to go to the police."

"Has he?"

"I believe so."

Then Cinnamon already knew about Hannah's set-to with Nick. Good. It wasn't my responsibility to inform her. Once she started grilling Hannah, she'd find out about the other altercation.

I bit into my frozen treat and hummed my appreciation.

"Jenna, what are you thinking?" Bailey asked.

I told them about the first disagreement. I added that I'd seen Hannah attacking the ground with the shovel between her property and the Baldinis'. "I was wondering whether she visited Nick later that day and whether they went at it a third time. Maybe things got out of hand."

Katie twirled a napkin on the table. "Killing him would have resolved the water rights issue."

"Would it have?" I asked. "Nick's death might put his estate and any possibility of divesting property on hold." I bit into my second dessert. The frozen raspberry in the middle added just the right pizzazz.

"I think she killed him," Bailey said.

"Not so fast," I said. "Until now, you thought Alan did. And just because Hannah argued with Nick doesn't mean she killed him, even if I did find her bead on the verandah."

"It was *her* bead?" Bailey said.

"According to Dolly, Hannah made a necklace of them."

"What bead?" Katie asked.

While explaining, I showed them the evidence on my cell phone. "However, it was a single bead on the patio, not an entire necklace."

"What if Hannah went to confront Nick? What if they struggled and the necklace broke?" Bailey pushed her ice cream treat away and tapped the table with her fingernail. "The bead puts her at the scene of the crime."

"Not necessarily," I said. "It's possible that Alan's crow brought the bead from Hannah's property, and she never set foot there at all." I didn't add my suspicion that Dolly could have planted it there. Why spread a rumor? We needed more facts.

"Who overheard the other disagreement?" Katie asked.

"Sean Beaufort."

"Isn't he the husband of the woman who makes pottery?" Bailey asked.

"Yes, he is," Katie said. "Melody is a darling woman."

"You know them?" Bailey swung her gaze in Katie's direction.

"I've met all the vendors at the fair. We share sales secrets and tell tales about quirky customers. It's tradition."

Bailey pouted. "Why am I not up to speed?"

I patted her hand. "Because you haven't gone back since you received Nick's call."

"Well, I'm tired of being out of the loop. I'm convinced Hannah killed Nick, so I'm contacting Cinnamon." She leaped to stand.

I grasped her by the wrist. "Whoa, nelly! Why are you determined to see Hannah arrested? You like her. I've seen the two of you poring over cookbooks and savoring the recipes. And laughing. Not to mention you enjoy her wine."

"Because . . . I don't know." Bailey wrenched free. "Because lately she's become more sullen."

Katie said, "Maybe taking care of her grandmother and the vineyard has become too much for her."

"Exactly. When Nick took her on, she snapped." Bailey flicked her fingers.

"C'mon," I said. "Hannah is no pushover. She comes from solid stock like you and me. We don't *snap* for no reason."

"Maybe she's restless," Bailey reasoned.

"Maybe the vineyard's losing money," Katie suggested.

I said, "If that's the case, why would she want to buy Nick's? Wouldn't she rather sell hers to him? I'll bet he would have been eager to own both properties. He had friends in high places. He could have arranged a loan."

Katie returned to the pastry station, hoisted a pastry tube, and started squirting the cheesecake concoction into the chocolate-lined ice cube trays. "I know Hannah pretty well. I was friends with her brother, Hugh."

"You were?" I joined her and eyed the melted chocolate. How I wished I could dip my finger in the bowl. "When? He must be eight years older than you."

"Six. And don't look at me like that. We weren't an item." She shimmied her shoulders. "We were in a cooking club. He's a chef now in Paris."

"So I heard," I said. "I also learned that he left the wine business because he was allergic to grapes."

"That and he's a teetotaler. He doesn't drink alcohol."

Bailey pursed her lips. "Why is someone who abstains referred to as a teetotaler? The word doesn't start with *T-E-A*."

Katie snorted. "There are a few answers for that. I like the one that claims the letter *T* starts the word *totaler*, and like the phrase *to a T*, the letter emphasizes how strongly one abstains, but it's spelled with the lowercase *tee*. However, another tale asserts that certain advocates would make followers who pledged total abstinence sign with a capital *T*."

Bailey knuckled Katie's arm. "You're a history geek."

Katie roared. "And proud of it." She pressed fresh raspberries into the ice cube trays and topped them with more of the cheesecake mixture.

"Back to Hugh." Bailey patted her thigh impatiently. "Is it possible he sneaked into town and took up arms against Nick on behalf of his sister?"

"Hugh will never come back to Crystal Cove," Katie said. "Not until his grandmother kicks the bucket. They had a huge falling out when he didn't enter the business. She is a vindictive woman." She drizzled melted chocolate over the remaining sin-in-a-cup cubes and popped the tray into the freezer. "I'm telling you, Hannah didn't do this. I feel it in my gut."

# Chapter 9

Despite Katie's gut feelings, Bailey was convinced that she had to contact Cinnamon and bring her up to date. No matter how hard I tried to dissuade her, I couldn't stop her. She dashed out of the café and across the parking lot toward the street.

I raced into the shop and asked Tina if she was managing all right. She was. I assigned her two duties: to set out tomorrow's children's art project in the corner featuring watercolor art sprinkled with salt and to make sure Tigger was okay.

She said, "Can I put him in a timeout if he shreds anything? What is going on with him?"

"Teenage hormones maybe?" I quipped. "Honestly, I'm not sure. I'll put in a call to our veterinarian soon. In the meantime, yes, if you can corral him, you can put him in timeout. However, use the phrase *uh-uh* as a warning. I'm not into saying 'Bad kitty.'"

"You've got it."

I promised her an early end to the day, which delighted her, and chased after Bailey.

Though I was typically faster than her, the cumbersome Maid Marian costume slowed me down. The folds were catching around my calves. I didn't want to lose my new wreath, either. Aunt Vera may have anchored it to my head, but a hatpin or two wouldn't hold very well in a foot race. I caught up to my pal as she was bustling north on Buena Vista.

"Where are you headed?" I shouted.

"It's three o'clock, which means Cinnamon will be having iced coffee at Latte Luck Café." Cinnamon had once confided to us that she visited the easygoing place daily to pick up the local gossip. "She is as predictable as a grandfather clock."

I lurched into the café right after Bailey. As anticipated, Cinnamon was sitting at her usual table. On the nearby wall hung a sepia-toned picture of the Theater on the Pier. Similar pictures of Crystal Cove in the 1920s graced all the walls. Cinnamon was sipping her usual drink through a straw. The glass was frosty, so she must have recently taken her seat. To my surprise, Katie's boyfriend, Keller, was at the table with her. Pushing six and a half feet, he'd had to fold himself into the bistro-style chair. A thatch of unruly brown hair hung down his forehead. His eyes were focused on Cinnamon and pinched with concentration.

Not one to stand on ceremony, Bailey marched between the wooden tables, pulled out an empty chair at Cinnamon's, and sat. Cinnamon, who had the patience of Job when it came to some things, did not take kindly to the intrusion. She peered down her nose at my intrepid pal. Bailey didn't flinch. She waved for me to join them. I hovered nearby.

"Hey-hey, Jenna and Bailey," Keller said, his serious demeanor lightening a tad.

I nodded a greeting.

Cinnamon blew out an exasperated breath. The air flipped up her bangs. She finger-combed them into place. "Sit, Jenna. No one likes the old saying *Three is a crowd.*" She stared pointedly at Bailey and back at me. "Nice outfit, by the way. Maid Marian?"

"Good guess."

"I have insider knowledge." She winked. "Okay, everyone, you'll all take turns. I imagine you have something to share, Bailey?"

"I do," Bailey said.

"After he speaks, it'll be your turn." Cinnamon refocused on Katie's fiancé.

"So like I was telling you . . ." Keller reiterated what Katie had told us at the Nook about Nick and Hannah arguing over water rights issues, and Hannah offering to buy out Nick.

Cinnamon leaned forward on her elbows. "But no threats were exchanged."

"No, ma'am."

"No, 'I'll kill you if you don't agree.'"

Keller offered a toothy grin. "That only happens in the movies, doesn't it?"

"Did either of them touch the other?" Cinnamon asked. "Was there any physical contact?"

"No, ma'am."

"Got anything more to add?"

"No, ma'am."

Cinnamon leveled her gaze at Bailey. "Your turn."

Bailey blushed, obviously realizing her account was actually *my* account. "Jenna can tell it better."

I filled Cinnamon in on seeing Hannah at the bottom of the hill on the day Nick died. I recounted how Sean Beaufort had heard Nick and Hannah bickering. To him, it sounded like the same topic of dissent: water. "Sean heard Hannah say, 'You owe me,' and Nick countered with, 'Do not.' According to Sean, they split up after that. Has he reached out to you?"

"He's coming to the precinct later to file a report."

*Why not immediately?* I wanted to ask but knew better. Like every other vendor at the fair, he couldn't afford to lose business by being absent.

Keller said, "I heard Hurricane Vineyards is undergoing some financial strain."

"Who'd you hear that from, Mr. Landry?" Cinnamon asked.

"One of my customers. I can't remember who. It was yesterday. I was on the Pier. Let me think." He tapped his forehead between his eyebrows. "Aha. I remember. Old Jake. He bought a double scoop of coffee crunch. He had just purchased one of those foot-press thingies from Hannah's booth, and we got to talking."

I flinched. Cinnamon did, too. One of those *thingies* was the murder weapon.

"Why would Jake know about Hannah's or Nick's business?" Cinnamon asked.

Old Jake saved my father's life years ago; in return, my father taught him to invest. No one is quite sure when Jake arrived in Crystal Cove. Back then, he was a drifter. Now, although he may be the wealthiest man in town, he still loves to drive a tractor fitted with a huge rake and clean up the beaches each morning.

"Jake knows everyone's business," Keller said. "He's sort of like you. He goes to coffee shops and listens and learns."

Cinnamon shifted in her chair, clearly uncomfortable that everyone knew her routine.

"Water rights are important when it comes to running a vineyard," I said.

"I agree." Bailey jabbed a thumb in my direction. "Which makes Hannah a main suspect."

I threw her a withering look and said to Cinnamon, "I didn't notice a stream or anything on Nick's property, but maybe there's an underground source of water he tapped into, and Hannah believed it belonged to her family. That might explain why she said, 'You owe me.'"

"Do you think Nick was that inscrutable?" Cinnamon said.

"I'd like to think he wasn't"—I leaned back in my chair—"but I told you about Hannah digging by their property lines. Maybe she was looking for proof that Nick was siphoning off water."

"Excuse me." Keller cleared his throat. "A thought just dawned on me. She offered to buy Nick out. How could she do that if Hurricane Vineyards is under financial strain?"

Cinnamon frowned. "All of this sounds like a gossip mill gone amok."

"Nick wouldn't sell," Bailey insisted. "I'm sure of it. You said so yourself, Jenna. That vineyard has been in his family for generations."

"Okay," Cinnamon thwacked the table. "I'll look into Hannah Storm, but I've got to tell you, I've known her for years, and I hold her in high regard."

"You know her brother Hugh, too, I hear." I cocked my head, ready to glean more.

"We dated for a nanosecond," Cinnamon said. "He had a huge chip on his shoulder in high school."

"So did you."

"Two blockheads don't make a tree," Cinnamon said.

In her teens, she had run with the wrong crowd. My father, at my mother's insistence, befriended her. At the time, he was participating in a Big Brother program. He took her under his wing and helped her focus on the future. After college, she considered going into social service work in San Francisco to help girls like herself, but then Pepper got sick, and Cinnamon moved home. The rest was history.

Cinnamon said, "For Hugh, discovering his love of cooking helped him get straight, but he didn't want anything to do with the vineyard. The pressure was intense from his grandmother to get in line, but he refused. Now, the bitter old woman exerts enormous influence on Hannah. Somebody has to keep the vineyard running."

"Could the grandmother have killed Nick?" I asked.

Cinnamon shook her head. "She has severe osteoporosis. I'd rule her out."

Bailey leaned forward, her gaze riveted on Cinnamon. If I knew my friend — and I did — she was intent on proving her theory. "What if she talked Hannah into doing the deed? Hannah was at Baldini Vineyards — on the verandah. Jenna has proof. Show her."

Cinnamon gave me the evil eye.

My cheeks warmed as I pulled my cell phone from my purse. "Chief," I began, "before you arrived, I spotted a bead on the verandah. I took a picture of it. I was going to pick it up but a crow — Alan's crow, I think — swooped in and flew off with it." I swiped the cell phone screen and pressed the appropriate buttons until the image materialized. "I checked with Dolly Ledoux, who told me she'd sold a stash of these beads to Hannah to make a necklace. Hannah was the only person to buy them."

Cinnamon inhaled and let out a long, exasperated breath. "My deputy informed me that you were looking into things."

"Not intentionally." I spread my hands. "I was there. At the vineyard. That night. I was observant. And then when I was buying a wreath at Thistle Thy Fancy —"

"She's always attentive to detail, Chief," Bailey said in my defense. "It's one of her best traits. That's why she soared in her position at Taylor & Squibb."

"I've heard enough." Cinnamon held up a hand. "Keep clear of this, Jenna."

"Sure, but if I learn something, you want me to tell you, right? Nick was my friend."

"And mine," Bailey said.

"And my aunt knew his family well. I can't believe . . ." I felt a hard yank on my heart. Another person I knew was *dead. Murdered.* Without warning, my thoughts flew to my deceased husband, David, and my friend Desiree and my therapist, Dr. Thornton. How many more of my friends and family would suffer in the years to come? Hopefully not like this. Never again like this. I pushed the morbid notion aside. "Nick was a good member of the community, Chief. Whether he had a gripe with all these people or not, he deserves justice."

Cinnamon polished off her iced coffee with a slurp.

"What about Nick's brother, Alan?" I asked. "Did you pin him down on his alibi?"

"I did."

"Where was he? Why did his bird fly to the verandah and squawk? I told you we heard the bird, right?"

"You did." She pushed her glass aside. "Alan was pranking his brother."

"Pranking?" I raised an eyebrow. "Are you kidding me? He's in his thirties, for Pete's sake."

"He was lacing a well on the property with frogs."

"Frogs?"

Cinnamon's mouth twitched ever so slightly. "He said Nick would go bonkers when he discovered the frogs because Nick mistakenly believed the frogs would contaminate the water, and therefore harm the wine-making process."

I glanced at Bailey, who frowned, not believing a word of it. I continued. "Could this have been the water issue Nick and Hannah were discussing?"

"I doubt it. A prank like that is not important enough to kill over."

"Did anyone see Alan carrying out the deed?" I asked.

"Not that I know of, but my people did find frogs. Dozens of frogs."

A bell jingled over the front door as my father entered the café or, rather, swept inside, the purple cape of his apothecary costume flowing behind him. "Good day, daughter," he bellowed as if he were onstage. He made a beeline for me. "I have come for a libation."

For most of my life, I had feared my father. A former FBI man, he could be cryptic and a tad icy. No more. Now he was warm and jovial and appreciating life. My mother's death had taken his spirit; his relationship with Lola had boosted it tenfold.

My father was strikingly handsome, in an aging silver fox way, which prompted many of the women patrons to watch him stride across the café. He—typical Dad—was oblivious. He greeted the others at our table.

Cinnamon said, "Looking dapper, Cary."

He blew a kiss to Bailey. "How is the fair maiden who dost marry in a week?"

Bailey shrank in her chair.

I put a comforting hand on her shoulder and swallowed hard. "Dad, didn't Lola tell you?"

"Tell me what?"

"Haven't you listened to the news or picked up a newspaper?"

"What's going on?" He dropped the accent and bravado. "I was in the city yesterday on business. I just got back to town an hour ago and am stopping in to get a coffee before meeting Lola on the Pier."

After retiring from the Bureau, Dad bought a hardware store. It was small but serviceable. What business could he have been conducting in San Francisco? He didn't need to purchase a second store. Maybe he'd met someone from Habitat for Humanity. He donated a lot of time to the organization. I pushed the distracting notion aside and quickly told him what had happened to Nick and how Bailey's wedding was in limbo.

He blanched. "I had no clue, Bailey. Your mother obviously wanted to speak to me in person and didn't want to leave the news on a voice mail." He pecked her on the cheek. "My poor girl. If you need to chat, I'm available, but right now I should go to your mother. You seem to have plenty of support."

Bailey agreed.

As he made his exit, gathering his apothecary cape so it wouldn't catch on the door, a series of words scudded through my mind. Apothecary — druggist — *drugs*. I flashed on the Post-it notes on Nick's computer, and turned to Cinnamon. "Chief, one more thing. Nick affixed a bunch of Post-it notes to his computer. One said *Get MEDS*. Do you know what medications he was taking?"

"He didn't die of an overdose, Jenna."

"I know, but given his irritable behavior over the past few days, maybe his blood pressure was high or his heart was bad. There was a heart symbol —"

"I saw the notes," Cinnamon said. "And we talked to his physician. He wasn't on any medications. He was a health nut. No sugar. No GMOs."

"Maybe the meds were for Alan, then. After his accident —"

"That's it. We're through here." Cinnamon pushed away from the table. The feet of her chair screeched on the floor.

"Did you know Nick and Dolly broke up?" Bailey blurted. "Do you have suspects of your own? Do you —"

"Miss Bird," Cinnamon said sternly, no longer referring to Bailey by her first name. Friendship was off the table. "I've questioned Mr. Baldini's business associates and learned of any outstanding debts, and I've talked with people involved with the fair. Believe me, I'm doing my due diligence. Gossip does not solve a crime, got me?" She addressed Keller. "Mr. Landry, thank you for your information. As for you two" — she waggled a finger between Bailey and me — "steer clear. I'm warning you." She shot a snide look at me.

I waited until she departed before mimicking the look.

# Chapter 10

When Bailey and I returned to the Cookbook Nook, I gave Tina the rest of the day off, as promised.

"Really?" she exclaimed. "I mean, no lie? I'm over the moon. I used to go to the Renaissance Fair every year with my . . ." She chewed her lower lip.

*With her uncle,* I guessed. I knew how much she missed him. Nearly every day she wrote to him.

"I haven't had time to visit the Pier yet." Tina did a turn and flapped her costume's apron. "Do I look all right?" In fair-speak, she added, "Pray, tell me the truth. Utter no lies."

"You look adorable," I said.

She knitted her brow. "Adorable *'tisn't* the word I seek."

"How about saucy?"

"Yes. Saucy and sassy." She did another twirl.

I laughed. "Are you meeting up with someone? A beau?"

"He's not a beau yet, although I have my hopes up. He delivers love sonnets."

Aha. The gawky messenger in the Shakespearean outfit.

"But even if he's not around, I cannot wait to spy some swordplay." She did a parry and counter-parry. "Avast, lads, ye are no match for me." She giggled. "Plus, I absolutely must tear into a roasted turkey leg."

"Go on," I said. "Skedaddle. Have a great time."

She slung on a cross-body purse and hurried out.

Bailey said, "What I wouldn't give to have that kind of energy."

"You usually do. You're still stewing about Cinnamon's dismissal."

"How well you know me."

I stroked her shoulder. "We need to get this shop in order." With all the sales and foot traffic, I needed to tidy bookshelves. I slipped into the storage room and queued up "A Fairy's Love Song," which was a solo by an enchanting harpist. The effect was calming. Perfect. When I emerged, I said to Bailey, "You take the sales counter and slap on a smile." She liked to chat with customers and loved the sound of the register's *cha-ching*. "Also, while there's a lull, why don't you search for another wedding venue? See if Nature's Retreat is available," I suggested. "Chef Guy might have some persuasion there."

"Chef Guy." Her eyes grew misty. "Nick had such delicious suggestions for what the chef would cook for the wedding. I suppose I should ask for the menu from Alan at some point." She sidled behind the counter and straightened the free bookmarks that we offered. "Say, do you think Alan would consider letting me still have the wedding at Baldini Vineyards?"

"Would you want to?"

"No, I guess not. Who needs to start a marriage surrounded by bad vibes, right?" She pressed her lips together and popped them open with a *smack*. "But maybe. I mean, it's such a beautiful place. I've been dreaming about the event every night. Nick would want me to have it there, don't you think?"

"I don't know."

She sighed. "Yeah, me, either. I'm so conflicted."

Tigger trailed me for the first few minutes as I moved from bookshelf to bookshelf, reorganizing books by theme and author. It never ceased to amaze me how often customers pulled a book out of a slot and replaced it in a completely different slot.

When I ambled to the front of the shop, Tigger retired to the children's area at the rear of the shop. Seeing as there were no kids or customers nearby—he loved company—he curled into a ball and instantly fell asleep. Had Tina given him some kind of chill pill? I'd forgotten to ask if he'd acted up while I was gone. Did that make me a bad cat mommy? I made a mental note to contact the veterinarian before the end of the day and set to work.

Regularly I put books that were related to the week's theme on the specialty tables. One of my favorites in the current mix was *The Medieval Kitchen*, which had colorful illustrations and useful tips for cooks who intended to reproduce feudal meals within a historical framework.

In addition, I had drummed up a number of nonfiction accounts about the Renaissance Fair. The one that most of our customers were drawn to was *Well Met: Renaissance Faires and the American Counterculture*. The book spelled out when the idea for the fair came about and how it had matured.

Then, of course, there were the fiction books that appealed to me. I featured *Cloche and Dagger: A Hat Mystery* and *A Killer Ball at*

*Honeychurch Hall* because both were set in England. I added *Spells and Scones: A Magical Bakery Mystery* for the obvious reason—it featured scones. All three were mysteries.

As I placed them on the table so buyers could see the lovely cover art, I contemplated our current Crystal Cove mystery: who killed Nick Baldini and why? I didn't want to suspect Hannah, Alan, or Dolly, but who else was there? Granted, Cinnamon said—

*Cinnamon.* I moaned softly. She would hate that I was trying to work the issue. How could I not? Wasn't it my citizenly duty to help the police solve the crime so Bailey and my aunt, and the rest of Crystal Cove, could find peace?

Who had Cinnamon contacted so far? She said she had been in touch with Nick's business partners. Did she mean vendors, bottlers, and white oak barrel suppliers? How about those that provided the vineyard with new vines? Or his foreman and the men and women that worked the land? There were so many people involved in keeping a vineyard up and running. Had she questioned the people connected to the fair? Each year, the mayor and Nick had worked in tandem to get the fair up and running. There were stalls and stages to erect and barkers and musicians to hire. If Nick really was more volatile than any of us knew, maybe he had come to blows with one or more of them.

I didn't ignore what Flora had said about Nick arguing with Melody Beaufort, either. Had they been playacting or fighting? I had asked the mayor about Melody's history, but I hadn't inquired whether squabbling was part and parcel of their fair repertoire. I dialed Z.Z. but reached her voice mail. Quickly, I left a message saying that I'd like to talk when she had time.

If Melody hadn't met Nick until recently, I couldn't imagine her having a reason to want him dead. Why didn't she have a social media footprint? In her line of business, even creating something as simple as a Pinterest or Instagram page, like artists did to display pictures of their art, seemed vital. Maybe Rhett and I should take a pottery class, as he suggested, so I could learn more about her.

*Can it, Jenna. Cinnamon has it covered.*

Sufficiently chided—for now—I straightened the shop for another fifteen minutes and then said to Bailey, "I'm grabbing something cool to drink at the Nook. Want anything?"

She waved me off, too busy handling three customers, all of whom were purchasing a stack of books and gift items. I was happy to see how much better she seemed. Her eyes glistened with energy, and her gift of gab was effortless. *Work,* my father often reminded me, *is good for the soul.*

As I entered the Nook, I spotted Pepper and Flora sitting at a table for four near the plate glass window with a view of the ocean. Both were wearing identical pink-beaded tops. Each was enjoying a tumbler of a sparkling liquid with wedges of lime.

I slipped up to them and said hello.

Flora patted the seat of a bistro-style chair. "Join us."

"Just for a minute." As I sat, my skirt, thanks to friction, tangled with the hem of the white tablecloth. I smoothed both and settled back in the chair. "I have to return to work in a sec. What are you drinking?"

"Pellegrino. So refreshing."

"Looks good."

A brunette waitress heard me say so and said, "I'll bring you one in a sec, Jenna."

"In a to-go cup," I added.

"Jenna" — Flora toyed with the crystal vase that held a single white rose — "I heard you beat me to it."

"To what?"

"Telling the police about Nick and Melody Beaufort's spat."

"How did you hear?"

"I informed her," Pepper said. "My daughter stopped by the shop before returning to work. She's concerned about you, Jenna."

"Aw, that's nice," I said with a teasing lilt in my tone.

"She's not concerned in that way," Pepper warned.

"Don't I know it. I seem to rub her the wrong way."

"You and everyone else." Pepper glanced at Flora, who tittered. "Between us, she never played well with others in the sandbox."

The waitress delivered my Pellegrino in a plastic cup with a lid and straw and moved on.

"Say, Pepper," I said as I unfolded a white cloth napkin, "did you ever see your tenant and Nick Baldini together?"

"Sean doesn't mingle much."

"How about Melody?" I asked.

"Once. Doing that fair-speak thing. They were right outside my booth on the Pier. He and two others were fighting over which one would take the fair maiden to the king's ball. Of course, Nick, the king, said he had first rights. The others overly emoted their disappointment. One said, 'Be gone, ye paunchy, idle-headed mold-warp.'" Pepper snorted. "I love saying *mold-warp*."

Flora repeated the term; her cheeks flushed.

"The whole time Melody blushed like a schoolgirl," Pepper went on. "She fiddled with her hair and uttered, 'Please sir,' or 'If you will, sir.'"

Flora said, "I'm sorry I missed that. I love all the drama at the fair. Not the *real* drama, mind you," she hastened to add. "Not the murder. But the playacting is fun and lively. Although lately, all I seem to be running into are puppetry people bopping each other over the head."

"*Punch and Judy,*" Pepper grumbled. "How I hate that stupid show. In this day and age, why are we letting children see that kind of abuse?"

"I agree," Flora said. "We should talk to Z.Z. about it. Be pro-active. Change it up."

"Great idea." Pepper thumped the table.

Returning to the issue that piqued my interest, I said, "Pepper, do you know how long the Beauforts have lived in the city?"

"A year or so."

"Where else have they lived?"

She raised an eyebrow. "Why are you so intrigued by them?"

"Z.Z. said they came from Ohio."

"They might have. I wouldn't know."

"Didn't they fill out paperwork for the Airbnb rental?"

"Yes, with the parent company. I merely required that they have good credit."

I picked up my cup and rose to leave.

Pepper grasped my wrist. "Word to the wise, Jenna. Don't buck my daughter. She won't take kindly to it."

"I would never think of bucking her."

"Isn't that what you're doing, asking all these questions?"

I wrenched free of her grip. "Pepper, Nick Baldini was a friend of mine and of so many others in this town. Not to mention Bailey's wedding has to be postponed. The sooner this tragedy is solved, the sooner our town and friends can heal, wouldn't you agree? You of all people know how solving the murder of Dr. Thornton helped others. You were instrumental in the capture of her killer."

"I wasn't . . ." She paused. "Well, maybe I was." Before Pepper had stumbled upon my standoff with a killer, she had made it her purpose in life to thwart me. Ever since we'd worked in tandem to foil the murderer, however, we had coexisted nicely.

"Do what you have to do," she said. "My lips are sealed."

When I reentered the Cookbook Nook, my aunt was slipping into the storage room, shaking her head to and fro. Sensing something was wrong, I followed her. Tigger bounded to his feet and trailed me.

I pushed through the curtain. "Aunt Vera, are you — "

She whirled around. Her face was ash white.

My stomach snagged. I hurried to her and threw my arms around her. "What's wrong? You're shivering."

"It's nothing." She wriggled free.

"Talk to me."

She whisked off her turban, set it on a shelf, and fluffed her hair.

"Aunt Vera, c'mon. Something has you spooked."

Picking up on her angst, Tigger rubbed against her ankles. He looped his tail around her legs. She scratched him beneath his chin. "You sweet adorable cat." She stopped doting on him and eyed me. "Jenna, dear, you know how much I loved the Baldini family. I've known them so very long."

I nodded.

"Well, I did a tarot card reading" — she withdrew a packet of tarot cards from the pocket of her lavender caftan — "for Alan Baldini." She spread the cards and fanned herself.

"You saw him at the fair? Did he tell you that Cinnamon questioned him?"

"No. He was there performing with his crow. He looked a little sallow, and his eyes were decidedly hollow. He mumbled something about the show *going on*. He said Nick would expect nothing less, but I could see his heart wasn't in it." She removed the top three cards from the deck and set them on the desk. "He begged me for a reading. After paying a farthing, he asked if I saw love in his future."

"You didn't see love, though, did you?"

"No."

"Please don't tell me you pulled the Death card."

"*That* and more." She showed me the three cards she had drawn on his behalf: the Three of Pentacles as well as Death and Devil cards. She waved the Three of Pentacles, which showed three people discussing a property structure, basically implying that work needed to be done or renovations needed to be carried out. "If a person draws this, he could be coming into property. With Nick dead . . ."

I got her drift. Since both of their parents were dead, Alan was the lone survivor. He would inherit Nick's portion of the vineyard, unless Nick had divested of it another way.

"The Death card, as you know, can be highly misunderstood," she said, "but when it shows up in companion with the Three of Pentacles, I felt a fear beyond all fears. Death can stand for the ending of a major phase of your life."

"Losing your brother."

"It can also represent the beginning of something far more valuable."

"Inheritance."

"It might mean you have to close one door in order to open another."

"Murder."

She nodded. "It's horrible, don't you see?"

I opened my arms, palms up. "Cinnamon questioned Alan. She's letting him roam free. She's convinced he didn't do it."

"Is she?" Vera said. "Maybe she let him go because she doesn't have the goods on him yet."

"Listen to you. *The goods*, like this is a scene out of a gangster movie." I squeezed her arm affectionately.

"Maybe she set him loose so he might reveal himself." She worried one of her dangling earrings between her fingertips.

"The third card is the devil. What does that represent in conjunction with the other two?" The card depicted a satyr that was half man and half goat.

"Often times the devil becomes the scapegoat that we blame for troubles in life, meaning Alan might be innocent." She shuffled the tarot deck and reinserted it into her pocket. "If he is, then who killed his brother, and is Alan in danger?"

"Cinnamon says she has a number of suspects in her sights."

"Is Hannah Storm one of them?"

"Why do you ask?"

"She came to me for a reading, as well. Right after Melody Beaufort rushed off and before Alan arrived. Hannah was nervously itching her palms throughout the session. She said the police had questioned her."

*Good.* Maybe Cinnamon had discovered why Hannah had been staring through binoculars at Nick and whether she had lost a bead.

"I like Hannah a lot," my aunt said. "I'm worried for her."

"What cards did you turn up?"

Aunt Vera pulled a single card from her other pocket.

I recognized the Empress card, which featured a full-figured woman—the archetypal Earth Mother—in a gold gown with blond hair. She had a peaceful aura about her.

"That's a good card," I said.

"Not if it's upside down." She twisted it. "In reverse position, it means the recipient is dealing with confusion, maybe even indecisiveness about the direction of a relationship."

I took the card from her and held it upright. "Perhaps this has to do with Hannah and Nick. I was wondering whether she was interested in Nick or he in her," I explained. When I was telling her about the bird swooping in and flying off with the bead, I paused. Why was there only one bead on the verandah? Did Alan's crow, as I'd theorized earlier, bring it from Hannah's property, meaning Hannah was never there?

Aunt Vera said, "The card also signifies Hannah might be finding it difficult to work cooperatively with others."

"She and Nick had a couple of disagreements over water rights."

"Hmm," she hummed softly.

"What other cards did you draw for her?"

"The Eight of Cups, which signifies disappointment and abandonment, and the Two of Pentacles reversed, which implies difficulty and discouragement."

"Perhaps those pertain to her family. I hear she's got her hands full with her grandmother, and her brother is living in Paris. What do you know about them?"

"The Storms have a long history in Crystal Cove. Her great-grandfather, Hugh, for whom her brother was named, relocated from

England. The Storm surname is interesting." My aunt shuffled to the water cooler beside the desk and filled a paper cup with water. The water tank burped as she downed the liquid. "In olden days, it was given to someone with a blustery, stormy temperament. This comes from a long history of Europeans giving surnames attributed to nicknames. According to tales, Hugh Storm, or *Stormy*, as he was called, was such a fellow. He enjoyed his liquor, but he fell in love with wine. He went to Europe and hunted down four old vines. Using the cloning technique, he kept the vineyard prospering. As you know from the vineyard tour we took last year, a clone is a single vine that has been selected from a *mother vine* to which it is identically similar."

"So the Storms tinkered with nature."

"All vintners tinker with nature. With the varied rains and drought that we have experienced, the key to keeping a vineyard going is to tweak and try something new. Stormy was passionate about what he did. He passed that fervor onto his son, rest his soul, who passed it on to his daughter Hannah."

"Not to Hannah's brother."

"No." She heaved a sigh. "Such a pity. Young Hugh left town with a chip on his shoulder the size of a hundred-year-old vine. Hannah had to carry on alone. It's not easy running a vineyard."

"I've heard her grandmother can be quite a tyrant. Cinnamon went so far as to call her bitter."

"She wasn't always that way. When her beloved husband was alive, she was a fun woman to be with. Quite intelligent. A good storyteller. The loss of a spouse can turn a soul dark." Aunt Vera tossed the empty paper cup into the trash can. "It doesn't help that osteoporosis has crippled her so much that she clings emotionally to Hannah." My aunt's eyes brimmed with tears. "She always took such pride in her husband's accomplishments. She doesn't want anyone to ruin his legacy."

"How sad." I handed her back the Empress card.

Aunt Vera rotated it and studied it, dragging a finger along the length of the gown. "So pretty, isn't she? But what is her fate?"

# Chapter 11

After closing the Cookbook Nook and dropping Tigger at home, I met up with Bailey at the entrance to the Renaissance Fair. Dusk was setting in, and torches were lit along both main avenues. The glow gave the area an ethereal, otherworldly look, which made me feel like I'd entered a magical town.

Bailey had already purchased a wreath for her hair and corncob on a stick for a snack. She offered me a bite. I grabbed hold of the stick and dug in. The treat tasted smoky. Butter oozed onto my fingers. I was glad she had brought napkins; otherwise, I would have licked every drop off my fingertips.

When I handed the corncob back, she said, "I spoke with Chef Guy. He thinks the rose garden at Nature's Retreat is a perfect setting for a wedding. What do you think? I'm meeting up with Tito after he's done interviewing a few of the vendors. We have to decide what to do next."

"I think the rose garden would be lovely."

"No view."

"The magnificent flowers will make a beautiful backdrop, and you can keep your green-and-red theme. Plus the food will come straight from Nature's Retreat kitchen, so you know there won't be any slipups."

"When did you become Pollyanna?"

"In the last hour. I asked Glinda the Good Witch to grant me a wish."

Bailey laughed. So did I. When we were ten, she and I had read *The Wizard of Oz* at the same time. Both of us had imagined ourselves as Dorothy. We adored Glinda. Who didn't?

"Guy isn't sure if the garden is available, though," Bailey said, "so I'm waiting for a callback."

"Hi-ho!" Tito strode toward us, sans crier's bell. No doubt, it had become a hindrance when doing his interviews.

I poked my friend. "There's your lover. Go. I'll stop in and see Rhett."

I entered Bait and Switch Fishing and Sport Supply Store and spotted Rhett in the camping section, which featured camping gear, dozens of fishing rods, and a glass-enclosed display case of multi-use tools. Displays of backpacks and hiking boots hung on the walls.

Rhett was tightening the straps of a backpack on a lanky male customer. A few other backpacks lay on the floor. The customer gave Rhett a thumbs-up gesture, shrugged off the pack, and headed to the checkout desk with his selection in hand.

Rhett saw me and sized me up with a sexy grin. *If I could bottle that look.* Luckily, it was etched in my memory. He sauntered to me. "My lady, Maid Marian, what brings thee to the fair this fine evening?"

"To beg a sweet kiss from you."

"I must oblige." He pecked me on the cheek.

"Do you have time for a quick meal? I was thinking before dinner we could sign up for a pottery class like you promised."

"Sure. Let me wrap up a few loose ends here. By the way"—he picked up the unwanted backpacks and slung them onto the stand with other similar carriers—"our dedicated chief of police stopped by today."

"What did she want?"

"To find out more about Nick—for example, who worked with him at the fair and who might have had a feud with him. She's asking every vendor."

"Glad to hear it."

"I also got an earful about you tracking her down during her coffee break, like I could rein you in." He dragged a knuckle along my jaw.

"Yeah, well." I felt my cheeks flush. "It was Bailey's idea."

"Did you race her to the café?"

"I tried, but I had to slow down because my wreath was jiggling like crazy."

Rhett guffawed. "What did you learn?"

"Not much. You know Cinnamon. Tight-lipped and by the letter."

He donned his Robin Hood hat, told his clerk that he was taking a much-needed break, and clasped my hand. A moment after we exited, I spotted Melody Beaufort hastening toward the ladies' room. Her cheeks were tear-stained.

"Melody," I shouted, hoping I might be able to provide comfort, but she didn't slow.

A barker in a cherry red jacket and pantaloons tramped past us yelling, "Come one, come all. The event of your lives is about to take place. What is it, ye ask? Why, 'tis tea with the queen!"

The queen, looking regal in an elaborate gold gown with a gold-and-white accordion-style collar, followed him. Two guards, dressed like those at Buckingham Palace, and a half dozen maidens trailed her.

"Who's playing the queen?" Rhett asked me.

"If I'm not mistaken, she's the same actress who played the Queen of Hearts. Once a queen, always a queen."

"Isn't that a Queen Elizabeth getup?" Rhett asked. "Aren't we in Henry VIII's time period?"

"I'm sure there are lots of time warps at the event. Haven't you seen the steampunk patrons?" I patted his arm. "Try not to get caught up in the details of reality, my love."

We passed a small booth named Braids for Maids, where vendors were braiding the hair of girls of all ages with ribbon. Even a few boys with long tresses were getting in on the fun. I was glad Tigger wasn't with me. He would have had a field day with the ribbon.

Directly across the boardwalk was Beaufort's Beautiful Pottery. I made a detour to the stall, dragging Rhett along. Sean, in his dashing Petruchio costume, stood at the sales desk. Three customers sat at pottery wheel stations.

"Good e'en, kind sir," I said to Sean. "Wouldst be possible for us to enroll in a lesson on the morrow?"

Sean shook a finger. "You don't have to bother doing the fair-speak thing with me."

"But it's fun."

"Honestly? I find it a pain. Melody loves it, so I indulge her." He picked up a pad. "What time? We have spots at ten and two."

"Ten?" I glanced at Rhett. He nodded.

Sean scribbled our names in the pad. "Got it."

"Hey, Sean, I saw Melody rush past me," I said. "I don't mean to be nosy, but is she all right? I think she was crying."

"She's fine. Got something in her eye."

"Tell her I look forward to learning how she makes her pots."

"Will do, but don't get your hopes up because"—Sean flicked his fingertips—"it's magic."

"Like smoke and mirrors?" I teased.

"Exactly. She doesn't give away her secrets."

Enjoying our walk, Rhett and I moseyed toward the far end of the

Pier, passing a series of activities including juggling, archery, and the Dragon Swing—an adventuresome ride on a gigantic green dragon. A line of people waited at each venue.

"What piques your fancy for dinner?" Rhett asked.

"I was thinking of having hawker's mush."

"Pray tell, what's that?"

"Spinach-and-wild-rice pancakes topped with hollandaise sauce."

"Intriguing."

We moseyed to that stall and fetched two portions. While sitting on a bench with a view of the beach and ocean, we ate to our hearts' content. The hollandaise sauce was luscious and just the ticket on a cool evening.

"Say, isn't that Alan Baldini on the sand?" Rhett asked.

Alan looked quite handsome in his falconer's outfit of black trousers, black suede vest over a muslin chemise, and plumed hat. Sporting a falconer's elbow-length leather gauntlet on his left arm, he was showing the group how his crow would fly in a circle and come back to him. Once that task was completed, Alan selected a woman in the group. With the woman's blessing, he ordered the crow to fly off and, upon its return, land on her shoulder. The crow obeyed. On its new perch, the crow boldly plucked a trinket from the woman's hair adornments and took wing. Alan commanded the bird to return to its perch. When it did, he grabbed hold of the bird's leather jesses, retrieved the woman's treasure, and gallantly handed it back to the woman.

As the spectators cheered their approval, I pictured the bead I'd found on Nick's verandah and wondered whether Alan had coaxed his bird to put it there to frame Hannah.

Alan wrapped up his demonstration and made his way to a staircase leading up to the Pier.

"Show's over," Rhett said. "It's time for me to return to work, fair maiden. Customers are hankering for wares. You continue on. I'll see you on the morrow." He lifted the hair off the nape of my neck and kissed the hollow. I about swooned.

"Till then," I murmured.

Without Rhett by my side, I strolled along South Street drinking in the marvelous items for sale. At Sabersmith, I sorted through amazing metalwork, ancient coins, pewter pitchers and cups, and decorative knives in leather sleeves. Beside Sabersmith was Celtic Dreams, a booth that offered gorgeous jewelry and silk scarves. At Dragon's Quest, I browsed exotic hand-blown glass dragons, complete with fiery eyes and ornate tails and claws. None were cheap; most went for over a hundred dollars. The purple-headed dragon with red eyes was mesmerizing.

Near Mum's the Word Diner, I cut through to North Street and entered Mistress of the Fairies. The entire stall was decorated in tones of green—moss green flooring, forest green silk banners, and kelly green shelving displaying finished products. Flora was seated at a mosaic bistro-style table working on an ethereal small garden that was decked out with flickering lights, blue picket fence, and wishing well.

"Nice work, mistress," I said. "Who 'tis the buyer?"

"I don't ken yet. As I told you—"

"Each garden picks the buyer."

"Though in this competitive market," she said, drooping the fair-speak, "I'm selling less than I expected."

"Really? There seems to be plenty of foot traffic."

"Most people are taking pictures to post on their Instagram sites. Go figure."

"Be of stout heart, mistress," I said, taking up the fair-speak again. "May luck be with thee."

"And with thee, Maid Marian."

Outside her booth, I paused when I spotted Alan hovering near Ye Olde Wine Shoppe. The crow was not on his shoulder. He was fingering one of the winepress tools. My insides knotted. Was he reliving the experience of bludgeoning his brother? I was surprised that Hannah was still selling the items. Maybe she was ignorant of the fact that one had been used as a murder weapon. It hadn't been mentioned in any of the newspaper articles.

I drew near and heard Alan say, "Are you sure?"

"I haven't seen it," Hannah replied.

"Seen what?" I asked Alan. "Did you lose your bird?"

He swung around and zeroed in on me. "No, the bird's in its crate. I lost my gauntlet. Who are you?"

"It's me, Jenna."

"Sorry." He fanned a hand. "The glow from the torchlights behind you obscured your features."

The lights weren't very bright. Maybe he was strung out with angst. Over the past year, before his mother passed away, he had come into the shop often to buy her gifts and knew me pretty well.

I said, "Alan, moments ago you were wearing your gauntlet. On the beach. Maybe you dropped it there, or maybe you put it down when you stowed your crow in its cage."

"That's my main glove. I've got that one. My backup one is missing. The last time I saw it was the day . . . the day . . ." Tears pooled in his eyes. He curbed them with a knuckle. "When you were there."

*The day Nick was murdered.*

"Alan, keep calm," I said, though I was feeling anything but calm. Had he worn the gauntlet so his fingerprints wouldn't show on the winepress handle? Was he afraid the police would discover the glove with Nick's blood on it? "I'm sure you'll find it. Why did you ask Hannah if she'd seen it?"

"I thought maybe I'd dropped it in the vineyard or something. Her workmen might have—" His voice crackled with tension. "I don't know."

A customer approached Hannah.

As she dealt with the transaction, I said, "Alan, the day Nick died, Bailey and I heard you two arguing. Nick said it was a brotherly disagreement. I heard him yell, 'Over my dead body.' That made you so mad that you quit."

Alan sagged. "I didn't quit. I would never quit."

Hmm. That was what Nick had said.

"Tell me about the quarrel, Alan."

He glanced over his shoulder. Hannah was still involved with her customer. "I told Nick I was in love with someone and wanted to date her, and he got worried. He didn't think I should ever marry because of . . . the accident."

"You were hit by a lacrosse stick."

"That's right."

"What did it do to you?"

"Gave me a swelled head." Alan attempted a humorous smirk, but it made him look malicious. "In all seriousness, I used to get angry and have outbursts, and . . ." He worked his tongue inside his mouth. "And other stuff."

Other stuff *is certainly vague,* I mused.

"The doctors can't fix the problem," he admitted.

"What do you do for the anger?"

"I take medicine. It helps. I haven't lost my temper about anything in a long time."

"Except at Nick."

"That's different. Brothers . . ." He flapped a hand, like Nick had. "Working with birds of prey helps. It gives me focus. That's why I became a falconer. I own a lot of birds, but I primarily bring Crow to the fair."

"That's his name?" I said. "Crow?"

"Isn't that utter nonsense?" Hannah rejoined the conversation. "Naming a bird Crow. Honestly, Alan." She clucked her tongue with disdain, but her eyes sparkled with amusement as she greeted a pair of customers and guided them to the wine-tasting bar.

"What do you do at the vineyard, Alan?" I asked.

"I balance the books and pay bills and such. I'm good with numbers. The blow didn't take that away from me. Although that won't change things in regard to the trust."

"What trust?"

"With Nick dead, everything goes into the Baldini Family Trust. Given my condition, my father didn't think I was the best person to manage the estate long-term. Nick knows . . ." He faltered. "He *knew* that I didn't have the brawn for physical work, so he put me in charge of bookkeeping. The foreman, Frank, and a few others do the heavy lifting. I suppose the trust will hire someone to take up where Nick left off. An attorney rang me, but I haven't phoned him back."

I mulled over that information for a moment. If he didn't inherit outright, then he didn't have a financial motive to want his brother dead, did he? "Alan, when we overheard you guys arguing, Nick threatened to reveal your *history.* Did he mean he'd tell the woman you had your eye on about your outbursts?"

"Sometimes Nick flew off the handle and said I was unsteady, but I'm not, and he knew it. Truthfully, I don't think he approved of the, um . . ."

"Woman you fell in love with?" I asked.

"You're in *love,* Alan?" Hannah asked, joining our conversation again.

"Yeah. I—"

"With whom?"

Alan scuffed his toe on the burlap carpet.

"Any woman would be lucky to have you," Hannah said, her eyes twinkling with impishness.

Alan's neck turned splotchy. He licked his lips self-consciously.

"Sorry," Hannah said, clearly realizing she'd embarrassed him. "I've got to attend to another customer. I'll be right back."

Had Nick and Alan fallen for the same woman? Maybe Nick told Alan to back off because he wanted her for himself. Did that drive Alan wild with jealousy? No, despite my earlier musings, I couldn't see him lashing out at his brother. He was docile and frail and downright sweet. After their set-to, he had coaxed his bird to taunt Nick with swooping antics. Would a killer do that?

I said, "The police said you pranked Nick that night by lacing the well with frogs."

"Yeah, we were always goading each other."

"Maybe he hid your missing glove," I suggested.

"I hadn't considered that."

"Where did you find all the frogs that night?"

"I . . ." He faltered. "I bought them. At a pet store." His eyelids fluttered. Was he lying? "When I was putting the frogs in the well, I saw Hannah in the field. She was on her property, but she could probably vouch for me."

"Are you sure it was her?"

"Positive. I'd know her anywhere. Five eight. Slim figure. She was wearing black, but she always wears black. And she had on a broad-brimmed hat."

"You saw all that in the dark?"

"Yeah, I'm good with shapes. Besides, she sneezed. She's got allergies." He shrugged. "I have to admit, wearing the floppy hat at night was sort of odd, but she can be goofy, you know?" His voice had a dreamy quality, and I suddenly understood why he had grown embarrassed a moment ago.

"Alan, are you in love with Hannah? Is that why you and Nick were going at it?"

He lowered his chin and didn't respond.

"Are you lying about having seen her in the vineyard?"

"No way."

"To give her an alibi?"

His mouth drew thin. "She was there. It was around six o'clock. She was sprinting. Her grandmother keeps her on a tight schedule. Ask her."

I pivoted to do so, but Hannah had disappeared. So had the customer. I peered down the boardwalk and saw Sean Beaufort strolling toward his booth.

"Hey, Sean. Did you see Hannah Storm pass your way?"

He spun around, shielded his eyes from the torchlight, and shook his head.

When I turned back to address Alan, he had vanished, as well.

• • •

Later that night, settled at home for the evening, I threw together a quick meal of stir-fried shrimp—I often keep shrimp on hand in the freezer—artichoke hearts, baby tomatoes, chives from my miniature herb garden, and kalamata olives. In less than ten minutes, I was dining like royalty. Tigger finished munching kibble and quickly decided that the area between the kitchen table and the living room window was a racetrack. He darted back and forth a dozen or more times.

"What's going on with you, kitty?"

All of a sudden, he became motionless. A statue. His nose twitched.

"What's wrong?"

He eyeballed the living room window and hissed. He never hisses.

Heart pounding, I set my fork on my plate, muted the album of Judy Garland classics that I was listening to, flicked on the exterior lights that my father had installed on the cottage a few months ago, and seized the poker from the fireplace tool set. I peered out the bay window and stiffened. A figure in black was dashing toward the ocean, away from the cottage. Alan said Hannah always wore black. Come to think of it, I couldn't remember seeing her in any other color. The figure looked about the same size as her, but lots of people were about her size, including me. And lots of people wore black.

Even with the glow of exterior lights, I couldn't nail down whether the figure was man or woman, and I sure as heck wasn't going outside to find out.

Instead, I dashed to my cell phone and dialed 911.

Within two minutes, Marlon Appleby showed up at my door clad in street clothes—plaid shirt, jeans, and tennis shoes. His shirt wasn't tucked in.

"That was fast, Deputy."

"Let's just say I was the closest responding policeman."

I glanced past him. His Jeep was parked by my aunt's house. Were they . . . ? Had they . . . ? I felt my cheeks flush.

"What's up?" He scrubbed his five-o'clock shadow.

I filled him in.

Keeping calm—was he ever not calm?—he inspected the outside of the cottage. It took him a few minutes to complete the tour.

When he returned, he said he couldn't make out any discernible footprints. "It was probably a beach bum or a peeping Tom. They're usually harmless. Looking for food in the trash or searching for bottles they can recycle for cash. Lock up and go to sleep."

"Yes, sir."

He touched my shoulder. "If you need anything or have another fright, I'll be right next door."

Well, that answered my question. Yes, they *were* and they *had*. My cheeks burned hotter than I could have imagined.

# Chapter 12

On Friday morning I ate a fruit-protein smoothie, fixed a button on my Maid Marian costume, donned the outfit as well as the garland—I was getting adept at sticking in hatpins—and hurried to the Cookbook Nook with Tigger. I wanted to make sure things were set up properly before I left for my pottery class with Rhett. Tina and Bailey had beaten me to the shop and were busy at the crafts table getting ready for the onslaught of kids who would be coming in for the watercolor painting class. Bailey was teaching it. A few months ago, on a balmy day off, I'd taught her the salt technique. She had taken to it like a pro.

Today, however, she wanted to concentrate on fairies because they fit the Renaissance Fair theme. She had preprinted drawings of fairies that the children could paint. Before the paint dried, the children could sprinkle on salt. When the art was finished, the salt would glimmer in certain light. Perfect for fairies' wings, Bailey said. I suggested she put an array of our unique saltshakers near the table. Maybe parents would purchase one for their budding artists. We still had a couple of silver-plated guardian dragon saltshakers, three adorable wooden beer mug shakers, and a half dozen metal pheasant shakers. All of the thimble-style shakers with depictions of the Middle Ages had sold out the first day. I hadn't considered purchasing any fairy-themed shakers and made a mental note to do so for our next Renaissance Fair event.

Needing a snack before I set to work, I joined Katie in the breezeway. She was putting out slim slices of room-temperature meat pie. The aroma was incredible.

I took one and mumbled between bites, "Yum. I really like the carrots, onions, and herbs. What are you calling this?"

Katie pointed to her handwritten sign: *Heathen Cakes.*

"Cake? But it's pie."

"It's a long story, but the term *cake* comes from the old phrase 'Let them eat cake,' which really wasn't referring to cake, as in a sweet confection, but to flat bread, or a poor man's food. This pie is a peasant dish, hence the word *cake* ascribed to it."

"Whatever the origin," I said, "our customers will love it."

"I hope so, and now I'm off to the fair," she said. "Reynaldo will be in charge of the café."

"How's he working out?" I asked.

"Like a dream."

"A very handsome dream."

"Yes, he's a bit distracting. Not to me. I'm in love with Keller. But the waitstaff is definitely googly-eyed about him." She flapped the air. "I don't care as long as he keeps turning out great food." She strode to the front door. "Too-ra-loo."

"Oh, no, you don't, Katie," my aunt cried. "You may not steal my line, you varlet." She skirted around the sales counter but had to halt when the folds of her mauve caftan snagged on the corner.

Katie blew her a saucy kiss and exited. Aunt Vera pulled free and hurried after her.

I caught up to my aunt before she could depart. "Hold on a second."

"What do you need, dear?"

We stood near the entrance. A customer passed us and nodded *hello*.

"I wanted to ask you about those tarot readings you gave to Alan and Hannah."

"The first was to Hannah, the next to Alan. Actually the first was to Melody" — Aunt Vera used a finger to reorder the names — "but she ran off."

"Right. Do you remember if Alan was hovering about, as if he were trying to listen in on Hannah's reading?"

"Come to think of it, yes." She adjusted the strand of her knotted lariat-style necklace, which had skewed toward her left arm. "How did you know?"

"I think he has a crush on her."

"How sweet."

"Maybe he wanted to overhear if love was coming into her life."

My aunt frowned. "Her reading certainly didn't imply that. Nor did his. Now, Jenna" — she pursed her lips — "you and I both know a reading doesn't determine one's fate."

"Yes, of course."

"If he's in love with her, he has to tell her."

"I think she might be in love with him, too — that is, if I'm any good at reading the signs."

"Wouldn't that be marvelous? Not that you can read signs. I'm sure, given time, that you will, but wouldn't it be lovely for the two of them to find one another?" My aunt folded her hands together.

Bailey poked me in the ribs. "What are you two chatting about?"

I was delighted to see how cheery she looked in a lemon yellow sundress. Maybe her mood was brightening. "Good morning, sunshine."

Bailey flicked her dangly sunflower earrings. "It's okay, isn't it, not wearing a Ren Fair costume?"

"You look darling and rested."

My aunt said, "To answer your question, Bailey, Jenna thinks Alan Baldini might be in love with Hannah Storm."

Bailey's eyes widened. "You don't think he killed Nick over that, do you?"

My aunt gasped. "Was Nick in love with Hannah?"

"I don't think so," I said.

"Nick had his eye on someone," Bailey said. "Do you know if Hannah is seeing anyone, Vera?"

"I wouldn't have a clue. She certainly didn't mention it at her reading."

I said, "Nick claimed the woman whose heart he wanted to win wasn't free, and if Hannah isn't in a committed relationship—and I got the feeling she wasn't by the way she was flirting with Alan—then that would rule her out."

My aunt nodded. "Dolly, by obvious elimination, is out of the equation." She wiggled a finger in front of my face. "What's going on in that brain?"

"I had the fleeting notion that Nick might have set his sights on Melody Beaufort, but seeing as they'd recently met . . ."

"Love happens in a flash." My aunt flicked her fingers like fireworks igniting—*pow, pow, pow.* "It did for me the first time, and even for you, Bailey Bird."

Bailey gave my aunt the stink eye. "No, it didn't. Not the first time. Ugh. Talk about a disaster. And if you're referring to Tito, *ahem*"—she cleared her throat—"if you'll recall, I couldn't stand him."

"Until he stood in for our magician," I said. "It didn't hurt that he was sending you secret mementoes to win your heart."

Bailey nodded. "Yeah, he's a quirky guy, but he's *my* quirky guy."

My aunt eyed me. "Tell me, Jenna, how long was it before you knew you loved Rhett?"

"An instant. But I was single."

"Except you weren't."

I screwed up my mouth, ready for a retort, but let it go. At the time, I had believed that I was a widow, but then David resurfaced in my life. Now he was gone forever. The memory of the two of us when we were happy brought tears to my eyes.

• • •

I barely arrived at the Pier in time for the ten o'clock pottery lesson. Parking had been rough. Melody and Sean, who were in costume standing by the register, greeted me as I entered. I waved *hello* and headed for Rhett, who was already there, along with four other students. Each was sitting at a pottery wheel station at the rear of the tent. Rhett had saved a spot for me. I wove in between the display tables and the steamer trunk and settled onto a stool beside him. His skin was shaven; the shirt of his Robin Hood costume appeared freshly washed. I drank in his musky scent as he pecked my cheek.

"Good morning," I said.

He set his mouth close to my ear and whispered, "Good morning, love. I dreamed about you."

"I hope it was a good dream."

"You kept playing hard to get. I was exhausted after chasing you."

I smirked. "I don't play hard to get and you know it. Are you sure it wasn't the other way around, me chasing you?"

"I think we should discuss our dilemma and how to end it."

"Do ye now?" I said coyly, falling into fair-speak.

"Aye, I do. Over a very romantic dinner."

"I shall wait with bated breath."

"Hi-ho, everyone," Melody said and clapped her hands. "Let us begin." She righted the apron that covered her dress, which was gold but different from the one she'd worn the other day—no hint of burgundy lace or inserts, its skirt adorned by a sheer ecru lace overlay. "Welcome to Beaufort's Beautiful Pottery. I'm Melody Beaufort." She circled the area, making eye contact with each student. "How many of you have taken a pottery course before?"

Rhett and I raised our hands. So did two of the other students.

Rhett whispered to me, "She didn't ask if we were any good."

I giggled and elbowed him to hush.

A matronly woman to my right, who was clad in a silver gown and sported three strands of diamond necklaces, waved to catch Melody's attention. "I want to do what you do, Ms. Beaufort. I want to make long-necked porcelain vases."

Melody affectionately brushed the woman's shoulder with her palm. "I appreciate lofty goals, but a word of warning. It might take you a while to master. I studied for many years before I could become proficient."

"With the same teacher?" the woman asked.

"No, I had three different teachers."

"Three?"

"Two were quite good."

"And the third?"

Melody paused; her forehead pinched as she searched for a word. "Was brilliant but complicated."

"Well, I'll take as many classes as it requires," the woman said. "Now that I'm divorced, I'm building a new life for myself in the city."

"Building a new life can be a challenge," Melody said. "Believe me, I know."

"Do you offer private instruction?" the woman asked.

Rhett nudged me. "This gal must have deep pockets."

"I'm sure she does," I murmured. "Look at the necklace she's wearing."

"You don't think the diamonds are fake?"

"I'm pretty sure they're not." I knew the difference thanks to an advertising campaign I'd managed for Glitter, a high-end jewelry store. The store's owner had coaxed me to try on dozens of rings, necklaces, and bracelets so I could decide which to feature in the ad. To educate me, she had compared the real thing to paste for hours on end.

Melody said, "Of course I offer private lessons. However, today we're starting with the basics. I'm going to teach you the coil method."

For the next few minutes, she explained the process, which was a simple way to teach newbies, like us, how to build bowls, vases and other shapes by forming the clay into sausage-like ropes.

Halfway through Melody's speech, Sean approached her and placed a white lace shawl over her shoulders. Then he tenderly tucked a loose hair behind her ear. She thanked him and proceeded.

As attentive as he was to her, I was afraid I wouldn't be able to get her alone and ask the questions that were plaguing me: why didn't she have an Internet presence other than her website, and had she known Nick before meeting him this week?

During her chat, Melody provided pictures of items we could create. Rhett chose to make a small vase. I hoped to produce an oval pot. Melody showed us how to keep our fingers flat and meld the coils after we'd placed two or three of them together.

At the end of the session, as Melody was directing us to add finger textures to the upper rims of our creations, the messenger in the royal blue Shakespearean outfit rushed into the booth. Upon closer inspection, he wasn't as gawky as I'd thought. He was lean and ropy and rather cute. No wonder Tina was interested in him.

"What, ho! I have a missive," he bleated.

Melody inhaled sharply. Sean tried to muscle him out.

"Sire, please. The missive is not for thy bride. 'Tis for the lady in silver. Forsooth, I shall have to forfeit my position if I do not deliver it. I have seven mouths to feed. Please, sire, have pity on a beleaguered soul." The messenger couldn't have been more than twenty-one. His spontaneous playacting, as though he were a family man, was charming.

"Fine. Sure. Go ahead. Sorry, ma'am," Sean said to his patron.

The messenger hurried to the diamond-bejeweled woman, bent at the waist, and placed the scroll tied with ribbon across his palm. "For thee, my lady."

She took it and read it, and a grin spread across her face. "Ooh," she cooed as she pressed the letter lovingly to her chest.

When the messenger departed, Melody sank onto a stool, her eyes glistening with moisture, her hands clenched tightly in her lap.

"Melody?" I rose to console her.

Sean blocked me. "Let her be. She wells up whenever someone is happy."

She didn't seem *welled up*. She appeared distraught.

Sean said loudly to the group, "Folks, now that you've completed your projects, set them on one of the trays with the receipt I gave you upon entering. We'll fire them overnight, and you can pick them up tomorrow. Thanks for coming. Feel free to browse."

He sauntered to Melody and dropped to one knee. He said something in a hushed voice. Melody nodded, wiped her eyes, and, gathering the folds of her skirt, exited the tent.

I sighed. My quest to get answers from her would have to wait.

A short while later, after enjoying another quickie lunch of shepherd's pie at the diner—it was fast becoming one of my favorite comfort foods—Rhett and I emerged into the sunlight. I didn't mind the harsh glare because I was thrilled that the spring rain, which had been predicted for this week, had missed us and gone north. It was a gorgeous, cloudless blue-sky day.

"Heading my way?" Rhett jutted his thumb in the direction of his store.

"I think I'll stop in and see Katie before going back to work."

"Enjoy yourself. This was fun." He kissed me on the cheek and strode away, immediately swallowed up by the mob.

I headed toward the Nook's Pasties booth but startled when a scraggly young pirate in a thigh-length leather vest, striped shirt, and pantaloons burst from Ye Olde Wine Shoppe. He nearly knocked me down, so I barked, "Hey!"

He didn't slow and he didn't apologize. He sped toward the far end of the Pier.

Hannah burst from her stall, one hand planted on a hip and the other brandishing a corkscrew. "And stay out!" she shouted. Dressed in her smoky black gown, she looked formidable.

I dusted myself off and crossed to her. "Are you okay?"

"I'm fine. How are you? Did he run into you?"

"Almost."

"Come in." She beckoned me. "Have a sip of wine. I have a bottle open."

"It's a tad early for me."

"Suit yourself, but a little pinot noir can calm the nerves." She retreated inside her stall.

I followed. "What happened?"

"That thief tried to steal a corkscrew. He hid it under his vest. The nerve." She offered a sly smile and hitched her thumb. "But I spotted him in the angled mirror." A mirror hung in the corner and gave her a clear view of the stall. "I wrenched it from him and told him you don't mess with a Storm." She straightened the mugs on her display table and guided me to a stool by the petite oak bar. She poured a glass of water and pushed it toward me. "Why are you staring?"

"Am I?" I supposed I was. I couldn't help thinking that I'd seen someone about Hannah's size running from my cottage. I slid onto the stool and rested my arms on the countertop.

"You're still staring."

"Last night, were you on the beach outside my place?"

"No. I was with my grandmother. Why? Did someone spook you? You know, another girlfriend in your neighborhood has complained about a prowler. Maybe you should ask Old Jake to keep an eye on your place for a day or two. He adores you." She moved to the barrel of winepresses and twisted the tools, heels inward. "These things get so snarled up. Putting them in order keeps me on my toes." She snickered and repeated, *"Toes.* Ha! What a punster. Can you believe that I've sold over twenty?"

"Twenty. That's a lot." I swiveled on the stool. "Hannah, I'm not sure I should say anything, but . . ." I hesitated. Sooner or later she would find out. She would have to. "Did you know that one of those was used to kill Nick?"

She blanched and staggered backward, a hand to her chest. "No," she rasped.

"The police didn't tell you?"

She shook her head.

"But they questioned you, didn't they?"

"Yes. Someone heard Nick and me exchanging words at the fair, and a witness saw me digging near our property lines earlier in the day."

Apparently, Cinnamon hadn't revealed that I was said witness.

"Were you truly angry when you and Nick went at it?" I asked. "Or were the two of you acting?"

"I wasn't angry at first. I'd heard he wanted to sell his place, so I approached him."

"That had to be a rumor. He would never sell."

"That's what he said. I'm not sure who started the gossip. Nick blew a fuse. He said even if he were to sell, he would never make a deal with me because of what my grandmother did. That made me lose my cool."

"What did she do?"

Hannah huffed. "It doesn't matter."

"Yes, it does. Your family history matters because . . ." I jammed my lips together.

"Because why?"

*Cool, Jenna. Now you've stuck your foot in it.*

"Were you at his house that night?" I asked, switching tactics. "An ornate bead from your necklace was found on the verandah where he was killed."

"How would you . . ." Her eyes widened. "Of course. You were there. You and Bailey found him. That had to be horrible."

"It was." An image of Nick lying on the floor popped into my mind. I pushed it aside and focused on Hannah. She hadn't denied that she was there.

Hannah sighed. "I might as well tell you. I've already told the police. Yes, I was there that evening, around five. After not finding anything troublesome at the property line, I wanted to apologize for hassling him in public."

"Twice."

She rolled her eyes. "Boy, everyone's tongues must be wagging, huh? Yes, twice."

"Go on."

"I also wanted to apologize for whatever my grandmother did. For years, Nana—I call her Nana—claimed that Nick's grandfather diverted water from a natural spring beneath our property, which forced us to have to transport water. She said that raised our costs by a mile."

"Is that true?"

"Hold on." She flattened her palm to ward me off. "A couple of days ago, when I got back from Europe after visiting my brother for a week, Nana swore that she saw Nick walking the property with an inspector while I was gone. She told me Nick's crew had changed the fencing line because they'd found another spring to tap into. I seethed and stewed and finally confronted Nick at the fair. He denied everything. He said he never walked the property, never brought an inspector to check things out, never moved a fence, and never tapped a spring—ever. He tried to calm me down."

"You said he *owed* you."

116

"Owed me an explanation. He said he didn't. He said it was Nana's fault because she carried a longtime grudge against the Baldinis. I hated hearing that so I stewed some more. When I met up with him again outside the ice cream store, well . . ."

The scene Keller had witnessed ensued.

"I was a boor. A bully. Nick stormed off. But I wasn't convinced by his Mr. Innocent act. That was why I was in the field, to scope out what might be going on."

"You were digging with a shovel."

She blinked. "So it was *you* who saw me and told the police."

My mouth went dry. "Yes. Bailey and I had gone to the vineyard to discuss her upcoming wedding."

"Wow, she was going to have her wedding there? She'll have to change the site now, won't she? Poor thing."

I nodded. "She's put out some feelers."

"Good. I've always wanted to hold weddings at Hurricane Vineyards, but Nana won't hear of it." Hannah muttered something that sounded like *stubborn*. She fanned the air. "Back to Nick and me. Later, after finding no evidence, I rode my bike to his place to apologize. We met on the verandah. A few minutes in, I started to hyperventilate because I was so ashamed. He steadied me by the shoulders. Somehow his fingers caught in my necklace. In an instant, the strand broke apart. I'm an inept amateur jewelry maker. He helped me gather the beads. One must have rolled out of view."

Hannah's admission let Dolly and Alan or possibly his crow off the hook. No one had planted the bead to frame her.

"I didn't kill him, Jenna," she said, her tone filled with sincerity. "Over the next few minutes, Nick and I discussed my grandmother and why she'd always hated his grandfather. Pride? Jealousy? The Baldini property is slightly bigger than ours. Its yield is much greater. Whatever the reason, we made amends, and I went straight back to my place to have it out with Nana. I railed at her for a good hour."

"Can she corroborate that timeline?"

Hannah lowered her chin. "No. She's old. She fell asleep mid-rant. And neither can the nurse. I released her the moment I got home. But I was there. I swear it." She fisted her hand and pounded it into her palm. "Wait. I saw Alan in the field around six. I don't know if he saw me. I waved from the second-story window."

"Really?" I cocked my head. "Alan said he saw you in the field at that time."

"What? No! I was in the house. Like I said, I had ridden my bicycle to Baldini Vineyards. I wouldn't have taken it through the fields. The foreman saw me pedaling up the hill, and the housekeeper watched me set it in the bike rack." She sighed. "I suppose both sightings would be too early to corroborate that I was home at the time Nick died."

"Alan said he'd recognize you anywhere."

"Well, he's mistaken. He didn't see me. Not in the field. But I did see him. How could I miss him? He had that silly bird on his shoulder."

"Did you see anyone else in the field?"

"I can't say that I did."

If Alan wasn't lying, then who was on Hurricane Vineyards' property that night?

Hannah folded her hands in supplication. "Jenna, you've got to believe me. I wouldn't have hurt Nick. I would have taken him to court if I'd needed to prove he was appropriating our property. Nana might have tried to mislead me, but my father taught me the proper way to conduct business. In fact, I did contact a lawyer before approaching Nick about buying the vineyard. He was supposed to be drawing up an offer. You can check with him, not that it gives me an alibi, but it substantiates my story."

# Chapter 13

In the early afternoon, when I returned to the Cookbook Nook, I discovered that the children had come and gone and adults had taken their place at the rear table. Dolly, in an olive green medieval gown—she featured so many Renaissance-style dresses in her shop that she could wear a different one every day—had signed on to lead a second class. Today, she was teaching five women and one gentleman how to make Celtic jewelry. Storage trays holding a vast assortment of beads sat in the middle of the table. Her students were reviewing printouts of possible designs.

"Hi, Dolly," I said, drawing nearer to study the beads. I loved the silver tubes and Irish knots, but my favorites were the long, twisted pendants with a single stone set in the middle. They reminded me of an opal necklace David had given me a month after we'd started dating. It was now nestled in the bottom of my jewelry box, never to see the light of day again.

"Afternoon, Jenna." Dolly gave me a wink, but I noticed her eyes were puffy and she had developed a rash around them, probably from crying so often. Had she told Cinnamon her alibi?

Luscious, comforting music started to play through the speakers. My breathing settled into a steady rhythm.

Seconds later, Aunt Vera emerged from the storage room. "Like the tune, dear?"

"Love it. It's the Viking one, right?"

"Good memory."

I recalled the album because its lengthy title was worthy of a cookbook—*Medieval Viking Magic Fantasy for Celtic Folk Lute and Classical Guitar.*

"This tune is 'Saga of Viking Ship in Irish Sea.' Can't you just see the ships floating across the water?" She mimed the swell of the ocean in front of her.

"I can, indeed." I tilted my head to assess her—weary eyes, thin taut mouth. She was anything but lighthearted. "How are you feeling about your misgivings over Alan's and Hannah's tarot card readings?"

"Alas, I know I can't fix everything, dear." She forced a smile. "I do my best, but ultimately fate takes the lead."

"Cut it out, Vera." Bailey scurried from behind the checkout counter and flicked my aunt on the arm. "Don't lie to Jenna."

"Lie?" my aunt echoed.

"Lie. Fib. Tell an untruth." Bailey aimed a finger at my aunt. "Those two readings have you shivering in your Birkenstocks." She leveled her gaze at me. "Jenna, your aunt has been moping about ever since she returned from the fair. We've got to do something. We have to find Nick's killer."

"Don't worry." I steered the two of them back to the sales counter. "I've sent Hannah in Cinnamon's direction."

"Do you think she's guilty?" Bailey asked.

"No, I think she's innocent. She has an alibi."

"Then what good does it do sending her to the police?" Bailey huffed. "What's her alibi?"

I explained.

Bailey folded her arms. "That sounds iffy."

My aunt agreed.

I nodded. It did. "However, she saw Alan and his crow, which corroborates her story, right?"

Bailey shrugged. "I suppose, but if she didn't kill Nick, then who did?"

"I don't know."

Grumbling, Bailey slipped behind the counter and started organizing the prepaid orders, each secured by a rubber band and a notecard signifying who had bought what. "By the way," she said, a growl in her tone, "bad news. Chef Guy contacted me. Nature's Retreat isn't available."

"I'm sorry to hear that."

"So I've bitten the bullet and contacted Alan about holding the wedding at Baldini Vineyards."

My aunt stifled a gasp. I steadied her with my hand.

"If the police find out who killed Nick," Bailey continued, "and if Alan will let me have it there, is it gross beyond gross? Be honest."

"You do whatever you want, Bailey," I said.

"Yes, dear," my aunt said, rallying. "It's your day."

"Tito and I were thinking that it might bring positive karma to the vineyard if something joyful happened there."

*Can a place that has suffered a murder heal?* I wondered. Yes. A killing had occurred right outside the Nook Café's kitchen door, yet the shop and café were thriving.

"That sounds reasonable," I said. "Doesn't it, Aunt Vera?"

"Absolutely."

"Bailey, did Alan tell you to contact whoever is in charge of the Baldini Family Trust?"

"I didn't speak with him. I left a message. The family has a trust?" Bailey's eyes widened. "Argh. An executor will put the kibosh on everything."

"Not necessarily. A trust is designed to make unbiased financial decisions on behalf of the estate."

"Hold it." Aunt Vera wagged a hand. "If Alan doesn't inherit outright, then he can't have a motive to want Nick dead."

"Whew!" Bailey flicked imaginary worry sweat off her brow. "That takes a load off of my mind. I like Alan."

I wasn't sure I agreed with my aunt's logic. Money isn't always the reason for murder. Jealousy might rank right up there for Alan if he believed Nick had his eye on Hannah, but seeing Bailey and my aunt looking so relieved made me think twice about offering an opinion.

"Jenna, my love." Gran, a vivacious silver-haired woman who has the most extensive cookbook collection I have ever seen and a healthy bank account to fund it, sidled up to me. "I could use your help, dear."

I excused myself from Bailey and my aunt. "Good day, Gran."

Gran's real name is Gracie, which she hates. After her adult son died suddenly, she relocated to Crystal Cove to help her daughter-in-law with the children. The daughter-in-law told the story a tad differently. She hadn't wanted Gran to spend the rest of her years alone in the bitterly cold Northeast.

"Is your family with you?" I laced my hand around the crook of her arm.

"Not on this excursion. I need some *me* time." She offered an impish grin and steered me to the front of the store. "I'm trying to decide which of the fiction books I want to dive into. I was thinking about reading those noir novels you have on hand about Crispen Guest. Would I like them?"

I had added a few *not so cozy* mysteries to the mix this week because fairgoers often enjoyed darker material. Crispen Guest was a disgraced former-knight-turned-detective in the Middle Ages. I'd read the series and had fallen in love with him. He reminded me of an edgy but approachable swashbuckler.

"You read across genres," I said. "If you don't like the books, bring them back and I'll give you a full refund."

"Deal." She gathered up a set of three.

"There aren't any recipes in them," I teased.

"Ah, but there might be a recipe for being entertained, and that, my love, is always my goal." She tweaked my cheek.

"By the way, I love the pendant you made." I circled a finger toward her jewelry.

She caressed her new Celtic pendant necklace, which went beautifully with her stylish linen dress. "Thank you. Dolly is an excellent instructor, although she was a bit tart with one of the students. You might suggest she harness her temper."

I recalled how Dolly had demolished the shelf in her store and winced. "Will do."

"Also, between you and me," Gran lowered her voice, "she was gushing about Nick and telling us how much she loved him, but one of the women told me, confidentially, that she'd heard Dolly and Nick going at it a time or two." Gran coughed out a laugh. "That very same woman, if you can believe it, then had the gall to brazenly ask Dolly if she had an alibi for the night. I sputtered in amazement, of course." She put a hand on my arm. "As you know, blunt is not my style."

I did.

Gran pressed a hand to her chest. "Dolly didn't bat an eyelash. She said she was home that night fashioning wreaths."

"She said the same to me."

"Aye, there's the rub."

"How so?"

"I live close to her, and I was walking my dog around the time of the murder, and I didn't see any lights on at her house. Not a one. Now, perhaps there's a room in the back where she works; therefore, the lights would be dim if she was conserving energy. I can't be certain. Would you know?"

"I haven't a clue."

"If you want the opinion of an old woman like me—"

"I do."

"Tumultuous relationships often wind up in bad straits."

As Gran ambled to the sales counter, my gaze swung to Dolly. She was focused on beading, her head bowed. What had her relationship with Nick been like? Had he ever hurt her? I couldn't imagine. To me, he seemed like such a kind soul. On the other hand, people had witnessed him having a number of confrontations this week. Had Dolly ever hit him? Why had she lied about being home alone? Maybe she went to Nick's and, incensed by a jealous rage, slugged him with the winepress. Did I honestly believe that was possible? Right now, she appeared calm and in control, but I'd read somewhere that cold-blooded killers were skillful at hiding their emotions.

"Hi-ho, sister." My father strolled into the shop with Lola on one arm and a toolbox slung over the other. "Hello, daughter." They made a handsome couple, he in his purple apothecary costume and Lola in her matching purple-and-white queen's costume complete with silver crown.

My aunt greeted them each with a hug.

"Vera, I've come to repair the shelving in the storage room and, Jenna, I've come to give you this." Dad set his toolbox on the floor and popped outside. When he reentered, he was carrying an elaborate three-level kitty condo, complete with a carpeted living space, ramps, and sisal rope toys.

My mouth dropped open. "Wow! Did you build it, Dad?"

"With my very own hands." He set it on the floor. "Your aunt said your little guy has been having quite a go with his claws lately."

"Tina told me," Aunt Vera said quickly, her cheeks reddening.

"I don't care who blabbed, I love it."

My father threw open his arms for a hug, which made me laugh. Who was this warm and cuddly man? As a girl, sitting on his knee was akin to riding a sawhorse—totally lacking in warmth.

I stepped into his embrace and pecked his cheek. "Thank you."

"If it works out well"—he stroked my hair—"I'll build you another for your cottage." He released me.

"Really?"

"Cross my heart. Now, lead the way to the storage room. Your aunt said a few shelves were toppling. The dowels aren't secure. Lola, I'll be back soon."

"Have a blast," she said.

He hoisted his toolbox and pushed through the drapes.

I set the kitty condo by the children's table and encouraged Tigger to come out from beneath a stool. At first he was reluctant to investigate. When he began to frolic, I joined my father.

I switched on additional lights in the storage room. "Better?"

"Much." He opened his toolbox.

"Are you having fun at the fair?"

"You bet. I've never participated in the past, and for the life of me I can't fathom why not. Acting like an entirely different person is quite entertaining. The costume doth make the man. Now"—he surveyed the area—"which shelves do you need me to fix?"

The word *fix* gave me pause. I pictured the note on Nick's computer: *Fix it.* What had he needed to fix?

"Ah, here we are." Dad faced a set of bookshelves with one shelf clearly askew. He removed a set of pliers and a pin hammer from his kit. Then he unloaded the cookbooks from the shelf and, using the pliers, plucked out the offending dowel. He replaced it with a fresh one and tapped it in place with the hammer. After returning the books to their spots, he concentrated on another shelf.

"Dad, did you help Nick Baldini with any repairs?"

"Why do you ask?" He wagged the pliers at my nose. "No, let me guess, you're investigating, aren't you? Haven't you learned—"

"I'm not investigating. I'm postulating."

"Postulating." He snorted.

"Cinnamon is doing a good job, I'm sure, and I believe she'll solve the crime, but Bailey is still contemplating getting married there, and since I saw and heard things the night Nick died—"

"Has Bailey considered the bad karma?"

"She thinks solving the case will erase it."

He brandished the pliers. "You're scrunching your nose. You disagree?"

"I'm not sure what I think, but I won't tell her she can't. It's her wedding."

He rested the hand with the pliers on one hip. "Go on. What did you see that has you badgering me for answers?"

"I'm not badgering. Whitney badgers." Whitney is my oh-so-perfect sister who lives in Los Angeles with her oh-so-perfect daughters and husband. "I'm asking nicely. Prudently."

He snorted again.

"Did Nick hire you for any future projects?" I asked. "He had a note that said *Fix it* on his computer."

"I've repaired things at the vineyard in the past, but I haven't done so in over a year. Maybe he had a problem with his computer." Dad pivoted and resumed replacing dowels, one at a time. "Perhaps he meant he needed to fix a relationship."

*With Dolly?* I wondered.

My father added, "Maybe he meant he needed to rig something so it would have the ending he desired, like a bet or a transaction."

A gust of air swept into the storage room as Mayor Zeller poked her head through the drapes.

"Jenna, there you are." She stepped in. "Sorry to bother you. Hello, Cary."

"Z.Z." My father nodded. "Nice to see you."

"I recently listened to your voice mail, Jenna," Z.Z. said. "I apologize that it's taken me so long to respond. However, seeing as I was at the café setting up a dinner reservation, I thought I'd track you down rather than call. What's up? Have you discovered something more about Nick? I know you've been investigating."

"What? No, I haven't."

"Hannah said you were asking questions."

My father let out a stream of air. "She's not investigating, Z.Z. She's *postulating*."

I threw him a caustic look. "Very funny."

"She's concerned," the mayor said. "I admire that about her. Don't you, Cary?"

How I wanted to hug her, but I maintained my dignity. "I do have a question," I said. "About Nick and Melody Beaufort."

"Melody?" Z.Z. flapped a hand. "I told you the other day that I don't know much about her. You can't possibly think that sweet girl had anything to do with Nick's death."

"She's hardly a girl," I said. "Pepper said she's close to forty."

"True."

"As I said before, someone overheard Nick and Melody bickering. I'm curious to know whether that was part of their scripted fair exchange?"

"Lots of characters make up their own storylines. What was the disagreement about?"

"Nick asked if Melody recognized him. She called him a rogue and madder than a hatter."

"That sounds like shtick to me," Z.Z. said.

"Did it go any further?" my father asked.

"Flora didn't say so."

"Flora." Z.Z. *tsk*ed. "I wouldn't think twice about anything she said. She probably padded the story when she related it to you. She always wants to be the center of attention."

I nodded. Flora does have a penchant for elaborating. "You said you hadn't met Melody before this fair."

"Melody and many others. There are regulars, of course, but each year we have newcomers. Like every other vendor, the Beauforts filled out a contract for their space. We ran a background check. It was clean." The mayor lifted a book from the pile that my father had removed to repair a shelf and recited the title. *"The Craft Beer Bites Cookbook: 100 Recipes for Sliders, Skewers, Mini Desserts, and More—All Made with Beer.* Is this any good, Jenna? You know how I love my beer."

"That came in yesterday, so I haven't had time to flip through it, but all the reviews are great. Some of the recipes have a number of ingredients."

"*Pshaw.* I don't mind a long list. That gives me a reason to make a grocery store run." She tucked the cookbook under her arm. "Now, back to Nick. If you want my frank opinion, I'm afraid that Alan did his brother in."

"Why?" I asked.

"You know about his past, the bop to the head. He hasn't been quite right since. He gets emotional. In fact, after we taped the instructional video, Alan exchanged words with Nick. 'You are not the boss of me,' and such. And did I tell you about my meeting with the estate's attorney? Not a meeting. We ran into each other at the fair. He was telling me that Alan has taken Nick to task many times in his office. Once, he slugged Nick in the throat."

I gasped. "Why?"

"Because Nick referred to Alan as the baby in the family. It was petty, of course, but Alan didn't take kindly to the insult."

I recalled Alan glowering at Nick as Rhett and I were leaving the fair-speak taping. His gaze had sent a shiver down my spine. "Bailey and I overheard the two of them having a falling-out on the day Nick was killed," I said. "Alan quit."

"Quit?" the mayor asked.

"Apparently, Nick paid him as an employee."

Z.Z. raised an eyebrow. "Isn't he a half owner?"

"He doesn't inherit outright, even though Nick is dead. The vineyard goes into a trust. Didn't the attorney mention that to you? After the accident, that's how their father set up the estate. He was worried that Alan's injury might worsen."

Dad pulled another dowel from his toolbox. "I've had lots of interactions with Alan. He's a decent guy. He didn't do it."

I snapped my fingers. "Hey, Dad, maybe *fix it* meant Nick wanted to mend the relationship with Alan after their blowup."

He wagged the pliers at me. "Good guess."

"Z.Z.," I said, "Alan has a pretty solid alibi. Hannah Storm saw him in the vineyard at the time of the murder. Cinnamon corroborated that. She said he was pranking his brother by putting frogs in the well. She found lots of . . ." I hesitated.

"What's wrong?" the mayor asked. "Your face turned sour."

"What if Hannah is lying? I told her Alan had seen her in the field, and she said he couldn't have. She was with her grandmother in the house. I asked if her grandmother could verify that. Hannah faltered. She said her grandmother had fallen asleep. That's when she added that she'd seen Alan. Maybe they're both lying. Alan could have dumped the frogs into the well at another time."

Z.Z. said, "Why don't you ask Alan again? See if he'll amend his story."

Dad grumbled. "Why don't you call Cinnamon, instead, and let her figure it out?"

# Chapter 14

I murmured assurances to my father that I would do just that—far be it from me to anger the kitty condo master—and exited the storage room with the mayor. After she purchased her book and departed, I honored my father's wish and dialed Cinnamon. She was not available because she was handling a petty theft. I left a message about Alan and Hannah and did my best to convince her that I wasn't sticking my nose into her investigation. Would she believe me? Probably not, but a girl could dream.

Bailey approached the sales counter and rested her elbows on it. "I spoke with Alan and asked him to meet me here."

"I encouraged her to," Lola said as she strode to the sales counter with two mini meat pasties in hand. "If you don't ask, you'll never know. Better to do so in person." She offered one of the pasties to Bailey, who accepted it and downed it quickly.

"And?"

"He's on his way."

Pleased to see that Tigger was enamored with his ultrafancy scratching pole, I let him be and shifted to the display window. A marionette was out of place. One of the children from the morning's session must have played with it. Bailey and Lola followed me.

I hitched my head toward the rear of the store. "How's Dolly's workshop going?"

"She's putting on a good face," Lola said, "but I can see she's sad."

Bailey agreed. "I think she's happy with the turnout, however. Nearly everyone has asked for her business card as well as the location of her stall on the Pier."

Lola hooked her thumb over her shoulder. "Jenna, is it okay if I check on your father? We have plans to meet another couple for dinner, but I don't want to disturb his concentration."

"You won't. Dad can do repairs with his eyes closed." As she departed, I said to Bailey, "Would you mind organizing the books on the front table? They've toppled over."

"Will do."

I returned to the checkout counter and asked Tina how sales were going.

"Swimmingly." She pulled up an Excel program on the computer and showed me the list of transactions for the day. "I think the Renaissance Fair has been the biggest draw for Crystal Cove this year."

"It does seem to be a favorite," I said.

"Did I tell you that I saw a terrific swordfight yesterday? Between a man and a woman. Both were dressed as pirates. I was amazed by how much power the woman had and how crafty she was. She swung that sword—*whoosh, whoosh*." Tina mimed the action, nearly taking me out. "She even did a flip before felling him."

I glanced at Dolly and wondered how crafty she might have been. Had she slipped into Nick's house after Hannah met with him? Maybe she stole Alan's gauntlet so she'd leave no prints on the murder weapon. Would a raid of her home turn up vital evidence?

"Bailey," a man said from the front of the shop.

I spotted Alan in his falconer's costume, sans hat and glove, heading toward me.

"Over there, Alan." I pointed. "You walked right past her."

Bailey stole up behind him and tapped him on the back. "I know I'm short, but are you blind?" She scooted around him and planted her hands on her hips.

Alan's face tinged crimson. "Sorry. Why did you want to see me?"

"I hope you don't think I'm crass, but—"

"Oh, Alan." Dolly propelled herself off her stool and threw herself at him. She clutched him in a bear hug. Tears sprang from her eyes and spilled down her cheeks. "Where have you been? I haven't seen you."

Tigger paused on the ramp of his new playhouse, either fascinated or stupefied by Dolly's outburst, I wasn't sure which.

"Why haven't you returned my calls?" Dolly gushed. "What are your plans for the funeral? You've got to let me help."

Alan wriggled to free himself but couldn't. She had pinned his arms to his sides and wasn't willing to release him. He raised his chin as if he couldn't breathe.

Realizing Dolly was oblivious while in the throes of anguish, I leaped to Alan's rescue and gently pried her off of him. "Dolly, give him a little space."

"Oh, yes, of course. I didn't mean . . ." She stepped away and laced her fingers together. "It's just that I want to help. I miss your brother so much."

Alan cleared his throat. "I don't know when the police will release his body, Dolly."

"Will you bury him in the family plot?" she asked.

"Of course. Beside Mom and Pop."

"At any rate, you could have a memorial service," she suggested. "There are so many of us who need to mourn him."

"You can do so privately," Alan suggested.

I got the strange feeling that Dolly craved to do something *publicly* so she could show how much she had adored Nick. Maybe I was being snarky.

"Besides," Alan went on, "I don't know who to invite."

Aunt Vera entered the shop via the breezeway. "We'll help you with that, Alan."

He ran his fingers through his hair, clearly relieved. "Thanks. I appreciate that." He swung his head left and right as if trying to take in everyone who had surrounded him.

"Dolly, dear, come with me." My aunt guided her back to the crafts table while crooning calming words to her and promising another tarot reading.

When she was out of range, Alan exhaled. "Now, Bailey, why would I think you're crass?"

"What if we still want to hold our wedding at your vineyard?"

"Honestly? I think that would be terrific." He rested a hand on her shoulder. "Nick would, too, I'm sure of it. He'd been talking about your wedding for weeks. He had some surprises planned. He had grown very fond of you."

Bailey blushed with the compliment.

"But aren't you worried about bad mojo?" Alan asked.

"I was, but I'm not anymore."

*Amazing how the setback of losing not just one venue but any venue could change one's mind,* I mused.

"The way I see it," she went on, "if I make a good memory on the premises, then the bad memories can fade. Not quickly, of course. We'll all miss Nick for a long time, but think about it. My good memories could open the door for more happy couples to hold weddings there, which would benefit you and enhance the vineyard's, um, *mojo*." She glanced at me, aware she was blathering.

I smiled like an indulgent parent.

Alan said, "I must warn you that I don't know much about these things, so I'll have to hire someone to help me out."

I said, "I'll bet Hannah Storm would be willing to help you."

"Why Hannah?"

"She has always wanted to hold weddings at her vineyard, but her grandmother wouldn't let her."

"That's a great idea." Bailey squeezed his arm.

"About Hannah," I said, glancing over my shoulder to see if my father was close to emerging from the storage room; he wasn't. "Have you told her how you feel?"

"How I . . ." Alan gulped. "No."

"I think she likes you, as well."

His face brightened.

"By the way," I continued, "she said she saw you in the field the night Nick died, but that she wasn't there, as you claimed. She was in her house looking out the window."

Alan scratched his ear. "I could have sworn it was her. Guess I was wrong. But the fact she saw me is good, right? That confirms my alibi."

"Unless you're covering for each other."

"I'm not . . . I wouldn't . . ." he sputtered. "I heard someone, Jenna. I truly did."

"You *heard* someone? You said you *saw* Hannah. Were you trying to give her an alibi because you glimpsed her leaving your house?"

"No. I did see someone in the field. Wearing a hat." He outlined his head with a finger. "But . . ." He lowered his chin and drummed his fingers on his thigh. Then he looked up. "I have a confession."

My stomach did a flip-flop. Bailey glanced at me, her face pinched with worry. I sensed someone creeping up behind me and caught a whiff of floral perfume. *Tina.* Apparently, she wanted the skinny. Could I blame her?

"Go on, Alan," I said.

"You know about my accident."

"You got hit with a lacrosse stick. It affected your brain. You have outbursts."

"Right. Well, ever since that day, I can't see faces."

Bailey said, "So you're blind?"

"No, I have prosopagnosia"—the word spilled off Alan's tongue—

"or what is known as face blindness. Adults who have the condition as a result of a brain trauma, like me, can be retrained to use other clues to identify people. I use shapes and sizes, and I'm good with voices. For example, I know that your voice, Jenna, is lower and calmer than Bailey's and"—he plucked his hair—"Bailey's hair is spiky like Hannah's. Your aunt wears a turban. These things help me."

"So why did you walk past me a second ago?" Bailey asked.

"I realize you're short, but at a distance, Jenna can look about the same height as you. I can tell height when I'm close to you and measuring you against me, and with that garland on Jenna's head, her hair looked sort of spiky."

"Alan," I said, "I'm afraid this means you can't corroborate where Hannah was."

"I guess not, but I saw someone in the field. I swear. The person was running and breathing hard."

"Who knew about your illness, Alan?" I asked.

"Nick, but he kept it quiet. That's why we were going at each other when you overheard us. I told him I was in love with Hannah. He said I couldn't marry her."

"'Over my dead body' were the words he used," Bailey said.

"Because she's the competition," I added.

Alan sighed. "I told him we're rivals, not enemies. He scoffed at me. He said—and I'm paraphrasing—'You don't know anything about her and what her family did.' I said, 'Her family? Don't you mean *our* family? We diverted water from a well long ago.' He screamed, 'No, we didn't!' I'd heard Hannah tell the tale, so I said, 'We forced the Storm family to invest in transportation of water.' Nick said, 'That's a lie that her grandmother concocted.'" Alan ran a finger beneath the collar of his shirt. "To hear him tell it, Hannah's grandmother lived and breathed for her husband. When he died, she dreamed up all sorts of crazy stories. I told Nick that Hannah was nothing like her grandmother. He wouldn't agree. Plus, he was concerned that my illness might turn worse, and that I shouldn't marry. Ever. 'Why saddle someone with that?' he asked me more than a dozen times."

"That's why he threatened to tell the history," I said. "*Your* history."

"He hoped I'd back down because I didn't want people to make fun of me, but I didn't care." Alan brandished a hand in front of his face. "It's disconcerting that I'm this way, but now that you know, it's sort of freeing."

"I'll bet," I said.

Alan faced Bailey. "Call me and we'll set up an appointment. You'll come to the vineyard, and we'll go over everything. I'll have Chef Guy there, if you want, and I'll get a wedding planner who can deal with all the stuff Nick was going to handle."

"Ask Hannah," I suggested again.

"Maybe I will." Alan trudged out of the shop.

When he was gone, I corralled Bailey and Tina. "Do you know what this means?"

They nodded.

"There was someone else fleeing through the vineyard," I murmured. "But who?"

I felt like someone was studying me and turned to scan the shop. When I realized Dolly was staring daggers in my direction, a shiver swizzled through me.

# Chapter 15

To my surprise, Dolly didn't confront me. In fact, as she left, she thanked me profusely for allowing her to lead the beading clinic. Rationally, I decided to table whatever that weird look was that she'd thrown me. Perhaps hearing Hannah's name had rattled her.

Even so, when I arrived home with Tigger, I checked all my doors and windows — being security-conscious was becoming second nature — and I telephoned Rhett. I didn't reveal everything I'd learned from Alan and the mayor, and I didn't mention the unsettling gaze from Dolly. I didn't want him to worry about me. Heck, *I* didn't want to worry about me. The more I reminded myself that everything was normal, the more I believed it. Of course, as a girl, I'd also believed that ducking under my bedspread meant my parents couldn't see me. I asked Rhett if we could meet for early-morning coffee, but he couldn't. He had arranged to take a group on an ocean fishing trip. I made him promise to come to Aunt Vera's for dinner on Sunday evening. Our family had a standing Sunday dinner date. He agreed and blew me a kiss before signing off.

After I hung up, I whipped up what I decided to call a *pan pasty* — a pasty without the crust. I made it by using less than ten ingredients, which included ground turkey, potatoes, veggies, herbs, and a dash of Parmesan cheese. Easy comfort food. Simple for me to make. While it baked, I listened to Judy Garland singing Gershwin tunes and dabbled on one of my paintings in progress. Whenever I am distressed — and I was definitely bothered by not knowing who had killed Nick — painting helps me unwind. I was gifting this particular piece of art, which was an image of my sister, brother, and me frolicking on the beach as kids, to my father as a surprise for his birthday.

Mid-brushstroke, I heard a rustling and a *thunk-thunk-thunk* coming from the bedroom. My pulse kicked up a notch. Was someone trying to get into the cottage through the window? I seized the fireplace poker for the second time in two days and crept to the bedroom door. I released the breath I was holding when I realized that Tigger, the sneak, was rummaging through my vintage colonial sewing kit. I must have left one leaf open when I'd fixed the button on my costume.

*Thunk-thunk.* My rambunctious cat was tossing out spool after spool of thread.

"Tigger, stop."

He froze, his paw in the air and his eyes as big as saucers.

I replaced the poker and hurried to him. "You scared me, you little devil. I thought we had an intruder. I—" I balked. Did I truly believe Nick's killer would come after me because I'd asked a few questions? On the other hand, someone had lingered outside my cottage the night before. Coincidence?

Anchoring my fingers beneath his front legs, I lifted Tigger out of the box. His purring vibrated down my arms. I snuggled him close to my body, more for my comfort than his. "What is eating you? Is it me? Are you picking up on my angst?"

I'd meant to call the veterinarian and had forgotten. Now, I didn't hesitate. I picked up the telephone on the nightstand—I have a landline because my aunt insists upon it—and dialed the vet's office. An after-hours answering service picked up. The woman, who had a kind, elderly voice, asked if I had an emergency, which I didn't. I explained that my cat was getting into all kinds of trouble and asked her to please have the vet return my call.

The woman chortled. "How old is your cat?"

"Close to two."

"Ah, the terrible twos."

"Do you mean cats are like babies?" I asked.

"No, but they're into everything all the time, like babies. Whenever my cats act up, I've called the behavior the terrible twos. FYI, the behavior might last a good fifteen years if you don't get a scratching post and a variety of kitty-safe toys."

I thanked her for her advice, and after hanging up, texted my father. I begged him to build me another kitty condo *pronto*.

With Tigger on my lap—he was being *darling kitty* so long as I scratched him—I ate a portion of the casserole and read a few chapters of the hat shop mystery that I'd brought home from the store. When I crashed into bed, Tigger hunkered on the comforter near my feet.

I drifted to sleep with three thoughts: Alan was in the clear; I hoped Hannah was telling the truth; and I couldn't point a finger at Dolly without knowing more. So she had stared nastily at me. Big deal.

• • •

When I awoke Saturday morning, I checked my cell phone first thing. Cinnamon had not contacted me. Had I honestly expected her to?

On my way into the shop, I caught sight of Nick's foreman, Frank Nelson, a weathered seventy-year-old who had worked for the Baldini family for years. He was descending the stairs from Surf and Sea, a surf shop on the second floor of Fisherman's Village. Brilliant morning sunlight highlighted his salt-and-pepper hair. His yellow swim trunks made his muscular legs look dark tan. His black Speedo swim T-shirt clung to his taut torso. He was carrying a neon orange surfboard under one arm. Frank was a regular at Surf and Sea and bopped around like an eternal teenager. How he had the energy to surf after a six-day workweek amazed me.

We locked gazes and he heaved a sigh.

"Hey, Jenna."

"Good morning, Frank. Give me a sec." Tigger was wriggling in my arms. I crossed to the Cookbook Nook, opened the door, set him on the floor, and returned to greet Frank properly. "Beautiful day."

"Indeed, it is. I like your Maid Marian costume."

"Thanks. I'm afraid I have to resort to Fabreeze for the underarms."

"Everyone has to by now."

"How did people ever live without washing machines and air-conditioning?" I joked.

"Got me."

I nodded at his surfboard. "Are you going surfing?"

"Sort of. The boys and I are meeting on the water to pay tribute to Nick." His face grew grim. "I still can't believe he's dead. The police say they're making headway on the case, but I don't know. They asked me and my crew for our alibis and ruled us out."

"All of you?"

"Uh-huh. We were in the cellar checking out last year's harvest. We do that every April. We must have tapped a hundred barrels that afternoon and evening." He switched his surfboard to his other arm. "I don't know who else the police have questioned. Word is that you and Bailey found Nick."

I nodded. "We were with our boyfriends."

"It was bad, huh?"

"It wasn't pretty." Tears threatened to spring from my eyes. I tamped them down.

"Alan said whoever killed Nick whacked him with that winepress. That's sick." He scrubbed his hair with his fingertips.

Cinnamon wouldn't be pleased to know that Alan had shared that tidbit. It still hadn't appeared in the news.

"I remember Nick joking around with the one he bought," Frank went on. "He suggested we make them ourselves and sell them in the tasting room. He said we'd probably clear more profit from them than the wine."

"Is the vineyard in financial trouble?"

"Nah, Nick was kidding. He was a real joker. As a matter of fact, we're on an upswing. The latest crop is going to be killer." Frank wriggled his nose. "Sorry. Bad choice of words."

"Gallows humor, whether intended or accidental, always seems to crop up after a death, doesn't it?"

"Yeah."

Silence fell between us. Frank shifted feet like he was eager to end the chat.

"Frank, before you head to the beach, answer me one question. Did Nick mention that he wanted to sell the winery?"

"No way. It's a family business. A legacy. Every year, whether the meteorological gods complied, he had high hopes for a great return. Always positive, that guy. A real romantic. The world lost a good soul when he died."

"Yes, it did."

After another brief silence, Frank saluted and said, "Nice seeing you, Jenna. If you don't mind, I'm going to head down." He hustled along the corridor between the café and Beaders of Paradise to the stairway leading to the beach.

As he vanished from view, a woman said, "Morning, Jenna."

I spun around. Pepper locked her smart car and strode toward me, her gait sprightly. The Bohemian fuscia-colored frock she was wearing swirled around her calves. I bit back a laugh wondering when the lumbering sourpuss I used to know as Pepper had morphed into this amiable, life-loving person.

"Good morning," I said.

"Isn't it a beautiful day?"

"Indeed." If not for the fact that I'd been discussing Nick's murder with his foreman. *On to better subjects, Jenna.* "Say, I hear you're dating the haberdashery guy."

Pepper's cheeks flamed crimson. "Who told you?"

"Dolly might have let it slip."

"Mold-warp," Pepper mumbled, then a grin spread across her face and her cheeks tinged pink. "It's true. I am. He's such a delightful man. We have so much in common. We like the same books and the same food. He's even done some beading."

"Has he really?"

"For his teenage nieces. They love jewelry. Isn't that sweet?" Jauntily, she started toward her shop.

As she did, I recalled our chat the other day, when she had uncharacteristically grown quiet. "Pepper." I caught up to her. "The other day you were fidgety, like you wanted to say something more."

She tilted her head. "Which day was that?"

"When I showed you the bead I'd found at Nick's house."

She dragged her tongue along her upper lip, deliberating. "Did you find out if it was from Dolly's collection?"

"Yes, it was." I didn't add that Hannah had purchased it and lost it on the verandah at Baldini Vineyards. "Did you want to tell me something else about the bead?"

"No, I don't think so." She tapped her chin with a fingertip. "Aha! I remember now. We were discussing Nick. Well, not really discussing *him*, but the fact that he was . . ." She hesitated.

"Murdered."

She surveyed the parking lot, and though the three parked cars were vacant, she lowered her voice. "You know I don't like to talk out of school, but . . ." She wasn't much of a gossip even if some of her fellow beaders, like Flora, were. "That afternoon, I caught Sean and Melody bickering. At my house. I'd come to bring them lasagna. I thought they might like something homemade. I knocked and called out when I entered, but they must not have heard me because they kept at it. They were in the backyard. I could see them through the kitchen window."

"What were they fighting about?"

"Camping."

"*Camping?*" I repeated.

"Sean said he needed to protect Melody because if Nick found out—"

"Found out what?"

"I don't know. Melody shouted, 'He won't!' Sean said something I couldn't make out. That's when Melody announced she was going for a walk on the beach."

"In her fair costume?"

Pepper shook her head. "No, Sean was dressed in his handsome blue one, but she had changed into short-shorts and a tank top. She flew out the back gate. Sean made his way toward the kitchen. Feeling guilty for listening in, I zipped out the front. I didn't want either of them thinking I was spying on them."

"Camping," I repeated.

She bobbed her head. "All I could conclude was that perhaps they were transient—you know, living house to house through the Airbnb program—and Sean feared that if Nick found out, he might decide their credit wasn't good and deny them their stall at the fair. Nick wasn't that way, of course, but Sean couldn't have known that, being new to the circuit."

"Transient," I repeated.

"Moving over and over can be quite stressful. It creates hiccups in a loving relationship. Believe me, I know from experience. My husband and I were quite the travelers, but when Cinnamon was born . . ." She let the sentence linger. Cinnamon's father, the rat fink, left the day she was born. Pepper flitted a hand. "It's best to leave the past in the past."

As I entered the Cookbook Nook, it dawned on me that perhaps Pepper might be wrong in her conclusion. What if the word *camping* meant something else, like Ren Camp, which was highly important to Nick. He had oodles of photos on his Facebook page about his experiences. Was it possible that, way back when, he had met Melody at Ren Camp? Was there a secret that might hurt Melody if Nick put two and two together? When he'd confronted her the other day, he'd said: *Dost thee not recognize me,* meaning he *did* recognize her. Or was he mistaken? She had rebuffed him.

Curiosity nagging at me, I settled beside the computer, woke it up, and clicked on the Internet browser icon.

Aunt Vera exited the storage room while adjusting the silver turban on her head. "Phooey. I can't get this darned hat to stay on straight. Help me out." She offered me two long hatpins.

I obliged and said, "There. All set."

"Thank you." She pecked my cheek and edged past me to open the register.

I brought up Nick's Facebook page, selected Photos, and waited while it loaded.

"Hello! I'm here!" Tina entered the shop and did a twirl, which made the skirt of her red polka-dot wrap dress flare out. No Renaissance costume for her today. "What do you see in my future, Vera?"

My aunt clucked her tongue. "You know that's not how I operate."

"True, but I keep thinking that if I ask, you might fine-tune that intuitive mind."

"I don't need to fine-tune it. I have ESP."

"Tosh." Tina scrunched her nose. "You do not. No one does."

"Yes, I do." My aunt frowned. She hates when people question her ability.

I was wise to keep my mouth shut. I considered her highly intuitive, but ESP? Does anyone truly have that?

"I want love, Vera." Tina tucked her purse beneath the register. "And I want my career, and I want to come into a ton of money."

"Then you'd better work hard for all three. Those do not fall from the sky." My aunt headed toward the café. "I'll be back shortly. Want a coffee, anyone?"

"No, thanks," Tina and I replied.

When the photos loaded, I clicked on Albums > See All and selected the very first Ren Camp album. I scoured the pictures, searching for images of fair-haired girls with cute turned-up noses. I saw lots of photographs of Nick. He had been an impish kid with an easy smile. There were plenty of snapshots of other children in costume. About half were dressed as royalty, and the other half as common folk. There were a few jesters and magicians, too. I didn't see Melody anywhere in the mix. I chose the next year's Ren Camp album and repeated the process.

"Want me to vacuum?" Tina asked.

"Sure, and tell me what we have planned for the kids' table today. I can't remember."

She twirled a finger in my face. "This morning, boys and girls are coming in to learn how to sew potholders. I'm teaching. Katie is providing homemade apple cider. It could get messy. This afternoon—"

"Forget the vacuuming and put out a plastic floor mat."

"Will do."

Bailey flounced in, her skin glowing and eyes bright. She stowed her purse beneath the counter with the rest of ours and tugged her turquoise sweater over her white jeans.

"You look happy," I said.

"Tito and I met Alan on the Pier for breakfast. We were too excited to wait any longer to finalize plans. The wedding is a go. Alan has already contacted Chef Guy."

"I'm glad you're feeling more positive."

"I'm over the moon. Now, if only the police would solve Nick's murder . . ." She peered over my shoulder at the computer screen and poked me with her finger. "You've learned something new, haven't you?"

"Nothing that has come to fruition." While browsing more albums online, I told her about the spat Pepper overheard.

"Hey, maybe Nick didn't upload all his photos. Remember how many albums he had in his kitchen? If we could peruse them, maybe—"

"That's it." I swiveled on the stool. "What if Melody went to the vineyard to remove images of herself as a girl?"

"And Nick found her rooting through his stuff and demanded an explanation, so she lashed out."

"She could have been the person Alan saw fleeing across the fields. She's about the same size as Hannah. At dusk, a floppy hat would have been enough of a disguise."

Bailey agreed. "But what motive could she have to kill Nick?"

"Maybe she's in the witness protection program, living under an assumed name. Maybe she didn't always go by Melody Beaufort."

"Well, that's a given." Bailey rolled her eyes. "She wasn't married back then."

"Maybe she wasn't named Melody ever, and that was why Nick

was pressing her. He felt he knew her."

"If she really had something to hide, why would she come to Crystal Cove and risk being discovered?"

"That could have been her husband's idea," I said. "To grow the business. Melody was discussing the problem with him when Pepper happened upon them."

Tina exited the storage room carrying a rolled-up plastic mat.

I sidled past Bailey and said, "Tina, let me and Bailey do that. You man the register."

"Sure." She dropped it on the floor with a *thud*.

"I saw Melody on the Pier," Bailey said, taking one side of the mat while I gripped the other. We unrolled the unwieldy thing and arranged it on the floor. "Waiting in line for the Shakespeare spoof to start. Sean wasn't with her. Go talk to her."

"I'll tell Cinnamon."

"Tell her what? You have nothing."

Together we slid the mat beneath the crafts table and stools.

"What if Sean has joined Melody?" I said, dusting off my hands. "He's so protective."

"Someone has to operate their stall. He'll be there. C'mon. I'm dying to know the truth."

The word *dying* sent a chill through me. "If you're so eager, you question her."

"As if. I don't have your style or your innate ability to get people to confide in you."

I made smooching noises and said, "Kiss my grits."

"Plus, you're dressed in your costume. You'll blend in."

I threw her the evil eye. "You, my wicked friend, are a fawning, flap-mouthed flirt-gill."

Minutes later, as I drove out of the parking lot, I could still hear her laughing.

# Chapter 16

During Ren Fair, the Theater on the Pier players put on a Shakespeare spoof, *Omelette: Chef of Denmark*, an over-the-top parody of *Hamlet*, three times a day. I'd heard great things about it from some of our customers but hadn't had a chance to take it in yet. I arrived at the theater right as the audience line started to move. It wasn't a long line. The early-morning show didn't draw the largest crowds. Melody was near the back, dressed in yet another gold gown, this one fitted with a gorgeous satin corset. She was sipping from a to-go cup of coffee.

I drew near and my heart began to hammer. What was I doing? How had Bailey talked me into this? Nervous laughter burbled inside of me. Who was I kidding? Bailey hadn't talked me into anything. I wanted the truth as much as she did.

"Good morrow, Melody."

"Good morrow." She dabbed her nose and eyes with a vintage handkerchief edged with crocheted lace. Had she been crying? Maybe, like Hannah, she was suffering from pollen allergies. The wind had kicked up.

"Might I join you?" I asked.

"Sure." She jammed the handkerchief into the pocket of her gown and tossed her coffee cup into a nearby trash can.

"Where's your husband?"

"At our booth. Saturday is a big day at these fairs."

I adjusted my crocheted purse on my shoulder. "Have you been selling like gangbusters?"

"Yes. It's been a boon. We've covered six months' rent in a week."

"Missive!" a man announced.

Melody swiveled her head.

I followed her gaze.

The messenger in the royal blue costume sprinted from Shakespeare's Poetic Inspirations and tore past us waving a scroll. I hoped he was getting lots of hefty tips for his efforts.

The line started to proceed into the theater.

I kept pace with Melody. "I've never seen this show. Have you?"

"A few times. It's quite fun."

"What's it about?"

"Two teams of authors, Danes and Scots, come to the Globe Theater to compete for the chance to provide the plot for Shakespeare's next play. Shakespeare, himself, will decide." Melody's mouth quirked up on one side. "Will he love the Danish concept, or will the Scottish team foil them?"

"Who wins?" I asked, taking two single-page playbills from an usher and handing one to Melody.

"I'll never tell." She winked.

The Theater on the Pier was set up like an old saloon. Patrons sat at cocktail tables. The cane-backed chairs featured red plush brocade to match the drapes on the stage. Wall sconces and chandeliers provided ambient lighting. Old-fashioned scallop footlights jutted up from the apron of the semicircular stage. The light emanating from them cast a warm glow.

"How quaint is this!" Melody exclaimed.

I led the way to a table for two. "You should come when they do karaoke night." The last time I'd attended, I learned that Cinnamon Pritchett could belt out a song like a cabaret pro. I settled into a chair and pulled the hurricane candle on the table closer so we could peruse the playbill. "Do you rent a stall at a lot of Renaissance fairs, Melody?"

"I've done a few."

*I*, she said, not *we*. Hmm. Was that significant? I said, "Nick Baldini sure knew how to put one of these together, didn't he?"

"He did, indeed." Melody's voice caught. "I can't imagine who might've wanted him dead. He seemed like a nice guy."

"*Seemed?* I thought you knew him."

She cut me a cautious look. "No." She faltered. "We met the day before the fair started."

"Isn't that odd?" I feigned casualness. "A friend of mine heard the two of you chatting, and she said your exchange sounded intimate. I told her you were most likely playacting, but she—"

"We were," Melody said hastily, not letting me finish my sentence. "Like I said, we barely knew each other. He was King Henry VIII, and the king—"

A waitress arrived with two glasses of water and stated there was a one-drink minimum.

I said, "I'll take coffee."

Melody said, "The same. With cream." When the waitress departed,

Melody dipped her finger into her water glass and then touched her right eye with her pinky, as if trying to remove an eyelash.

"What about the king?" I asked.

"King Henry VIII is a bit of a rogue, so he repeatedly makes a play for maidens while the fair is in session. The maidens are expected to snub him at all times."

"Is that so? I had no clue."

The waitress returned with our coffees and cream and packets of sugar. Melody doctored her coffee and we sat in companionable silence for a moment, sipping our drinks while reviewing the playbills.

After a moment, I said, "You know I could've sworn you knew Nick. I saw a piece of your pottery in his kitchen."

"He purchased one."

"Actually there were two in his kitchen—the piece he purchased and a vase holding a rose."

"Maybe he bought two. Sean could tell you."

"Maybe," I murmured.

"I was never at his house."

*Hmm. The lady doth protest too much,* I mused. *And too quickly.* "I didn't say you had been."

She sipped her coffee and watched me over the rim of her cup.

I added cream to my coffee and stirred it. "Melody, I have to admit . . ." I couldn't finish the sentence. Why not? In business, I've always been direct, but right now, being blunt didn't feel like the right tactic. Melody reminded me of a doll in a china shop, brittle and ready to topple at any second.

"C'mon. Out with it, you varlet," she teased. "I don't bite. Admit what?"

I took a deep breath. "I was wondering whether the scene my friend witnessed was more than playacting."

Her gaze narrowed. So much for good-natured banter. The rapid rise and fall of her cleavage revealed how tense she was. "What are you insinuating?"

"Did Nick hit on you?"

"No!" she cried. "He wouldn't. He was kind and sweet and roman—" She bit off the word.

"Romantic," I finished, repeating what his foreman had said.

Melody blushed.

My thoughts flew back to the evening when Nick and Melody and the others were making the fair-speak video. The messenger had raced into the tent and handed Melody a missive. At the time, I'd believed Sean had sent her a darling love letter, but looking back, maybe he hadn't. He'd snatched it from her and dragged her from the tent.

*Okay, dragged might be a little dramatic.*

"Melody, the night before the fair began, a courier from the poetry booth brought you a scroll. Did Nick send it to you?"

She didn't respond.

The overhead lights and wall sconces dimmed. The illumination from the footlights increased.

Under my breath I said, "Your husband wasn't pleased that you'd received it. He tore it from your hands." Come to think of it, he hadn't been pleased when the messenger had appeared in their tent during our pottery lesson, either.

Melody's lip started to tremble. She scrambled to her feet. "I'm not feeling well. I need to leave. Stay. Enjoy the show."

*No way.* I threw a twenty-dollar bill on the table for cover charge and pursued her out of the theater.

Sunlight blazed down on us. Hordes of happy people crowded the boardwalk. A trio of minstrels were playing guitars and singing "The Star of the County Down," a sprightly tune about the maid they had met at a fair. Their lilting tone was a stark contrast to the hasty pace of Melody's escape. Rossini's "William Tell Overture" would have been more appropriate.

"Melody, wait!" I shouted above the music.

"Leave me be." She trotted ahead.

"I canst," I replied, matching her medieval tone. If she was going to play a role, then I would, too. "Dost thee need the latrine?"

"Ye are a churlish, earth-vexing dewberry." She covered her mouth with her hand.

I kept after her, squinting against the glare. "Halt, and let me have my say."

"Never."

"Melody, stop!" I dropped the awkward language. "C'mon, talk to me. Pepper heard you and Sean arguing about Nick."

That drew her up short. She whipped around near Ye Old Toy Shoppe. "When?" she asked. A hank of hair fanned her face and stuck to her lipstick. She plucked it from her mouth and cast it over her shoulder.

Two moppets raced from the store carrying marionettes and bumped into Melody. Their mothers ordered them to apologize. They refused and ran off.

"The day Nick was murdered," I said. "You were in her backyard. She'd come to bring you dinner. She entered and called to you. Neither of you heard her, I guess. You were discussing a secret that Nick shouldn't find out."

"I have no secrets." Melody whisked out her handkerchief and blew her nose.

My breath caught in my chest. Was she the one Alan had heard sneeze that night? "Where were you the night Nick died?" I asked.

"How dare you ask for my alibi." She jammed the handkerchief into her pocket and defiantly lifted her chin. "I hardly knew the man."

"Alibi?" a man asked between coughs. "Who needs an alibi, hon?"

Sean swooped past me, a local pharmacy bag in his hand. He stepped next to his wife as he pulled a box of allergy pills from the bag. "I asked a fellow vendor to oversee the shop for a few minutes so I could get these. I hope you don't mind. I'm so stuffed up. It's got to be the pollen."

"Or a cold," she said, looking relieved that he had come to her rescue.

"I don't get colds."

She rolled her eyes in jest. "Me, either."

He chuckled. "Now, why aren't you in the theater?" He unpacked the pills and popped one without water into his mouth. "And what's this about an alibi?"

Melody frowned. "Jenna wants to know where I was when Nick Baldini was killed."

"Why?" her husband asked.

Melody swung her gaze to me. *If looks could kill.* "I was walking on the beach. Satisfied?" She sucked back a sob and hurried away, grabbing a fistful of skirt to make haste.

Sean said, "She's telling the truth. I was with her." He shoved the pills back into the bag and tore after her. "Honey, wait up!"

# Chapter 17

Disappointed that I hadn't garnered more information from Melody but satisfied that her husband had verified her alibi, I sped back to the Cookbook Nook. When I arrived, the place was hopping. Dozens of people, mostly women, crowded the aisles. I searched for another *twofer sale* sign but didn't see one.

I approached Tina, who had switched into a cheery all-yellow milkmaid outfit complete with white apron. "Don't you look adorable?" I twirled a finger. "Turn around."

She did. The skirt billowed. "Do you like it? I bought it at Dolly's shop on Buena Vista during my coffee break. Half price. Did you know she sold medieval costumes?"

"Indeed, I did, but it's a well-kept secret. The garlands and crafts are the lure. Speaking of lure" — I rounded the sales counter and started stuffing shopping bags with decorative tissue — "why are we jam-packed?"

"Ha! I knew you'd forget. The Cheese Lady is partnering up with Katie to share a cheese meat-pie recipe. She's bringing all sorts of cheese samples."

The Cheese Lady was none other than Charlene, who owned Say Cheese Shoppe, the charming store up the street.

"She opted not to have a stall at the fair since she's a one-woman operation," Tina added. "This is her way of participating. I can't wait." She rubbed her hands together. "I hear she's bringing manchego, cheddar, and Gouda — my favorite."

"All three of them?" I teased.

"Well, sure, but especially Gouda. I love the smoky flavor."

I nodded in the direction of a lean woman with thick black-rimmed glasses. "Who's that?"

"A saleswoman. She wants to show you cookbooks and fiction related to the Fourth of July."

"Does she have an appointment?"

"Nope. Do you want me to ask her to come back?"

"Yes, please. I've got so much to do today." We often ordered merchandise a month or two in advance, but I didn't have an ounce of room in my brain. Thoughts of Nick's murder were still running roughshod through it. Who had killed him? What was the motive that had pushed someone over the edge? A secret past, jealousy, or revenge? Or did Alan kill him to get control of the property—trust or no trust in place?

Tina saluted and said, "I'm on it."

Minutes later, Charlene, who was as boxy and peach-toned as the cooler she carted in, bustled to the sales counter. "Long time no see."

"Too long," I said and gave her a hug.

"There you are!" Katie exited the breezeway wheeling in a preparation cart. "Let's get cracking."

"We'll catch up another time, Charlene," I said.

"We'd better," she warned with a teasing shake of her finger.

Quickly, the two women gathered customers into an orderly circle around the preparation cart. Neither Tina nor Bailey had set out chairs. This was to be a quickie demonstration. Katie was already handing out preprinted recipes.

While the crowd quieted, I took the time to corner Bailey to tell her what I'd learned about Melody.

When I finished, she said, "Well, that's *that*. They have alibis."

"Unless one or the other is lying."

"True. Married couples don't have to testify against each other. Shoot." She clasped my hand. "Come with me. We have to hash this out over a snack. I'm starved."

"I'm not hungry, and we're going to be slammed once the demonstration concludes."

"Tina can handle the customers." Bailey signaled Tina. "Can't you?"

"You bet!" She offered a thumbs-up gesture.

Bailey steered me into the Nook Café.

The moment we entered, the aroma of warm maple syrup wafted toward me. My stomach grumbled. Guess I was lying about not being hungry.

After ordering each of us a cup of coffee and a plate of French toast, Bailey jutted her chin to the right. *"Psst.* Look who walked in."

I peered over my shoulder. Cinnamon entered the café with Bucky Winston, a handsome fireman who ought to be the poster boy for firemen everywhere. Somewhere along the way, his parents had hit the DNA jackpot. With him in a yellow polo shirt and jeans and

Cinnamon in her camp counselor–style police uniform, the duo looked like the All American couple.

"Get a load of the bauble on her hand," Bailey said. "That's an engagement ring if I'm not mistaken."

Cinnamon and Bucky followed a waitress into the café.

As they neared our table, I wiggled my ring finger. "Congratulations, you two."

Bailey said, "Yeah, congrats!"

"Thanks." Cinnamon signaled her waitress that they would continue in a second and pulled to a stop. Her eyes glistened as luminously as her ring.

"Hi, Bailey . . . Jenna." Bucky grinned. Even his teeth were DNA perfect.

If I didn't already have a gorgeous boyfriend, I might have swooned.

"What a beautiful halo diamond," I said to Cinnamon. "Have you set a date?"

Bucky hooted. "That's the big question. Getting a *yes* out of her was the easy part."

"Ha-ha." Cinnamon elbowed him. "Next year sometime. My mother wouldn't think of letting me do it any sooner."

I pictured Pepper managing the event for her no-pushover, adult daughter, and imaginary fireworks—not the good kind—exploded in my mind.

Bailey said, "Hey, Chief, I never asked and I'm not sure you'd tell me, but did you ever find out who Nick might have telephoned besides me, seeing as his cell phone was smashed? I mean, that had to be significant, right? I think the killer shattered it to disguise his or her identity."

Cinnamon raised an eyebrow. "Why would you assume that? It could have fallen on the floor and cracked in the scuffle."

"Nah." Bailey wagged a hand. "It was whacked on purpose. The brunt force was right in the center of the phone. Like someone jammed a heel into it."

Bucky mock groaned. "Way to go, Bailey. Ruin our date. Now her wheels are turning."

"They are not," Cinnamon said. "Okay, maybe they are." She regarded Bailey soberly. "Since you asked, my techie said he was able to retrieve a call list, and the last call before the one to you was made to my mother's house. Apparently, Nick was checking up on the napkin rings he'd ordered for your wedding."

"Your techie got that from a telephone number?" I asked.

Cinnamon's nostrils flared. "No. I spoke with my mother's tenants. Mrs. Beaufort told me about the message."

"Your mom is making napkin rings for us?" Bailey said. "That's nice." She gave me a cautious look that meant she wasn't so sure about that. She didn't like anything that was beaded other than dangly earrings and maybe the topmost edge of the bodice of her wedding dress.

"Why did Nick call your mother's house?" I asked. "Didn't he know your mother would be at the fair at that time?"

"I would presume he didn't want to bother her at work." Cinnamon made a move to continue on.

"Wait," I said. "Did you hear the message?"

Cinnamon knit her brow. "No, I didn't hear it. Mrs. Beaufort erased it. What's this about, you guys?"

I cocked my head. "What if Nick wasn't calling your mother?"

"What are you insinuating?"

"I think Nick and Melody Beaufort had a past."

Cinnamon sighed and nudged her fiancé. "Let's go, Bucky."

I leaped to my feet. "Hear me out. Please."

Bailey joined me, giving me the support I needed. Quickly, I explained what I considered to be true.

"Can you prove it?" Cinnamon asked.

"No. Not yet." Oops. *Not yet* implied I was investigating. *Bad, Jenna.*

Cinnamon arched her eyebrow. Needless to say, I did not add that I'd scared off Melody after asking her about her alibi, nor did I ask if Cinnamon had received my message about Alan and Hannah. *Loose lips sink ships.*

Bucky said, "How else would Mrs. Beaufort have known about the napkin rings, Jenna?"

"I don't know. I—" I snapped my fingers. "Wait! Yes, I do." I pictured the Post-it notes on Nick's computer. "There was a memo in Nick's kitchen. It read *p-slash-u napkin rings. P-slash-u* for *pick up.* What if Melody—"

"Chief, did you question your mother?" Bailey asked, cutting me off.

"I had no reason to."

An uncomfortable silence fell between the four of us. Cinnamon stared at me. I squirmed under her searing gaze.

"The notes are still there," she said. "I'll check them out, but that won't prove anything. Have you got something else to share? And yes, I got your voice mail."

The sarcasm in her tone was unmistakable. I didn't let it hinder me. "Did your mother tell you that she heard the Beauforts arguing about Nick? It had something to do with camping, and I think—"

"Uh, Jenna," Bailey said. "We already agreed. They both have alibis for when Nick was killed."

I swung my gaze between Cinnamon and Bailey. "Unless one of them is lying to cover for the other. Chief, your mother heard Melody tell Sean that she was going for a walk on the beach. But what if she didn't go for a walk?"

"Sean said he went with her," Bailey countered.

"Maybe he didn't."

"When did you ask either of them about an alibi?" Cinnamon's glower was as good as my father's.

My boss at Taylor & Squibb had been an ace glowerer, too. I didn't squirm. "I was at the theater for the production of *Omelette: Chef of Denmark* when I ran into Melody. We got to talking. Sean came upon us as she was sharing her alibi with me."

"Sharing?"

I nodded.

Cinnamon grunted. "Why would she think she needed one if she barely knew Nick?"

"Exactly my sentiments. Melody hurried off—"

"To get away from your prying questions?"

I matched her stare. "That's when Sean added that he'd gone walking with her, but what if he was covering for her?"

A couple of patrons tried to squeeze past the four of us.

Bucky cleared his throat. "Why don't we take this discussion outside?"

Cinnamon agreed and led the way.

We convened in the passageway between Beaders of Paradise and the café, and I replayed the spat Pepper had overheard between Melody and her husband. "Your mom said they were bickering about camping, but I think they might have been discussing Ren Camp." I gazed at Bucky. "That's Renaissance Camp, for the uninitiated."

"Got it."

"Nick was devoted to it," I said to Cinnamon. "He went every year as a kid. As an adult, he taught camps each summer. There are tons of photographs on his Facebook site."

Bailey added, "Jenna skimmed the photos."

"Why am I not surprised?" Cinnamon said, her disdain evident. "Did you see Melody Beaufort among them?"

"No, but—"

"That's it." She held up a hand. "I've heard enough."

"Let me finish," I pleaded. "What if Nick called Melody at your mother's house, and Sean caught them talking on the phone?"

"And he got jealous," Bailey offered.

"Okay, you two," Cinnamon said.

"Three," Bucky chimed. "I've got to admit jealousy is a powerful motivator. I've been jealous a time or two, especially when you have a private conversation with that handsome hunk Old Jake."

Cinnamon threw him a baleful look. Jake is well over seventy and as weathered as the day is long.

Bucky bussed her cheek, and her eyes instantly softened. Man, he was good at defusing her anger.

After a moment, Cinnamon said, "Can it, all of you. I'll follow up on this. It's obvious I won't get any rest until I do."

"How about speaking with your mother right now?" I hooked my thumb toward the beading shop.

"She's not there," Cinnamon said. "She's at the fair. I'll touch base with her after I eat. You"—she poked Bucky—"feed me."

"Yes, ma'am."

He slipped an arm around her waist and squeezed. She nailed his chest with the crown of her ring. He winced.

*Isn't love grand?* I mused as the two returned inside and proceeded to their table.

Bailey and I followed. We ate our meal while quietly rehashing our frustration. We wanted answers. We weren't getting any.

By the time we made our way back to the shop, Charlene and the audience had left. For the remainder of the day, I straightened and dusted shelves or I organized and took stock in the storage room. Midafternoon, I took a breather and watched Tigger enjoying his new digs. I sure hoped my father was constructing a duplicate for my cottage. What a find!

At six p.m., Bailey sidled up to me and said, "Are you up for a road trip?"

"Where to?"

"Baldini Vineyards."

I offered to drive, believing Tigger and I were accompanying her to a wedding-planning meeting with Alan.

Fifteen minutes later, as the sky grew dark and the first few stars came into view, we neared the property. When we reached a Y in the road, she directed me to drive southward, away from the main house.

"Why?" I asked.

She didn't respond.

At the juncture where Baldini Vineyards met Hurricane Vineyards, she cried, "Stop!" She plucked a pair of binoculars from my glove compartment and popped out of the passenger side. Why do I have binoculars? For the occasional whale sighting in the winter, of course.

Bailey had no intention of looking toward the ocean, however. She hightailed it through the Baldini Vineyards' gate. Without sunshine highlighting the area, the rows of vines looked scraggly and bleak.

"Where are you going?" I chased after her. "Slow down." Whatever she was up to, I wasn't willing to let her go alone.

"What you said earlier about the Beauforts lying for each other resonated with me."

"You won't see them here."

"I'm not concerned about them. I'm interested in Hannah and Alan."

I caught up to her and was ecstatic that the ground was firm. At least I didn't have to slog through pockets of mud. Medieval leather sandals are never good in mud.

"What if one of them lied to protect the other?" Bailey peered through the binoculars while fiddling with the lens adjuster.

"Alan didn't lie. He was simply mistaken. He believed he'd seen . . . *heard* . . . Hannah in the field. It must have been someone else." *Like*

*Dolly,* I thought, the only viable suspect on my list without an alibi.

Bailey threw out an arm to block me. "Aha! As I suspected. Look up." She thrust the binoculars at me. "Can you make out her house in the distance? Over the crest."

I positioned the lenses over my eyes. "Yes." Hannah's home is more of a mini castle with a couple of turrets and multiple chimneys. We were looking at the side of the house; the front was out of view.

"Focus on the second-story window. Hannah said she was looking out from it when she spied Alan, remember?"

I gasped. "There's only one window facing the vineyard, and it's boarded up."

"Right. Unless that window was covered over in the last two days — and it doesn't look likely; even in this dim light, the wood looks weathered — then Hannah lied about seeing Alan."

A bird cawed. I glimpsed overhead but couldn't make out a thing in the gloom. Suddenly a creature dive-bombed us. It came within inches of taking out my nose. I flapped my hands. Bailey flailed her arms.

"Crow!" a man bellowed. It was Alan. Even in the dark I could make out his hat with the feather. "Crow. Perch!"

The bird continued to soar.

Alan charged toward us, arm extended. He drew to a sudden halt. "Who's there? I see you."

But we knew he couldn't make out our faces. So we fled.

# Chapter 18

After dropping Bailey at her car, I drove home with Tigger, my insides in a knot. I considered calling Cinnamon to tell her about Hannah's lie but decided to sit on it. Why did she lie? She had to know her claim could be disproven. I needed an answer before I restored her to person-of-interest status.

Restless, I dabbled at the painting of my siblings and me for an hour. Tigger, equally agitated, chased a ball of yarn the entire time. For dinner, I ate a vegetable omelet. A short while later, I slipped into bed with my book. Unfortunately, I was too tired to read a page.

Sunday morning started with a *bang* followed by another *bang* and the roar of an engine. I dashed outside in my pajamas, Tigger at my heels.

Marlon Appleby's Jeep was speeding down the driveway. His taillights glowed red for a split second before he made an abrupt left onto the main road. Aunt Vera, who was clad in her robe and slippers, was on the side of her driveway. Paper garbage lay on the pavement at her feet, including a pizza box and empty bags of potato chips. She was putting the trash into the trash can piece by piece and slamming the lid after each deposit.

"Darned raccoons," my aunt muttered as she tossed in more junk. "Sorry if I woke you."

"I guess we should be glad we don't have bears in these parts," I quipped.

"Scavengers are scavengers. They're all after a free meal." She set two bricks on top of the trash can and wrapped her arms across her chest.

"Was that Deputy Appleby hightailing it away?" I asked, knowing full well that it was.

"Mm-hm."

I petted her shoulder. "What's really eating you?" Usually she was easygoing when it came to the raccoons.

"Marlon wants to get married."

*Geez. Is marriage in the air?* I bit back a giggle. "And you don't?"

"Why get married at our age? It's not like we're going to have children. And his grown children don't want him to get married, so why aggravate them?" She exhaled sharply. "Scavengers."

"Surely, you don't think Marlon is a scavenger," I teased. "Or his children."

"No, the raccoons."

"Why did the deputy tear out of here?"

She growled. "He's mad because I didn't go all girlie on him and gush over his proposal last night."

"Honestly?"

"No. He's ticked because I didn't say *yes*"—she snapped her fingers—"like *that*."

"But he stayed until the morning."

"Hoping I'd change my mind."

"Did you tell him you'd think about it?"

"I told him *no* a second time. Then he blew his top and asked if there was someone else. Men." She puffed out a *pfft* sound. "They can be so insecure and controlling."

"You reassured him that you loved him, didn't you?"

"I told him to *get real*." She sniffed.

No wonder he'd stormed off. At times my aunt could be thickheaded. I held my tongue.

After a long moment, she said, "I do love him, Jenna." A smile tugged at the corners of her downturned mouth. "For a large man, he sure can sprint fast."

I laughed; so did she.

"Call him," I said. "Mend his broken heart."

"He won't answer his cell phone. He never does."

"Then text him and add a few kissy-lips emojis."

"As if." She made another *pfft* sound. "He'll simmer down. In the meantime"—she kicked the trash can—"I'm furious with the raccoons." Giggling, she kissed my cheek. "See you at the shop. I'm looking forward to the magic show."

• • •

At nine a.m., Bailey and I, both clad in our fair costumes, bustled around the shop moving everything to the side—chairs, bookshelves, and display tables. We were expecting a big crowd.

Around eleven o'clock, Tito arrived in full Merlin the Magician regalia: white beard, black cone hat, and black robe lined with silver. I barely recognized him. Months ago, he'd stepped in as our magician when the one we'd hired had canceled on us, and we discovered what a whiz he was at pulling silk flowers out of thin air and lighting up his fingertips. That was the moment Bailey had started to fall in love with him.

"Good morning, everyone," he said as if on a huge stage. "I have arrived." He kissed Bailey and murmured *mi amor*, then he set up his staging area near the vintage kitchen table. He asked us to move a few bookshelves, but he didn't want us to set up chairs. Everyone, he said, should sit on the floor. It would make the event more intimate.

*And make you look a lot taller,* I mused.

Discreetly, Bailey and I positioned a few chairs at the rear of the room in case there were elderly people who couldn't manage the floor.

A half hour later, dozens of people flowed into the shop: grand-parents, parents, and children. To interest the adults, I'd set out a number of cookbooks with magic in the titles, like *The Magic of Mini Pies: Sweet and Savory Miniature Pies and Tarts* and *Candy is Magic: Real Ingredients, Modern Recipes*. Both had luscious pictures. Someday I wanted to attempt making a pie. Katie assured me that even if the pie shell stuck to the plate, no one would mind as long as the flavor was good. *Soon,* I promised myself. *Soon.*

For the children, rather than setting out magic-themed books, I'd purchased a number of magic sets and individually packaged magic tricks. Nearly all of them sold before Tito began.

After introducing himself as Merlin and telling the tale of himself as a great and powerful wizard, he started his show with a card trick. Following that, he did a cut-and-restore-the-rope trick to the amazement of all.

Bailey leaned toward me at one point and said, "Beneath his crusty exterior lives the soul of a kid."

"I couldn't agree more."

"I can't wait to be his wife."

"I know." I gave her a squeeze.

When the applause died down after a sleight-of-hand trick, Tito said, "Now I shall show you the magic of the rings. I need a helper." He chose a bruiser of a little boy who was dressed for the fair in a chemise and pantaloons and a not-so-medieval pair of Crocs. "Are you strong, young squire?"

"Aye," the boy replied.

Tito held up two eight-inch rings. He clanged them together. The sound was melodious. "Examine the rings, young squire. Are there any holes? Any gaps?"

The boy carefully examined the rings, his nose and eyes pressed so closely to them that he was staring cross-eyed. "No, sir."

"Watch carefully." Tito spanked the rings together and they interconnected. The crowd gasped in awe. Tito yanked his rings and they came apart. "Want to give it a try?"

"Yes, sir!"

Tito rummaged in his kit and produced a second pair of rings. He handed them to the boy. "Do as I do."

He held his two rings apart. The boy mimicked him. Tito clanged his rings together; they connected. The boy copied the motion, but his rings didn't interlock. He tried again and again but to no avail. *Clang, clang, clang.* Children in the front row plugged their ears with their fingers.

Tito removed the rings from his hands and said, "Sorry, son. Better luck next time. Magic doesn't work for everyone." Miraculously, he whisked a lollipop out of thin air and handed it to the boy. Then he thanked him for his service and directed him to retake his seat on the floor.

When Tito introduced his last trick, the Magic Funnel, he owned the audience. Many were leaning forward, elbows anchored on their knees, trying to discern how Merlin was performing his wonders.

Tito asked for another volunteer. All the children's hands rose in the air. He selected a little girl wearing a garland of white flowers. "Step right up, young miss." Her mother had to give her a little push. She stood shyly beside Tito. "Today, you and I are going to make water into wine."

"I don't drink wine," she said.

The audience tittered.

"Of course you don't," Tito said, "but you can make it for your mother." He waved to the girl's mother.

"She doesn't drink it, either," the girl said. "She's allergic."

Bailey nudged me. "Uh-oh. Tito is losing his patience. Look at him rubbing the underside of his nose. That's a tell."

"Let him be. It's good practice for him before becoming a dad."

She blanched. "Who said anything about us having children?"

Oddly enough, she and I had never discussed the matter. "Um, gee."

"I don't want kids. I would be a horrible mother."

"You're great with the little ones when we have children's projects."

"Sure I am—*here*—knowing I can send them home."

"Let's table this discussion for now." I pointed to Tito. "Watch your future husband perform a miracle."

Tito forced a big grin. "Okay, we'll make water into Hawaiian Punch. Is that better?"

The girl nodded.

He gave her a measuring cup filled with water and asked her to hold it. He then lifted the magic funnel. He held it by the handle and showed the audience the top and bottom of it. Then he set it mouth-side down on his table and spread his hands, front and back, for the audience—empty. He picked up the funnel, placed a clear glass beneath it, and said to the girl, "Ready?"

She nodded.

Waving his hand over the magic funnel, Tito said, "Eye of newt and teeth of boar, turn this water into punch forevermore. Pour the water, lass."

As she obeyed, Tito discreetly pressed on the topmost part of the funnel's handle. The water that poured from the bottom of the spout came out *red*. The audience applauded. The little girl squealed with delight. I imagined there was a hidden compartment in the funnel, and when Tito pushed the *magic* button, he dispensed dye from the compartment. Clever.

When all the liquid emptied into the glass, Tito picked it up and took a sip. "Ahh. Delicious juice. Bravo, young miss!"

"May I take a taste?" the girl said, hands extended.

"Uh, no. Sorry. 'Tis only for my lips." Tito's mouth twitched nervously. Obviously, he didn't want her drinking dye. If it had been *wine*, she wouldn't have asked.

I rushed forward, hands overhead. "Okay, that's it, folks. The show is over. I hope you enjoyed meeting Merlin the Magician.

Merlin, hand your assistant a lollipop, and thank you for a wonderful show! Everyone, may you have a magical day."

• • •

The rest of the day flew by. A half hour from closing, I said to Tina, "I've got to run. I forgot that I have to buy a cheese platter for tonight's family dinner before swinging by and picking up Rhett at his shop. His car gave out on him this morning."

"Go," she said. "Have fun. I can deal with the stragglers."

Four female minstrels with lutes, who looked like jesters in their mismatched checker-patterned and diamond-patterned costumes, had entered fifteen minutes ago. One was diligently leafing through each Renaissance-themed book we had in stock hoping to find a rare one for her mother. I had recommended *A Sip Through Time: A collection of old brewing recipes*, which contained over four hundred documented historical recipes for ale, beer, and the like, but that hadn't satisfied her. I then suggested *Eating Right in the Renaissance*, which took the reader through historical sources in a spicy narrative. She snubbed her nose at that, as well. Her companions, who I was pretty sure had imbibed a glass or two of mead before arriving, were occupying themselves by trying on aprons and checking out pepper shakers, which one exclaimed worked well as maracas.

"Don't worry," Tina said. "I won't let them break anything, and if they do" — she pointed to a sign above the register: *You break it; you own it* — "I'll demand cash." She pushed me gently. "Go."

"I'll return for Tigger as I make the loop."

"No worries. He's having the time of his life."

Indeed, Tigger was merrily playing with the ball affixed to the end of the sisal rope on his kitty condo.

I left and darted along Buena Vista Boulevard until I reached Say Cheese Shoppe, a darling place situated near the center of town. When decorating, Charlene had really taken the store's catchphrase to heart. The walls were plastered with images of cartoonish smiles and cameras, and mirrors hung everywhere to give the shopper the chance to test out a grin or two. Whenever I entered the place, I couldn't help but smile. I sidled past a table set with a mountain of jam and jelly jars and another piled with boxes of gourmet crackers. I considered purchasing a petrified wood cheese platter—Charlene had dozens of gorgeous platters—but decided against it. My aunt had plenty of serving dishes.

"Afternoon, Jenna," Charlene said, dusting her hands on her cheese-themed apron.

"Are you about to close?"

"Heavens, no. I'm staying open an extra hour. Fair folks like to slip in on their way back to their hotels and such. Business is booming. What can I get you?"

"Give me a sec." I peered into the cheese case, sizing up the various choices. "How is your daughter? What is she now, a sophomore at OSU?"

"Good memory."

"What's her major?"

"Goofing off." Charlene laughed. "Actually, it's botany. She's always been into plants. She wants to return home and save every endangered species in California."

"My aunt will be thrilled to hear that." Aunt Vera volunteers on the local coastal commission and various other ecological organizations.

"Either that, or she wants to own a garden store." Charlene wet a towel and wiped down the cutting counter. "Hey, I've been meaning to tell you, we have a mutual friend."

"Who's that?"

"Charlotte Bessette, the adorable woman who runs Fromagerie Bessette in Providence, Ohio."

"How did you two meet?"

"I was visiting my daughter and decided to go on an Amish Tour. When the tour concluded, the guide took us on a quick outing in Providence. What a charming town." She threw the soiled towel into a deep sink by the rear wall. "You know me. How could I resist going into a shop with the word *fromagerie* in its name? Over the past ten years, I've visited over a hundred cheese shops. I giggled when I heard Charlotte's name. Isn't it a funny coincidence that we both sell cheese and both have names starting with *CH*? She said you used to converse with her online."

"I haven't in a long while." I had reached out to her when Crystal Cove was hosting the Grilled Cheese Competition and the shop was featuring cheese-themed cookbooks. She'd offered some wonderful suggestions.

"Sadly, you won't. She had twins and is taking time off."

"Twins. How nice." I recalled Bailey panicking at the concept of having children and wondered whether she would reconsider. Granted, some people aren't meant to raise kids, but I thought for sure she'd be eager to.

"Speaking of Ohio, I met someone who hails from there. A lady named Melody. What was her last name?" She tapped her finger on the side of her face. "She came in the shop the other day."

"Melody Beaufort?"

"That's the one. Between you and me" — Charlene propped her elbows on top of the cheese case — "she sure doesn't sound like she's from Ohio. She has a California accent."

"Californians have accents?"

"Lordy, yes. You say some words very oddly."

"Like what?"

"You say Bowie knife with a long *o* instead of the *oo* sound, like moo. And you say cauliflower with a short *i*, as in sit. Most folks say it with a long *e*, like a collie dog." She twirled a finger. "Say caramel."

I obeyed.

She pointed. "See? You say it with three syllables. Most utter two syllables, like the middle *a* doesn't exist."

"Ha! You have an ear."

"Before becoming a cheese monger, I was going to be a linguist." She wagged a hand. "I know, I know. How does one relate to the other? It doesn't, but I fell in love with cheese, and the rest was history."

"Do you think Melody is a native Californian?" I asked, wondering again whether she might have known Nick at a previous time.

"Not necessarily. She's lived here for a bit. That's enough time to assimilate. Why, I've known people who have lived in England for less than a year, and they sound one hundred percent English. Like actors taking on a new role, they adapt and change their tone." Charlene hoisted a carving knife and slid it through a sharpener. "Melody and I were chatting about how my daughter would love to learn pottery. Melody suggested she check out the classes at an art school in Columbus. What was the name of it?" She tugged on her earlobe. "I remember. Clearlight. Lovely name. She said it has undergone a management change, but it boasts a terrific art program."

The chime over the front door jingled. Mayor Zeller entered, the folds of her innkeeper's skirt kicking up as she rushed toward us.

"Hello, Mayor, I'll be right with you," Charlene said.

"Actually, I'm here to see Jenna," Z.Z. said. "Tina told me you were here." She held out a clear DVD jewel case with a silver disk inside. "This is a fair-speak instructional video for you—a thank-you for participating. I'm on a mission to deliver them all by sundown. If you wish to share with friends, they can watch it online at the fair's website." She rattled off the URL.

"Wonderful," I said. "I haven't had time to see it yet. Did it turn out well?"

"Everyone is loving it. You have a nice little encounter with an elderly woman. Gotta run!" She scurried out the door.

Charlene clucked her tongue. "My, my, that woman never slows down, does she? She's a marvel. Now"—she pointed to the cheese counter—"what can I get you for tonight, Jenna? Have you made up your mind yet?"

I ordered a wedge of Brie, manchego, and Collier's cheddar. The last time I was in, Charlene had given me the full rundown on the history of that particular cheddar.

"No goat cheese?" she asked. "I've got your father's favorite. River's Edge Up in Smoke."

I frowned. "I don't always have to buy my father a treat, do I?"

"You don't, but you know how happy it makes him. How can you pass it up?"

True. How could I? The tiny ball of chèvre, which was wrapped in a maple leaf and spritzed with bourbon, was uniquely delicious. Maybe, by treating my father, he would make the second kitty condo sooner rather than later.

"Sold." I pointed to a colander filled with ugly tomatoes and various other fruits on the counter behind Charlene. "Are those tomatoes and apples for purchase?"

"They are."

"I'll take two of each. Do you grow them yourself?"

"Ha! I don't have a green thumb. These are from Pepper's garden.

She brings them in and I give her a pound of cheese. It's a fair swap. So many people, like you, want fresh goodies with their cheese. Sliced tomatoes and apples are simply the best." She set the tomatoes on top of the cheese case and pulled the Collier's cheddar from the case. As she unwrapped it, she glanced at me. She circled the tip of her carving knife in front of my face. "What's got your nose in a scrunch?"

"I saw ugly tomatoes like these at Nick Baldini's, sitting in a bowl above his kitchen sink. I'm wondering whether Pepper or Melody gave them to him. Melody is renting Pepper's house so—"

"No, no, no." Charlene brandished the knife. "I doubt Melody gave Nick anything but backtalk." She rewrapped the remaining cheese and returned it to the refrigerated case. "I saw him flirting with her out on the sidewalk before she came in the other day. She clearly wanted to slap him." Charlene shook her head. "Uh-uh. There was no love lost there, believe you me."

# Chapter 19

I trotted back to the Cookbook Nook to fetch Tigger and spotted Pepper entering Beaders of Paradise. Curious whether Cinnamon had questioned her about the telephone message from Nick, I hurried after her. I flew inside the shop before the door closed.

"Hi, Pepper!"

Though I'm not a beader, I love her shop. I didn't always. The first time I'd entered, the strands of seashell-shaped beads that served as a window shade attacked me. Now I find them as charming as the racks filled with string and twine and the jars and boxes packed with colorful beads.

She whipped around. "I'm not staying, Jenna. I've come to pick up more product. Can you return—"

"I'm not buying. I wanted to ask you a quick question. I heard Nick telephoned your house the night he died."

"This is the first I've learned of it." She reached into a closet and removed three plastic cartons of beads.

"Your daughter didn't tell you? Your tenant told her—"

"Cinnamon and I are not on speaking terms."

"But you're staying in her house."

"Which is why we're not on speaking terms. Familiarity breeds contempt." She set the containers on the counter and retrieved five spools of wire. "Apparently, my daughter doesn't like the way I keep the kitchen. What's wrong with leaving a few dishes in the sink? I rinse them."

"That means you don't know . . ." I balked.

"Don't know what?"

Heaven forbid I spill the beans about Cinnamon's engagement. "You should speak with her," I said feebly.

She *harrumphed* under her breath.

I pressed on. "Back to the phone call. Apparently, Nick left you a message about the napkin rings you're making for Bailey."

"Made," she said. "That I *made* for Bailey. They're done. And why would he contact me? We talked about them the day before he died. I'd promised to bring them Sunday—" She shook her head. "Today," she revised. "Maybe the police are mistaking it for a call he made to me the day before?"

"No, Melody Beaufort said Nick left you a message, but she erased it."

Pepper finger-combed her hair. "Why would she do that? She wasn't supposed to be answering my telephone. She and her husband both have cell phones. I'll ask her about it, although I suppose it doesn't matter. Nick is . . ." She sighed. "If you're wondering where the napkin rings are, they're in the guest room at my house. That's where I store all my completed projects. Bailey can ask the Beauforts for them if she's eager to see them. They're quite pretty. Some of my best work." She lifted the boxes of beads.

"One other thing," I said as I exited the shop before her. "Did you give Nick some of your ugly tomatoes?"

"No. All I promised were napkin rings."

"He had some on his counter."

"Dolly could have given them to him. She raises ugly tomatoes, as well."

As Pepper hustled to her smart car, my thoughts flew to Dolly. Did she visit Nick that night and lose her mind when she saw Hannah leaving, or better yet, did she enter the house and spot the distinctive second piece of Melody's pottery and suspect Nick of having not one but two affairs?

My cell phone rang. It was Rhett.

"On my way," I said the moment I answered. "Ten minutes." I lifted Tigger and hurried in my VW to the Pier.

After parking in a spot with a sign that read *Twenty Minutes Only* and cranking down the window so Tigger had fresh air, I hustled toward Rhett's sporting goods store. Before heading inside, I paused. Would Hannah and Dolly still be in their stalls? Should I—

*No. Not tonight.* I didn't have time to question anyone. Besides, Cinnamon might have already questioned them, and if I overstepped, she would cry like the Queen of Hearts, "Off with your head!" How I wished she would communicate with me. Why hadn't she? Maybe she didn't like the way I kept a kitchen, either.

• • •

Rhett and I sat on the rattan love seat on the lanai of my aunt's house. He was sipping wine. I was chowing down on cheese.

"Stop tapping your foot, Jenna," Dad ordered. He was seated in one of the many floral-cushioned chairs. Lola stood behind him gently rubbing his neck.

"I didn't realize I was." I stilled my legs and set my fourth slice of cheddar on a cocktail napkin. Neither the gorgeous setting sun nor the sound of the surf lapping the sand was doing anything to calm my overly active mind. On the drive over, Rhett and I had talked about persons of interest.

"More wine anyone?" Aunt Vera, wearing an exquisite silver-filigreed violet caftan, floated across the porch offering more sauvignon blanc to any takers. After she poured the last drop, she perched on the edge of a chair.

"Do you like the Up in Smoke chèvre, Dad?"

"It's fine." He stabbed a fingertip on the arm of his chair. "Care to tell me what's going on? What has you riled up?"

Rhett snickered. I batted his thigh with the back of my hand.

"I'll tell you what's bothering her, Cary." My aunt settled back in her chair and sorted the bangles on her wrists. "She's concerned about solving Nick's murder so Bailey and I and everyone else in this town can find peace."

"Here we go," my father said.

I glowered at him. "Solving the crime will help the vibes at Baldini Vineyards, Dad, so when Bailey and Tito get married—"

"Vibes." My father wiggled his fingers.

"Ignore him," Aunt Vera said. "Go on, Jenna."

Lola squeezed my father's shoulders.

"Ouch," he muttered.

"Cut Jenna some slack, darling. If she has theories about Nick's murder, I want to hear what she has to say."

Dad winked at me, and I realized he was simply doing what he did best—trying to get a rise out of me and everyone else.

I relaxed a tad and set my glass of wine on the rattan coffee table. "Okay, first, I know the police are doing their job. They've questioned a lot of people, including Nick's foreman and crew, all of whom have alibis. But I still feel that the prime suspects are Dolly, Hannah, Alan, and Melody Beaufort. Each have alibis, but they are tenuous."

"Melody Beaufort?" my father asked. "Isn't she new to town?"

"Yes."

"Why would she want to kill Nick?"

Aunt Vera twirled a hand. "Give us your reasoning for each, dear."

I nodded. "Let me start with Dolly. She said she was home making garlands, but Gran—she's one of our customers—lives near to Dolly. She was walking her dog about the time of the murder, and she didn't see any lights on at Dolly's house. Why would Dolly lie?" I splayed my hands. "Because she was furious that Nick had dumped her, so she went to confront him that night, and when she saw Hannah leaving—"

"Hannah was at Nick's house?" Lola settled into a chair and leaned forward, elbows on her knees, fingers laced beneath her chin. "How do you know?"

"She told me. She went to apologize for arguing with him in public. She said they parted on good terms." I paused. If she'd lied about seeing Alan, however, she might have fibbed about her meeting with Nick. On the other hand, she said the foreman, the housekeeper, her grandmother, and her grandmother's nurse saw her when she arrived home. Wouldn't one or all of them have noticed if she'd had blood on her clothing? How I wanted to believe she was innocent. Truth be told, I wanted to believe Dolly was innocent, too.

"Continue," Lola said. Prior to owning the Pelican Brief, she had worked as a defense lawyer. A few years ago, she had given up the practice. I always appreciated when she listened to me as if I were a worthy adversary.

"Maybe Nick let Dolly in," I continued, "and they rehashed the reason for the breakup. Maybe Dolly was satisfied, but when she saw a vase that Melody gave Nick as a gift—"

"How do you know she gave him a gift?" Dad asked.

"Actually, I don't, but I think she did. Even if she didn't, Dolly could have assumed"—as I had—"and she lost it. Rumor has it, when Nick broke up with Dolly, she destroyed a shelf in her shop with a baseball bat."

"That doesn't surprise me," my aunt said. "I've witnessed her temper firsthand. About six months ago, a salesman came into her shop and offered her subpar goods. She was not a happy camper."

"Did she hit him with a baseball bat?" my father challenged.

"No, but she let him have a mouthful."

"A mouthful is not—"

Lola waved a hand to quiet my father. "Jenna, tell us more about Hannah."

Rhett stroked my back and murmured, "You've got them hooked."

"We can hear you, young man," my father sniped.

"Not so young," Rhett countered.

My father threw him a menacing look; Rhett offered a huge, devil-may-care grin. The two of them had become good friends; both liked sparring.

I explained how Hannah had lied about being able to see Alan from the second-floor window.

"How do you know she lied?" Lola asked.

"It's boarded up and the wood doesn't look new."

"There's more than one window with that particular view of the Baldini property," Rhett said.

"Where? I didn't see one."

Rhett stabbed the air above his head. "In the turret. The corner tower."

"But wouldn't that be considered the third floor?" I asked.

"Sure, but calling it the second floor"—he joggled his hand—"might be a reasonable mistake."

I shifted in my seat. "Hannah said she was with her grandmother, who is an invalid. Why would Mrs. Storm be on the third floor? Do they have an elevator?"

"She's not an invalid," my father argued. "Where did you hear that?"

"Aunt Vera said she has osteoporosis."

"Perhaps she climbs stairs to strengthen her legs," my father said. "Did you ever consider that? Moving on." He brandished a finger. "Who's next on your list?"

I filled the group in about Melody and Nick's public spat. I added that Pepper had overheard Melody and her husband arguing about keeping a secret from Nick.

"A secret," my aunt repeated.

"Is Sean Beaufort a person of interest?" Lola asked.

I worked my tongue inside my cheek. "I suppose he should be, if he were a jealous man, but Melody repeatedly made it clear that she was not interested in Nick. Charlene, at Say Cheese, saw Melody nearly slap Nick."

"Sean is a cool guy," Rhett said. "Over the course of the past few days, I've had a few conversations with him."

"Cool guys have been known to kill," Lola countered.

"Nice women, too," my aunt said. "Jenna, you mentioned that Nick had a second piece of Melody's pottery. Are you sure about that?"

"Yes. I saw it the night—" My voice cracked, the memory of finding him so fresh that it stung. "The night he died. I asked Melody about it, but she swore she didn't give it to him."

My father gawked. "You asked her?"

"What about Alan Baldini?" Aunt Vera cut in. "He has a lot to gain from his brother's death. Do you think he made up the thing about having face blindness?" She rose to her feet and asked, "Who wants more wine?" She didn't wait for an answer and retreated into the house for a fresh bottle.

"Alan has face blindness?" Lola sounded astonished. "I don't understand why he would fib about that. It wouldn't support his alibi. More importantly, how often does he take the crow to the field? Hannah might have based her story on his schedule."

"He was there last night," I said.

"How do you know?" My father lurched to his feet, his voice gravelly with anger. "Were you spying on him?"

"No!"

"Jenna, tell the truth."

I tried to melt into the back of the love seat.

"That's it. I've heard enough!" Dad snapped. "You are taking risks you shouldn't take, young lady."

"I was with Bailey."

"Yeah, yeah. Tell it to the judge." He barreled down the rear stairs. "I'm going for a walk on the beach. Lola, are you joining me?"

"Yes, darling." She threw me a supportive look. "Don't worry. I'll calm him down." She raced to catch up to him.

"I'm still here, fair maiden." Rhett lifted my hair and kissed my neck. "Run the rest by me."

A shiver of desire coursed through me. Rhett laughed, knowing the affect he was having.

"You rogue," I chided. "That reminds me . . ." I dug into my tote bag and pulled out the DVD the mayor had given me.

"What's that?"

"A token of appreciation for helping out with the instructional video." I handed it to him. "Care to watch the two of us on film?"

"Using what? Neither of us brought our computers, and your aunt doesn't have a system."

"The mayor also posted it online." I fetched my cell phone, opened the Internet browser, and entered the link the mayor had cited. I pressed Play.

While watching the actors mingle, I said, "Hmm. How did Alan capture all of this if he can't see faces?"

"I would imagine he follows shapes and sounds."

"That makes sense. He did say he could determine who someone was by certain attributes like a haircut or headwear."

On-screen, Melody hurried up to an older frizzy-haired woman in lavender who was approaching Nick, aka Henry VIII. Seeing him alive tugged at my heartstrings.

Rhett tapped the cell phone screen. "Who's that woman in lavender?"

"I have no idea."

Melody gripped the woman's arm. "Nay, Mother, do not attack. Verily, I say he is not the scoundrel."

The older woman shot a finger at Nick. "By my faith, should I learn otherwise . . ." She glowered at him and did a U-turn.

Nick lingered near Melody and leaned in. He said something so softly that I couldn't pick it up. Melody lowered her chin and shook her head.

"Does she look scared to you?" Rhett asked.

"Scared?"

"Rewind it. Look at her eyes."

I rewound the video feed, switched up the volume, and hit Play.

Nick's voice was still faint, but we could make out, "Come now, Shannon, admit it."

Rhett was right. Melody's eyes glistened with fear. She glanced over her shoulder and back at Nick. "Stop," she urged in a whisper.

"'Tis I," Nick said, thumping his chest proudly, as Henry VIII might do. "You must remember me."

I paused the recording. "Why did he call her Shannon?"

"Maybe it's a name she gave herself for the fair, to keep the acting exercise separate from her identity as a potter? Keep going."

I pressed Play again. Nick gently swept Melody's hair to one side. He uttered a one-syllable word I couldn't make out. "What did he say?"

Melody batted Nick's hand and inched away.

"Wasn't that about the time her husband arrived?" Rhett asked.

"I think he came in a bit later."

"Even so, maybe Sean should be a suspect after all. What if he saw Nick hitting on Melody during the filming and he got jealous? I sure would be after observing that interplay."

I nodded. "I've been wondering if the missive the messenger brought in was from Nick and not Sean."

"What missive?"

"Don't you remember? Like the one you gave me." I related the scenario up to the point when Sean removed the scroll from Melody's hand.

The film skewed—an unprofessional, funky cut—and a new scene started. I wondered who had done the editing. Not Alan, if he couldn't discern faces. Maybe the mayor.

Rhett and I watched until the end. Neither he nor I appeared comfortable in our roles, which made us laugh.

"A career as an actor is not in my future," he teased.

"Mine, either."

When the video ended, I was still wondering about Nick having called Melody *Shannon*. Others said "Melody" throughout the taping. Was Melody her real name? Maybe she had reinvented herself, which was why she had no social media footprint.

In the search bar on my cell phone's Internet browser, I typed in *Shannon Beaufort*. Two profiles with that name materialized for Facebook, but neither of the profile pictures matched Melody.

"Do you know what her maiden name was?" Rhett took a sip of wine and set his glass on the coffee table.

"No clue." I opened Beaufort's Beautiful Pottery website and scoured the biographies for Sean and Melody. He was purely the money guy; Melody was the artist. There was no mention of their lives prior to starting the pottery business, nor any mention of her taking pottery classes in Columbus, Ohio, as she'd hinted to Charlene.

Who was Melody Beaufort? Why the secrecy? Why was I suspicious? Maybe Nick had been mistaken about her identity, and that was why she had rebuffed him.

I revisited the main Internet browser page, typed in *Beaufort's Beautiful Pottery*, and noticed a few links to reviews on Yelp. I selected one link after another. All raved about Melody's work. A headshot of the reviewer accompanied each review. I paused on one review written by a woman who looked similar to Melody, except she had dark hair. I recalled that Melody had dark roots. Had she bleached her hair to clandestinely review her own product? Was that the secret she needed to hide? Killing someone to conceal such an innocent ploy didn't seem reasonable.

One click on the photograph revealed that the reviewer's name was *Susan Shannon "Praise the Lard" C.*—the initial C being the way Yelp kept the last name private. Telling by the woman's other reviews, she was a serious foodie.

"Look, Rhett." I stabbed the name Shannon on the screen. "Is this Melody?"

"Can't be. The woman has brown eyes. Melody's are green."

"What if she were wearing contacts?"

Rhett shook his head. "This one's a lot older. Note the wrinkles around her eyes. Sister, I think. Maybe Shannon is Melody's maiden name."

"If so, that would mean Nick did know Melody before she was married. Why protest? Why—"

Loud bagpipe music resounded on the beach. A quite vocal group of medieval revelers carrying candles housed in paper cups snaked their way toward my aunt's house. Among them were my father and Lola.

The lead woman, barefoot and clad in a chemise and flowing skirt, broke from the pack and jogged up the stairs to the lanai. She snatched my cell phone, set it on the table, and gripped my wrist. "Down it goes, you varlets. No ether allowed. Time to party!" The woman tugged. She was strong.

Certain that my father had put her up to it and she'd never let go, I gave in, grabbed Rhett's hand, and off we went to have fun. Learning more about Melody Shannon Beaufort would have to wait.

# Chapter 20

An hour later, after celebrating with the Renaissance Fair revelers, we returned to my aunt's house. My father banned any discussion of Nick's murder. He threatened that if I defied him, he wouldn't give me the second kitty condo he was constructing. I complied. I am no fool.

Over a lovely meal consisting of a green salad, hearty beef stew, and Lola's homemade bread, we chatted about the fair. While enjoying coffee, chocolate tarts, and ginger cheesecake, we discussed the world in general.

Near midnight, I bid everyone good night, drove Rhett home, kissed him handsomely, and sped back to my cottage. Although I wanted to think about Melody Shannon Beaufort and the secret she was keeping, I was too tired, particularly after finding Tigger embroiled in yet another snarl—this time rainbow-striped ribbon. Where in the heck had he found it? I refrained from saying *bad kitty* and untangled him.

"Tomorrow . . ." I mumbled à la Scarlett O'Hara as I slipped under the comforter. I didn't have the energy to finish her go-to statement.

I slept heavily and awoke late Monday morning, a rarity for me—it was the chocolate tart's fault, to be sure. Running behind schedule, I had no time to think about Melody or anyone else. I merely had time to *do* . . . and fast. I downed a portion of my pan pasty, which was delicious for dinner and even more delectable heated up for breakfast, after which I dressed in capris and an ecru knit sweater. I couldn't muster another dose of Fabreeze on the Maid Marian costume and made a mental note: *next year, two costumes*. With Tigger in tow, I tore to work.

The moment I arrived at the Cookbook Nook, my aunt, who was wearing a lilac caftan I'd never seen before, and Bailey and Tina, who were clad in everyday clothing, like me, waylaid me and informed me there were fires to put out. Not real fires, but little catastrophes. Bailey said the books we had ordered for next week's theme hadn't arrived. She'd been distracted and had forgotten to put in the request. She was extremely apologetic. Tina informed me that the person who was supposed to help Katie disassemble her stall at the fair hadn't shown up, and Katie was on the rampage. My aunt was worried because more bookshelves in the storage room were straining under the weight of our wealth of cookbooks. In less than half an hour, I solved Katie and Bailey's concerns. For the remainder of the morning, I joined my aunt in the storage room trying to determine our next course of action. Metal shelving, we decided.

Close to noon, as I was amusing Tigger by pushing the sisal rope on his kitty condo to and fro so he could bat it, Marlon Appleby entered the shop. He stood inside the doorway looking massive and imposing in his green-and-brown hunter's costume. In his hand he carried a scroll like the one Rhett had given me.

Bailey joined me and pointed to Appleby. "What's with the deputy's getup?"

"He's been into the fair costume thing from the beginning."

"He's allowed?"

"One week a year."

She giggled. "Look at him scouring the shop. What's he looking for?"

"I think you mean *who*. No doubt, my aunt. He asked her to marry him. She turned him down. I think he's on the hunt."

"Ha-ha. Very funny. He's a hunter." She wiggled a finger. "I like his bow, by the way." It was a classic deep green American longbow. "And the quiver is a nice touch."

I agreed. "Aunt Vera," I cried. "You have a visitor."

My aunt emerged from the storage room carrying a deck of tarot cards. Upon seeing the deputy, she drew to a halt. Her eyes widened in panic. "M-Marlon"—she sputtered—"what are you doing here?"

He strode to her, knelt on one knee, and in a rich baritone said, "My lady, hear me out. Prithee, take my heart and soul."

Everyone in the shop stopped whatever he or she was doing. Many closed cookbooks or replaced kitchenware on the shelves, too enthralled with the unfolding drama to continue browsing.

Aunt Vera's face tinged pink. She rested the hand holding the tarot cards against her chest.

"And take this token of my affection." Appleby proffered the scroll by laying it gallantly across his other palm.

"Marlon, please." My aunt's voice was thin and strained. "You're embarrassing me."

"And you are embarrassing me, love of my life. I grovel, I beg, I would harness the sun for you, if I could. I have asked, but you have not given me a decent answer."

"Marlon, I already told you—"

"Bite thy tongue, woman, and let me finish. When, pray tell me . . ." He twisted his head in my direction and winked before redirecting his focus to my aunt. "When will you invite me to Sunday family dinners? 'Tis the sum total of my request."

My aunt burst into laughter. "You rogue. You scoundrel. On your feet."

"Not until you read my missive." He flourished the scroll.

My aunt withdrew it from his grasp, freed the ribbon, and unfurled the paper. She read the contents, and tears filled her eyes. I didn't know what it said, but whatever it was . . . was *good*. I couldn't remember the last time I'd seen her cry with delight.

Seeing her joy made me flash on Melody when she had received her missive. She had refused to reveal what it said or who had sent it.

My aunt tucked the scroll into the pocket of her caftan, held out her hand, and asked Appleby to rise.

He clutched her hands and said, "So? What is your answer?"

"Next Sunday. Don't be late."

"Until then, my beauty." He pecked her cheek and marched nobly toward the door.

"Wait," my aunt said. "Stay for cranberry scones. They're warm. Katie just set some out."

"Don't mind if I do." He offered her his elbow. She latched on, and the two strolled into the breezeway.

The customers went wild with applause as if they had witnessed a rare stage event. Quietly, I did a happy dance.

Bailey said, "Crisis averted."

"And how. Would you tend to the customers by the saltshakers? I'm going to neaten the Renaissance jigsaw puzzle." I headed to the vintage table and set the pieces of the latest puzzle into its box. Then I linked together a corner so customers would know they could begin anew. A number of regulars came in daily to concentrate on a puzzle. A few called it therapy.

"Jenna!" Dolly flew into the shop wearing a pair of jeans and a crisp white button-down shirt. It was a good look on her and I told her so. "Thanks. Is Chief Pritchett here?" She scanned the bookstore.

"No. Why would you think—"

"The precinct said she was at Fisherman's Village."

"Maybe she's in her mother's shop, though I don't see her cruiser in the parking lot. Why are you looking for her?"

"I'm ready to . . ." She let the sentence hang and licked her lips.

I tensed. Was she ready to admit that she had killed Nick? Was she here to turn herself in?

"I'm ready," she continued, "to fetch my things from Nick's place. It's time for me to put the past in the past. Then I'm moving to Los Angeles."

"Why?" I squawked.

"My business here is limited. I plan all year for the Renaissance Fair, and if I don't sell big—which I didn't this year—I'm deep in the hole. Face it, I'm a failure. I can't sell crafts. I can't sell garlands or costumes. Heck, I can't even raise any stinking vegetables in this perfect climate."

"What about your ugly tomatoes?" I asked.

"Not this year. They're all dead. Every last one of them. I don't know what happened." Dolly threw her hands into the air. "I'm a failure with a capital *F*! I've been thinking that in Los Angeles I might reinvent myself and—"

"Dolly?" A ponytailed woman at the sales counter spun around. Her doe-shaped eyes widened. "Dolly Ledoux? Is that you?"

Dolly peered at the woman. "Yes. Who are . . . Oh, it's you!" She rushed to the woman and embraced her.

The woman's shopping bag squished under the pressure. When Dolly released her, the woman dropped her bag on the floor and backed away. "Ready?" she said.

Dolly nodded.

Both began flapping their arms like chickens. "Cock-a-doodle-do," they crooned in unison. They extended their arms and tapped one another's fingertips. "Roosterettes rock and rule!"

The ritual complete, the Roosterette gathered her shopping bag and said, "You are not a failure, Dolly." She spoke with a Southern accent akin to Dolly's. "Do you hear me? Repeat after me: I am not a failure!"

"I am not a failure," Dolly echoed.

"Louder."

"I am not a failure."

"Positive is as positive does. Say it."

"Positive is as positive does," Dolly recited.

"There! Feeling better?" The woman tapped Dolly on the shoulder as if granting a fairy godmother wish.

Dolly beamed. "What are you doing here, Rhonda?"

"I'm traveling up the coast with my family. We're hitting all the sights in the great U.S. of A. Didn't know there would be a huge Ren Fair in town. Talk about traffic." She clucked her tongue. "I heard I absolutely had to come into this darling shop, so I let my teenagers sleep in, and here I am."

"You have teenagers?"

"Fourteen and sixteen!" She held up two fingers. "Take a selfie with me, sweet pea." She pulled her cell phone from her purse, squeezed next to Dolly, said, "Say cheesy-cheese!" and took a picture.

Dolly caught me staring at the two of them. "Jenna . . . Vera . . . everyone, forgive me. This is my softball teammate from high school, Rhonda."

"Teammate," Rhonda said. "Ha! I sat on the bench most of the time, but old Dolly here—"

"I'm not old."

"Neither am I. Forty is, after all, the new thirty." Rhonda knuckled Dolly on the arm. "You should have seen this girl hit the ball. Out of the park every time!" She thrust an arm into the air to demonstrate the arc of the ball.

I winced. If Dolly was innocent of murder, it probably wasn't good to keep hearing how powerful she was with a baseball bat. Reflecting on Nick's demise made me wonder: what did Dolly really want to take from his place? Granted, having been his steady girlfriend, she might have clothes tucked into his closets or dressers and truly wanted to pack up, but the cynic in me couldn't help questioning whether she had another aim. Maybe she wanted to divest herself of incriminating evidence, like Alan's missing gauntlet.

Rhonda's cell phone jangled. She glanced at the readout. "Sugar, I'm so sorry. I've got to go. The lions are roaring." She showed her cell phone to Dolly.

"Handsome boys," Dolly said.

"They're monsters, but I love them." She pecked Dolly on the cheek. "Remember, you can be whatever you want to be. If you need a pep talk, you look me up online. Use my maiden name dot com. I'm a life coach. And remember what I told you: Positive is as positive does. Say it at least ten times a day. Bye." She hurried out of the shop.

Dolly sank into a chair at the vintage table. "Wow, what a dynamo. Wish I had her cheery outlook on life."

I nestled into the chair opposite her and folded my hands on the table. "Dolly, why are you really leaving town?"

"What do you mean?"

"Your alibi for the night Nick died is—how can I say this—questionable."

"No, it's not." Dolly sounded indignant. "I already told you I was home doing crafts."

"Did you inform the police?"

"Yes."

"Did Chief Pritchett believe you?"

"Yes. Why are you asking?" She picked up two pieces of the jigsaw puzzle, linked them into the corner section I'd started, and searched for another piece.

"A witness said you weren't home. No lights were on."

Dolly leaped to her feet. "I was. I'm not lying. I—"

"What's going on?" Appleby asked as he and my aunt reentered the shop via the breezeway. Each was carrying a to-go cup and a miniature scone in a napkin.

Dolly rushed to him. "Deputy, I'm so glad you're here. I'm looking for Chief Pritchett. I want to fetch my things at Nick Baldini's house. I need her permission."

I leaped to my feet. "Dolly—"

"I don't have to answer to you, Jenna!" Defiantly, she folded her arms across her ample chest. "You have no right to question me."

"Question you?" The deputy threw me a baleful look. "You're not playing ace detective, are you, Jenna?"

"No, sir." My cheeks warmed, giving me away. "I was telling Dolly what I told Cinnamon . . . Chief Pritchett . . . on a voice mail, but I don't think the chief has had time to follow up. I would imagine she's been a tad preoccupied since getting engaged."

"Engaged?" Appleby whistled.

"You haven't noticed?" I pointed to my ring finger. "Plain as day."

"How did I miss that?" he muttered. "Well, that explains it."

"Explains what?" my aunt asked.

"Cinnamon has been . . ." He didn't finish.

"Absentminded?" I offered. "Like Bailey?"

"I'm not absentminded." Bailey joined our huddle.

"I beg to differ," I said. "A couple of things in addition to the book order have slipped by you." I ticked off three more items on my fingertips.

She huffed, but her eyes wavered. She knew I was right.

My aunt slipped her hand around Dolly's elbow and said, "C'mon, dear, I know you didn't kill Nick. What is your real alibi? Why are you keeping it a secret? We won't judge you, whatever the reason."

Dolly glanced between all of us and lowered her chin. "I'm not keeping it a secret. I told Chief Pritchett."

"Well, then . . ." My aunt leaned her head to the right.

"I went to another psychic." Air whooshed out of Dolly as if telling the truth had exhausted her.

My aunt released Dolly's arm.

"There, you see?" Dolly pointed at her. "I was embarrassed to tell you, Vera, because" — she gulped in air — "I was afraid you would be upset with me. And you are, aren't you?"

Clearly my aunt was flustered. Her lower lip started quivering. "Why did you feel the need to, dear?"

"I didn't believe you had envisioned my future correctly, and I wanted a second opinion." She focused on me. "And FYI, Jenna, Chief Pritchett has spoken with the other psychic to confirm what I've said. She knows I'm innocent."

"Honestly, Dolly, I'm relieved. I didn't want it to be you. I'm sorry for doubting you. I — "

"Stop," she said, cutting me off. "I get it. I've certainly made enough mistakes over the years, and you are known to be curious to a fault."

*To a fault?* I gulped.

Appleby snickered and tried, but failed, to hide a *gotcha* grin.

"Let me help you pack your things at Nick's," I offered. "It's the least I can do. Deputy, would you supervise?"

Dolly said, "It won't take long. Please?"

My aunt prodded Appleby. He shrugged his consent.

# Chapter 21

Shaken by her admission to my aunt, Dolly said she wasn't up to driving herself, so I offered to do so. We gathered the two empty suitcases she had packed in her Toyota Camry, set them into my VW, and followed Deputy Appleby in his Jeep up the hill to Baldini Vineyards. The bright afternoon sunlight, which was coming through the windshield at an oblique angle, made me squint, but I didn't mind. I was thrilled that Dolly was innocent.

"I'm thinking of opening an upscale dress shop in Los Angeles," Dolly said, looking idly out the passenger window at the ocean view. "With classics like Givenchy and Wang and—"

"Can you afford to do that?"

"I'll take out a loan."

"I've often wondered why you gave up your darling clothing business."

"I didn't give it up, exactly. I stopped buying current lines, renamed it, and allowed my product to become Ren Fair chic because . . ." She drummed the windowsill with her fingertips. "Because I wanted Nick's approval. I did everything to make him happy. When he came up with the name Thistle Thy Fancy, I accepted it to please him, even though I'd already decided upon the name the Prince and the Pauper."

"Cute."

"I know, right? Thistle Thy Fancy sort of limited me to garlands and crafts. Not many people knew to stop in the store for a gown or chemise." She swiveled to meet my gaze. "If I were really bold, I'd move to New York and try my hand at designing. You know the lyric, 'If I can make it there . . .'" She crooned the words. "But Los Angeles is a good choice."

"Why not move back to Louisiana?"

"Don't be crazy!"

I'd returned home to Crystal Cove and was thrilled that I had.

"I want to go someplace where I can get away from the memories," Dolly said. "Do you think an old dog can learn new tricks?"

"You're not old."

"True. As my fellow Roosterette said, forty is the new thirty." Her eyes pooled with tears, but she didn't let them fall. "I loved Nick so much, Jenna."

"I'm sorry I ever—"

"Forget it. Water under the bridge. You and your aunt have been stalwart for me for a long time."

When we pulled into the turnaround driveway near the front of the Baldinis' home, Hannah was standing on the porch between the stately columns chatting with Alan. Clad in black bicycle shorts and a snug matching T-shirt, she looked all of sixteen years old. A shiny charcoal-black Raleigh mountain bike leaned against the house by a trellis of bougainvillea.

Hannah turned as we pulled to a stop and shaded her eyes from the sunlight. Her eyes narrowed as Appleby, Dolly, and I exited our vehicles.

"Good day, Miss Storm," Appleby said, making his way to the door. "Out for some exercise?"

"I am, Deputy Appleby. Sitting around the stall at the fair isn't ideal for the waistline. Neither is eating a daily pasty. Are you here to speak with me or Alan?"

"No, ma'am. Miss Ledoux would like to remove any personal items she might have left here in the course of her relationship with Mr. Baldini."

Hannah's face relaxed. She nodded hello to Dolly and me.

Appleby said, "Will that be all right with you, son?" He shot a hand toward Alan and instantly pulled it back.

"Shake, Deputy." Alan thrust his hand toward Appleby. "I'm not blind, I just can't make out your face. P.S., I knew it was you before Hannah said a word."

"How?"

"The moment you climbed out of your Jeep. There aren't many men in town the same size as you." Alan held out a hand to Dolly. "Come in. Welcome. I haven't moved a thing since Nick died. At some point, I'll have to, but I can't cope with the change yet. You understand."

Dolly bit back tears. Appleby gestured for her to proceed.

Eager to chat with Hannah, I hung back, which made Appleby stop in his tracks. Dolly lingered, as well.

"I'm glad you're here, Hannah," I said. "I've been meaning to ask you a question."

Appleby grunted. If I didn't know better, I'd have thought he had learned the disparaging sound from my father.

"One question, Deputy," I muttered.

He waved for me to continue.

"Hannah, the other day you said you saw Alan in the field from your second-floor window."

"That's right."

"Okay, got your answer." Appleby crooked his thumb. "Inside."

I threw him a nasty look. "Sorry, sir, but technically that wasn't a question."

"What are you now, an attorney?" He huffed. "Go on."

"Hannah, the second-floor window that faces the Baldini property is boarded up and looks like it has been for a while."

Hannah swung her head to the left, as if she could see her house from that vantage point. She couldn't. She was trying to visualize it. When she turned back, her face drained of color. "I . . ." She faltered. "I made a mistake. I wasn't on the second floor. I was in the turret with Nana. That's a small room in the tower, on the third floor. It has a window."

Appleby's gaze sharpened. "What difference does it make, Jenna?"

"How could your grandmother be in the attic, Hannah?" I asked. "I heard she's pretty frail."

Hannah wagged her head. "She may have osteoporosis, but that doesn't slow her down. Her legs move rather well. She's from hard stock."

"You've hired a nurse for her," I stated.

"Because she's ninety years old and can be quite demanding. When she wants water, she wants it *now*." For emphasis, Hannah spanked the palm of one hand with the back of the other. "If I'm in the field or with a distributor or client, or like this week when I was at the fair, she had to have someone do her bidding. I didn't lie about having seen Alan in the field that night, Jenna." She eyed Deputy Appleby. "I know what he was wearing."

"How could you? It was dark."

"Yes, but I could make out his silhouette. He had on a hat with a feather. He doesn't always wear it when he's working with Crow."

"She's right. I don't always." Alan bobbed his head. "But that night I was. I'd gone straight from the fair to the shop where I bought the frogs, and I hadn't taken it off. I didn't go into the house and hang it in the utility room because I didn't want Nick to see me. I would've spilled the beans about the prank I was planning. Nick . . ." Alan heaved a sigh. "He could always strong-arm me into telling the truth."

Appleby swung his head from Hannah to Alan. "Did you two work out this exchange between yourselves?"

"No, sir, it's the first we've discussed it," Alan said.

Hannah agreed. "The very first."

"All-righty then," Appleby said. "Hannah, you're free to go, unless Jenna has any more official questions for you."

I didn't indulge the deputy with a retort. To Hannah, I said, "Did you spot the person that Alan saw in the field?"

"I didn't, I'm sorry to say. Timing is everything, isn't it?"

I regarded Dolly.

"It wasn't me." She threw up her hands. "The psychic confirmed to the police that I was with her. Besides, I wouldn't trudge through a vineyard if you paid me. Bugs." She flapped a hand. "Now, can we get going?"

"Alan, I've got to scoot," Hannah said. "See you at the fair tomorrow?"

"Sure will. Well, you'll see me, but I'm not so sure I'll see you."

She chuckled, joining him in the joke. "I'll be packing up midmorning," Hannah added, "so try to stop by before noon. Will you be bringing Crow?"

Alan shook his head. "The bird is about fair'd out, me-thinks."

"Come by yourself, then, and share a spot of tea with me, or taste Hurricane Vineyards' exquisite pinot noir. Critics say it's the best in California."

"We'll see about that," Alan quipped.

She pecked him on the cheek and hopped onto her bicycle. As she sailed down the driveway, Alan seemed to grow a foot taller.

Ah, love. What a wonderful elixir.

Appleby gestured with an open palm for Dolly to precede him through the main entrance. "After you, Miss Ledoux."

Dolly faced Alan. "All my things are in the bedroom."

"Make yourself at home," Alan said. "Feel free to make a pot of coffee, if you like. Beans are in the freezer. A coffee grinder, filters, and sugar are in the cupboard above the coffeemaker. Milk is in the fridge. I've got to see to Crow. I'm going to rebuild his interactive perch." He tramped toward the garage.

"Jenna." Dolly's eyelids fluttered. The tips of her eyelashes were moist. "You don't need to accompany me, but I'm glad you're here for mental support."

"I'll hang in the kitchen, then," I said. "Deputy, would you like some coffee?"

"That would be great. Black." He followed Dolly to the bedroom.

"Dolly, want some?"

"No, thanks."

I sauntered to the kitchen and prepared a pot of coffee. While it was brewing, I noticed that the ugly tomatoes in the colander—the tomatoes I was convinced that Melody had brought to Nick after Dolly told me her crop had failed—had aged quickly. Apparently, Alan knew nothing about chucking out rotten vegetables. Inside the refrigerator I noticed that a lemon, an aging zucchini, and an orange needed tossing. I smelled the milk and decided not to add it to my coffee. With Nick gone, perhaps Alan should consider asking the housekeeper to keep on top of things for him.

As I was pouring two mugs of black coffee, I eyed the shelves filled with photograph albums. Each had a small tab on it, denoting the year and subject matter. I did the math to deduce when Nick and Melody might have gone to Ren Camp together—somewhere between twenty-five and thirty years ago—and selected an album.

To make sure Deputy Appleby didn't walk in on my expedition, I decided to take him his mug of coffee first. I entered the master bedroom, which was richly decorated in gold and cream, and continued toward the walk-in closet to gauge how long it might take Dolly to collect her things. She was kneeling beside a multitude of shoes and a pile of clothes on the floor. *Poor thing.* No wonder she had felt bamboozled by Nick's rejection. She had literally moved in. She would need four or five suitcases to complete the task, not two.

I handed the coffee to Appleby and said to Dolly, "Water?"

"No, thanks." Tears were streaming down her cheeks.

I fetched a couple of tissues from the master bathroom and brought them to her—she murmured her appreciation—then I returned to the kitchen and removed the albums from the shelf. If I got caught nosing around, I'd say I was passing the time while reminiscing about Nick.

Flipping through the oldest of the albums, I saw many of the photos I'd seen on Nick's Facebook page. I paused when I noticed a picture of Nick as the king of the camp. He was crowning a dark-haired girl queen. Half of her face was obscured, but upon closer inspection, I could tell it was Melody; the green eyes and the turned-up nose gave her away. She was gazing lovingly at Nick.

As I perused a second album, I noticed more pictures of Melody, all in queenly regalia. In some, she stood in profile. In others, she coyly peeked over a shoulder. Was she camera shy or trying to avoid Nick, the photo buff, who was obviously smitten with her? In each of the shots, Melody was wearing a gold-toned gown that reminded me of the ones she had donned for the fair.

A shiver ran through me as a realization hit me. The gold gowns also brought to mind the gown the Empress was wearing on the tarot card that my aunt had pulled up in a reading. Aunt Vera believed she had drawn the card for Hannah, but directly prior, she had been giving Melody a reading until Melody prematurely ended the session. In reverse position, the Empress card signified that the recipient was dealing with confusion, maybe even indecisiveness about the direction of a relationship. What if Melody had been the intended recipient of the fortune? Maybe she had been struggling with a confusing relationship, like the one with Nick, or, better yet, the one with her husband.

No matter what the reason, my theory that Melody had visited Nick's place to root through the albums and remove evidence of her secretive past fell flat. The albums were intact.

I replaced the albums on the shelves and roamed the kitchen while sipping my coffee. I paused at Nick's computer, which looked the same as it had the night he was killed. I read the Post-it notes again, trying to discern something—*anything*—from them.

The to-do list was unimportant. The note saying *Fix it,* I decided, might have been a reference to mend the relationship with Melody. Maybe Nick had broken off their young romance and he'd wanted to beg her forgiveness. Or she had ended it, and he'd wanted a second chance. He'd suggested to Bailey and me that he needed to win a woman's heart.

The word *heart* stopped me cold. I snatched the note that read *Get MEDS* with the scrawled picture of a heart.

*Meds.* That was the word Nick had uttered softly in the fair-speak instructional video that Rhett and I watched. I hadn't understood it at the time, but now I was certain. *Meds* had to be a funky nickname for Melody Shannon. *Meds.* It denoted intimacy in a lifelong kind of way. Melody had been visibly upset that he'd used it.

I traced my finger across the Post-it. *Get MEDS . . . heart.* The juxtaposition had to signify that Nick had loved her and meant to win her over. Had they been boyfriend and girlfriend as preteens? Did they break up and lose track of each other? Was that why she hadn't recognized him as an adult? When did she meet Sean? When did they marry? I tapped the note again. Melody had dropped her maiden name. Why? As a matter of formality or anonymity?

Bailey said Saturday that if Melody had something to hide, then why risk coming to the Renaissance Fair? I'd suggested Sean might have made that decision, and Melody followed his lead hoping that aging and a different hair color would be enough of a disguise to fool Nick.

On the other hand, maybe she had wanted to be caught. *By him.*

I recalled the day Sean came into the Cookbook Nook to pick up the swan salt and pepper shakers for his wife. He said she was at the fair, except Dolly hadn't seen her there. Had Melody gone to the vineyard to see Nick? Bailey and I had met with him from 3:45 until 4:30 p.m. Hannah had gone to apologize at 5:00 p.m. Did Melody squeeze in a visit before Hannah arrived?

How had she gotten there? Sean had driven a car to the shop. Then I recalled Pepper saying that Melody and Sean were sports buffs. *Sean says exercise is good for the heart,* she told me. I supposed Melody could have hoofed it up the hill. It isn't a treacherous climb. Lots of people in Crystal Cove do it on a daily basis.

I imagined the reunion. Melody arrived with a piece of pottery as a gift—a token of peace. She planned to chat about old times—maybe even reveal the truth, whatever the truth was—but in the end, she got cold feet, told Nick to back off, and left. But Nick, unwilling to accept defeat, telephoned Melody at Pepper's house to request another meeting. Melody heard his voice via the speaker and answered. In no uncertain terms, he told her that he would find out why she was avoiding him. He would uncover her *secret*. Right then, Sean walked in. Seeing how flustered his wife was, he demanded she hang up. They argued. According to Pepper's account, Melody swore to Sean that she wouldn't tell Nick anything. She stormed out, saying she was going for a walk on the beach.

Did she return to Baldini Vineyards and demand that Nick's interest in her cease? Did he refuse? Was that when she lost it? She couldn't let him reveal her secret, whatever it was. She seized the foot-shaped winepress and wailed at him. Before leaving, she realized Pepper's home phone number was on Nick's cell phone, so she wiped the Recent Calls list and smashed the cell phone.

Catching sight of the to-do list attached to the computer made my breath snag: *pepper, p/u napkin rings*. What if my assumption when talking to Cinnamon at the café was right? What if Melody did kill Nick? What if she'd seen the note and, remembering that the rings in question were in Pepper's workroom, told Cinnamon that was the reason why Nick had called the house?

I revisited Pepper's account of what she had overheard Sean and Melody arguing about. Sean said he was worried that if Nick found out—

Found out *what*? I'd figured out her history with Nick. I'd figured out her opportunity for murder. What was her motive?

"Jenna, we're done, but I need your help," Dolly shouted from the master bedroom.

I hurried to her and skidded to a halt when I saw all the things piled on the floor that wouldn't fit into her suitcases.

"Guess I need some garbage bags," she said sheepishly.

I found a box of lawn and leaf bags in a cupboard beneath the sink in the utility room and withdrew three. As I stood up, I noticed the hat-and-coat rack. The gauntlet was missing, as I'd expected. Had any of the hats been taken? Had Melody put one on before fleeing on foot across Hannah's property?

# Chapter 22

While helping Dolly pack up the remainder of her things, I mentioned my theory about Melody and the missing gauntlet and the possibility of an unaccounted-for hat to Deputy Appleby. He didn't get angry. He didn't even offer a wisecrack. He said he'd pass my speculations along to his superior.

After stowing Dolly's suitcases and the additional garbage bags in her Camry—the car was crammed—I wished her luck with all the changes she intended to make in her life and reentered the Cookbook Nook. Three females in Renaissance Fair costumes were perusing the fair-themed cookbooks—the few that were still around; we had sold out of nearly all of them. I asked the women if they needed help. Overcome with giggling, they didn't reply. I concluded, from their red-faced and hushed conversation, that they were checking out some of the racier pictures in one of the nonfiction books I'd stocked. Low-cut bodices had been the rage back in the day.

I joined Tina at the sales counter. She was whistling while cleaning the cash register with a feather duster.

"Why are you so chipper?" I stowed my purse under the counter and took stock of the sales receipts for the morning.

"We have a new teacher at the culinary school. He's so-o-o much better than the other teacher, who"—she lowered her voice—"was kicked out for making an inappropriate advance."

I wrinkled my nose.

"Mm-hm. I agree. The powers that be caught him with his hand in the proverbial cookie jar." She mimed the action and whacked her wrist. "This new one, though, he's so handsome. When he's not cooking, he surfs or runs or even rides his bike. He's teaching us all sorts of techniques, like deglazing and dredging. Next, he's going to show us how to make chocolate. Ooh, ooh"—she wriggled her fingers—"and we learned a new term last night: *to seize*. It means water gets into the chocolate and causes it to become stiff and clumpy. Isn't that the coolest term? *To seize*." She thrust the feather duster like a sword. "Seizing is a no-no."

I sidled around her. "I think a certain someone has a crush on a certain teacher."

"Uh-uh, no way. He's twice my age. Besides, don't you remember that I have my eye on someone?"

"Right. The cute messenger."

"FYI, Bailey said she'll be back in a sec. She went to get a latte before she meets with Alan Baldini to talk about wedding plans. She'd planned to go to the vineyard, but he called and said he'd come here instead. He has errands to run in town. Your aunt" — Tina scanned the shop — "must be in the storage room."

"Too-ra-loo," Aunt Vera said, appearing from the breezeway carrying a sin-in-a-cup.

"Oops." Tina blushed. "Guess I missed her slipping past me."

"You're eating cheesecake?" I said to my aunt.

"I'm addicted. Have you had these?" She waved her treat near my face. "Devilish. Want me to fetch you one?"

"I need lunch before I down a straight dose of sugar."

"Katie's setting out some mini meat pies right now."

"Perfect." The pan pasty had filled me up for the morning, but it wasn't enough to keep me going all day. I headed in that direction.

"How is Dolly?" Aunt Vera asked.

"Yes, how is she?" Tina gazed at me earnestly. "She seemed distraught."

I halted. "She'll survive. She's determined to move to Los Angeles." On the drive back, Dolly had raved about Santa Monica. She had visited the area last year for a beading conference and had fallen in love with it.

"Heavens," Aunt Vera said. "It's all my fault for not giving her a better reading."

"It has nothing to do with you," I chided. "She needs a fresh start. Losing Nick has put a hole in her heart and a damper on her self-esteem. She wants to take a risk."

"A risk . . ." My aunt pulled a deck of tarot cards from her pocket. She shuffled them and chose three cards—what she liked to call a quickie tarot spread. Rather than lay them out on the counter, she studied them and reinserted them into the deck. "I do see a bit of derring-do in her future. Good. All positive. She has my blessing," she said, Dolly's disloyalty forgiven and forgotten. "I'll be right back." She ambled in the direction of the storage room, taking a moment at the kitty condo to give Tigger a kiss on the nose.

I continued toward the breezeway.

As my aunt pushed through the drapes, she added over her shoulder, "There's nothing quite as stimulating as taking a risk and building a new life. You of all people should know that, Jenna."

The words *building a new life* gave me pause. At the pottery class Rhett and I took, in response to something the matronly student had said, Melody claimed she had built a new life for herself. Why had she needed to? The classmate pressed Melody about her training. Melody hesitated, forehead pinched, as she groped for words to describe her third professor. What she had come up with was *brilliant but complicated*. What did complicated mean? Was he the reason she had left town and changed her name?

I sprinted to the computer and clicked on the Internet browser icon. A whirring symbol appeared. The modem was searching for a signal.

Tina peered at the display screen. "What are you doing, investigating?"

"Go back to work," I ordered.

"Can't. You're in my way," she sassed.

"Help the customers, then, you goofball."

"Goofball. Ha-ha. I like that. My uncle used to call me that." She tittered and left me alone.

The Internet gods complied and provided a signal. I typed *Melody Shannon* into the search bar. Like Melody Beaufort, she didn't have a Facebook profile or any other kind of profile online, but I was able to drum up images of her with dark hair, which meant she must have had a profile at one time, and friends or acquaintances had tagged her along the way. She appeared in group photos at Clearlight Art School of Ohio, as well as a fund-raiser for the local art community. In one, she was beaming and holding a crystal trophy consisting of two symmetrical shapes set on a walnut pedestal.

I zoomed in and read the inscription: *First Place ~ Ceramics; Ohio's Future Artists*. Melody was standing beside a distinguished man with salt-and-pepper hair and a square jaw—not Sean. He wasn't looking at the camera, however. He was gazing longingly at her. I read the caption: *Melody Shannon celebrating with Professor J. Daniel Loveland.*

Another photo featured Melody, Sean, and Professor Loveland.

Sean's obviously irritated gaze wasn't trained on Melody; it was fixed on the professor. The caption read: *Professor J. Daniel Loveland, Melody Shannon, and her fiancé, Professor Sean Ballantyne.*

*Ballantyne?* Not *Beaufort.* Sean had changed his name, too. Why? And why wasn't the fact that he had been a professor stated in his biography on their website?

I thought of what Tina had said about her former teacher. The powers that be had caught him with his hand in the proverbial cookie jar. Did Professor Loveland make a move on Melody? Did he force himself on her? Is that why she fled the state? Had Sean given up his career to help his wife escape the professor's advances? Was that why he'd changed his name?

I typed in *J. Daniel Loveland* and found a few articles relating to him. He had worked at several small colleges before heading up Clearlight Art School of Ohio. His LinkedIn profile read: *Experienced art teacher with a history of working in the arts and crafts industry. Skilled in ceramics.* Nothing overt there.

I delved further and gasped when I came upon a front-page article in the *Columbus Dispatch* dated ten years ago:

> *Professor J. Daniel Loveland found dead at the age of 52. The medical examiner discovered significant traces of arsenic in his bloodstream. The professor was undergoing no course of therapy that would require such heavy doses. The police are looking for an unidentified brunette female who was the last person to have visited his office, according to the art school's superintendent.*

Melody's name wasn't mentioned. Was she the unidentified brunette in question? Did she kill the professor? Was that why she had fled Ohio?

To double-check my theory, I did another search for Sean Ballantyne. Lo and behold, he quit his professorship at Ohio State University the day Loveland died.

Did Nick figure out Melody's secret? Did she believe he would expose her? I couldn't imagine he would have. He'd loved her.

I picked up the telephone and dialed Cinnamon at the precinct. I'd given Deputy Appleby a theory at the vineyard, but this was much bigger, and Cinnamon needed to hear it. The clerk informed me that the chief was taking a free day with her intended and couldn't be disturbed. I tried Cinnamon's cell phone. It rolled into voice mail.

"Dang!" I muttered.

"What's got you in a tizzy?" Bailey asked as she rushed into the shop carrying a to-go cup. A thin white film of milk lined her upper lip. I tapped my lip to let her know. She wiped off the milk and set down the cup. "Talk to me. You slammed down the phone so hard I thought it might crack."

I filled her in on my search and the added frustration of not being able to speak to Cinnamon.

"Temper, temper. The chief is allowed to have a life."

"Well said, Bailey Bird." Pepper strutted into the shop carrying a beribboned blue-and-silver box—Beaders of Paradise signature colors. "I gave my daughter ten wedding sites to peruse."

"You?" Bailey said.

"I'm well versed in the venues for weddings around here. I was once a bride."

*Ages ago, and not a happy one,* I mused, but held my tongue. My irritation was not with Pepper. Truth be told, it wasn't with her daughter, either. I craved answers.

"Did you suggest Baldini Vineyards, Mrs. Pritchett?" Alan asked as he strode into the shop. Apparently he had excellent hearing if he'd caught the thread of our conversation before entering the shop. "Nice beads, by the way."

I tilted my head, confused. He could distinguish beads but not faces? Were they in black and white? I definitely needed to learn more about face blindness.

Pepper fondled the septet of strands she'd donned over her crimson sheath. "Why, thank you, Alan. And no, I didn't mention your vineyard. I didn't think you would care to—"

"I definitely want to, Mrs. Pritchett. To honor Nick. He would want me to carry on the tradition. We'll hold a few weddings for special folks. Have your daughter call me." He sidled past Pepper to Bailey. "Ready for our meeting?"

"Wait a second," Pepper said. "I have a gift for you, Bailey." She held out the box. "These are the napkin rings that Nick requisitioned."

Bailey accepted them reluctantly. "That's so considerate of you."

"Don't thank me. Nick paid for them. Open it up."

Bailey glanced sideways at me, her angst evident. I gave her an encouraging thumbs-up. Slowly she unlaced the ribbons, lifted off the silver box top, and dug through a flurry of silver tissue paper. When she pulled out a napkin ring, she inhaled sharply. "Pepper, these are truly . . . beautiful."

I agreed. Pepper had woven tiny gold beads into a cluster of larger red and mossy green beads, all fitted together with three gold rings.

Bailey's eyes moistened. "Thank you. They're perfect."

Pepper beamed. "Nick was very specific. He had an eye for beauty, that man." She placed a hand at the base of her throat. "He wanted your wedding to be everything you hoped it would be. He said he wanted to have a wedding like yours" — her voice caught — "too."

Was she going to cry? I hadn't known Pepper long, but I couldn't remember her giving in to sentiment. I slung an arm around her. She wriggled from my grasp and veered toward the front of the shop under the pretext of looking for a new book.

Hannah strolled into the shop, the gold earrings she was wearing jingling merrily. "Hi, all. What's going on? Are you getting welled up because the fair is almost over?"

"No," Bailey said and fanned the air, close to tears herself.

"Heads up. When you go to shut down your stall, be prepared for dust." Hannah brushed off the thighs of her blue jeans and tugged on the hem of the crisp white shirt. "Remind me about the mess next year, Jenna, and ask me if I still want to participate." She chuckled and shot a finger at me. "Can you help me? I need a few recommendations for Central Coast wine books that I can sell at the vineyard. I don't want to compete with you, of course, so give me suggestions for a few titles that you don't carry, or I can buy them from you and mark them up. I don't care. I'm thinking of opening up the vineyard to tastings. Nana has always been against them, but we need to curry favor with the locals and tourists if we're going to remain viable."

"Feeling competitive, Hannah?" Alan said, emerging from behind Bailey, where he'd hidden the moment Hannah entered.

She pivoted. "Hey, Alan. I didn't see you there." She blushed.

"Um, no, not overly competitive. We won't do weddings and such. Private tastings is all I have in mind. Maybe three or four times a year. By the way, you didn't stop in for tea."

"I'm sorry. I meant to. I haven't . . ." Alan quit talking and edged toward her, his nostrils flaring in a happy way. "Say, I need a wedding planner to help out with Bailey's wedding. Do you know anyone who might be interested?"

"Let's put our thinking caps on." She slipped her arm through his and guided him into the breezeway, where Katie was setting out mini quiches.

Bailey hip-bumped me. "You're grinning like the Cheshire cat."

I giggled. "I'm happy to see the two of them bonding." My stomach rumbled.

"Hungry?"

"I'm craving a mini pie, but I don't want to disturb Alan and Hannah's budding romance."

Bailey chuckled. "Guess I'll have my meeting with Alan a little later."

"And I'll give Hannah book suggestions later, as well," I said. "It's sweet, don't you think?"

"Love is in the air."

"Excuse me, Jenna?" a man said.

I turned and spied Sean tramping into the shop carrying one of our gift bags and an aqua blue bag. He was wearing a T-shirt and khaki shorts and looked rather miffed. At me? At his wife? At the world? I had the urge to call him by his former name but nipped that impulse.

"Afternoon, Sean. What brings you in?" I asked.

"Here." He thrust the aqua blue bag at me. "You forgot to pick up your pottery creations. We're heading out soon. Melody is packing up at the Pier. I'm in charge of the house."

I accepted the bag, but I didn't open it, reluctant to display the pottery Rhett and I had made in front of a discerning crowd. Who knew how it had turned out after being fired in the kiln? "Thank you. That was sweet of you." I stowed the bag behind the sales counter.

"Also, I need to return something." He rummaged in the Cookbook Nook gift bag and withdrew the swan salt and pepper shakers he had purchased. The neck on the pepper shaker had broken. "I didn't drop it or mishandle it. I'd like a refund."

"I'm sorry. This rarely happens, but when it does, of course we offer a refund." I took the pair from him. "Would you like me to find out if we have another set for you?"

"No, that's all right. Melody wasn't enamored with them anyway." Sean sneezed and withdrew a tissue from his pocket.

"Still suffering from allergies?"

He nodded as he blew his nose.

"Have you tried Coricidin?" I asked. "It's the one thing that works for me. That and Dymista. It's a spray."

I noticed a sharp movement to my left. Alan had pulled up short, pausing at the entrance from the breezeway into the shop. His hand was on Hannah's arm, holding her back. His ear was craned in my direction. No, not mine. In Sean's direction.

Quickly, I pulled cash from the register and handed it to Sean. "Here you go. No harm, no foul. If you see anything else you like—"

"No time."

"Well, it's been lovely having you in town. I hope you'll come back next year. Please tell your wife it was a delight to take a pottery class with her."

"Will do." He offered a winning smile and exited.

I disposed of the used gift bag and set the broken swan pieces on a shelf behind the register, and then scurried around the counter to Alan and Hannah. He was standing stock-still in the arch of the breezeway. "Alan, are you all right?"

"Who was that?" he asked, his voice shaky.

"Sean Beaufort. You might remember him from the fair-speak instructional taping."

"Was he one of the players?"

"No, he's Melody's husband."

"He's the person I heard in the field."

"Are you sure?" I asked. "Because I've been wondering whether you saw . . . I mean *heard* . . . Melody."

Hannah said, "Why would you think that?"

"It's a long story, but I believe she might be on the lam for killing a man, and I think she might have murdered Nick to protect the secret."

"No." Hannah's hand flew to her chest.

Bailey drew near. "How would Nick have found out about it?

Melody just met him."

"As it turns out, they knew each other years ago when she was known as Melody Shannon."

Alan gawked. "Meds? Melody Beaufort is Meds?" He scrubbed his jaw. "Wow."

"You knew her, too?" I asked.

"Sure. I went to Ren Camp. She was the queen three years in a row. She and Nick were boyfriend and girlfriend until her family left town. She must have been fourteen then. Nick kept in touch with her for a long time, but sometime after college she went off the grid. Man, Nick pined for her." He shook his head. "No way Melody would've killed him."

I said, "She's the same size as Hannah."

"So is Sean," Bailey said. "About as tall as you." She held a hand up as if to measure me.

I flashed on Pepper talking about the Beauforts the day they moved into her house; she said they seemed perfectly matched. "Alan, why are you so sure it was Sean?"

"Remember how I thought it was Hannah because I heard someone sneeze? It was his sneeze I heard. Plus he smells like clay. I didn't recall that scent until now."

I put a hand on Alan's arm. "Is it possible that the person who killed Nick stole your gauntlet from the hat-and-coat rack in the utility room?"

"Gosh, you're right." He smacked his thigh. "That's where I left it. Crow did a number on it. I had to rinse it off and leave it there to dry."

I added, "I think the killer also put on a sunhat to wear as a disguise."

Alan drew in a deep breath. "How can we prove it?"

Bailey said, "Jenna, have you forgotten that both Sean and Melody have alibis? They were together at the time of the murder."

"Not necessarily," I said. "Sean claimed he was with her, but Melody ran off and didn't hear him say that, so she didn't confirm it. Maybe he was lying to give himself an alibi. I need to talk to her."

Bailey hitched her thumb toward the door. "Sean said he's going to Pepper's house to finish up. Melody should be alone in their stall. Let's go."

I asked Tina to close up shop, fetched Tigger and my purse, and was hurrying out the door with Bailey when the idea of taking Melody a gift came to me. If I had a reason to visit, she might not get spooked. I snatched a bag, decorative tissue paper, and a pair of long-necked salt and pepper shakers—they weren't swans, but they would have to do—and raced to my VW.

# Chapter 23

When we arrived at the Pier, the sun was setting and the parking lot was half full. The entrance to the fair was still adorned with drapery, but the barker wasn't greeting fairgoers. He was bidding them adieu.

Bailey and I, with Tigger in tow—it was too warm to leave him in the car—hurried ahead. The crowd had dwindled to a handful of people, mostly exiting vendors.

As we neared Beaufort's Beautiful Pottery, Bailey clasped my arm. "Hold up." She pulled me into Hannah's empty stall. "Did you see that?"

"What?"

"Sean just entered their tent."

"Shoot."

"Melody must have called him for help. Stay here." Bailey put a hand on my shoulder. "I'll slip past and see what he's up to. At the end of the center aisle, I'll make a U-turn and hurry back."

"No, don't—"

I reached for her. Too late. She escaped my grasp and sped past the Beauforts' stall. Sneakily, she glimpsed to her right before barreling ahead as if she were a woman on a highly important mission.

Two minutes later she returned, chest heaving from the exertion. "Sean is withdrawing cash from their steamer trunk. Melody is packing the remaining pottery in bubble wrap. By the way, the Pier is like a ghost town. The Beauforts might be the last to leave, though Mum's the Word is teeming with customers."

I gripped Bailey's arm and put a finger to my lips. Sean was saying something to Melody. I caught the words *Honey* and *Dolly*. "Why are they talking about Dolly?"

"Maybe they plan to frame her?"

To hear better, I tiptoed to the tent wall. Bailey followed me.

Sean said, "When I return, I'll strap the boxes to the dolly to transport them."

"Dolly as in *dolly*," I muttered to my pal. "Not *Dolly*. What a dolt I am."

"It was an honest mistake."

Suddenly, Sean took off at a run. Bailey and I dropped to the ground to hide. Tigger squirmed in my arms but didn't make a sound. Smart cat.

When I saw Sean's feet disappear beyond the center aisle of stalls, I scrambled to a stand and hitched my purse higher on my shoulder. "Come with me." I raced into Melody's booth.

Bailey followed and positioned herself at the edge of the tent to keep watch.

"Hi, Melody," I said.

She was positioned between the two display tables, a piece of pottery in one hand and a sheet of bubble wrap in the other. The front table still held pottery. More bubble wrap and reels of shipping tape occupied the rear table. Towers of packed boxes stood on either side of the sales counter. More boxes rested on the floor of the stall and beneath the tables, creating an unmanageable maze.

"Hello," Melody rasped. She sounded near exhaustion. With the hand holding the bubble wrap she smoothed her rumpled plaid shirt. "How can I help you?"

"Sean came to the shop to return the swan salt and pepper shakers, but he didn't look for anything to replace them. I thought you might like these." I offered her the hastily prepared gift. "They're not swans, but they have long necks, like your pottery."

"Thanks. That was sweet of you. You can set the bag . . ." Her gaze swung from the tables that held the pottery, to the steamer trunk near the sales desk with its lid open and upper compartments empty, to the worktable on the right side of the tent that held pottery tools, its pale blue tablecloth removed. "There," she said, choosing the latter.

I set the bag down. "May I ask you a question? It's about Nick Baldini and Ren Camp." It wasn't a smooth segue, but it would have to do. With Sean on-site, time was of the essence.

Melody stiffened, her hands poised above the box of bubble wrap. "Ren Camp? What's that?"

"You know what it is, where kids learn to playact for the Renaissance Fair. You and Nick attended for years. There are pictures of you as a young girl on his Facebook page, and more photographs of you in albums at his house. Back then, you were known as Melody Shannon."

Her face paled.

I set Tigger on the ground. He immediately vaulted into the steamer trunk. "Tigger, no."

"Let him roam," Melody snapped. "Cats are curious. It appears some cat owners are, too."

"You were the Ren Camp queen a number of times. You had dark hair back then." Seeing as she didn't deny anything, I continued. "Alan said you moved away when you were fourteen."

"Alan—" She glanced toward the boardwalk and back at me. Under her breath, she said, "Alan knows who I am? Why hasn't he said anything?"

"He didn't recognize you because he had a sporting accident years ago that left him with face blindness."

"Then how—"

"I told him."

She kept mum. The truth, without Alan's ability to verify it, wasn't going to scare her into a lengthier confession.

"Alan said Nick lost touch with you after college. Why?"

"Lots of people lose touch. We didn't have a future." Melody jutted a hip. "If that's all, please leave. I'm in a hurry to finish up and get out of here." She covered the pottery with bubble wrap and pivoted to fetch the shipping tape.

"When did you meet Sean?"

The question must have caught her off guard because she glanced over her shoulder at me, blinking as if trying to remember. "A year . . ." She shook her head. "No, a year and a half after I graduated. I was working as an art teacher at an elementary school."

"In Columbus, Ohio."

She spun around, a reel of shipping tape hooked on a finger. "How did you—"

"Was it a long romance?"

"More like a speed train." A bittersweet memory glimmered in her eyes and quickly vanished. She tore off shipping tape, set the reel on the table with the pottery, and secured her package. She stowed it in an opened box beneath the table and then picked up an azure-colored vase and a fresh piece of bubble wrap. "He saw my potential as an artist and offered to support me so I could take more classes."

"Did he encourage you to enter competitions?"

"No, that was my —"

"Professor? The one you said was *complicated*? I believe his name was J. Daniel Loveland."

Melody's hands started to shake. She nearly dropped the vase.

I caught sight of Tigger's tail rising from the steamer trunk and heard his claws digging. I ignored whatever damage he was doing and continued. "I saw a picture of you on the Internet with Professor Loveland, when you won the ceramics award for Ohio's Future Artists."

Melody moaned.

I said, "I'm sure you thought that if you changed your identity your past would vanish, but you can't expunge everything in the ether. Your sister's review on Yelp, for example. That's how I figured out your maiden name."

Melody's panicked gaze swung to the exit and back to me. "Why are you doing this?"

"I want to know who killed Nick Baldini. I want justice for him."

"I told you the other day that I didn't kill him."

"At the time, you claimed you barely knew him. That was a lie."

Bailey said, "*Psst,*" and made a gesture to hurry up.

Adrenaline zinged through my veins. "Is Sean coming?"

"I don't see him," Bailey whispered, "but c'mon. Get moving."

"Why are you worried about Sean showing up?" Melody's voice trembled.

I met her gaze. "When Nick saw you on the Pier the first day of the fair, he knew you instantly. He pursued you at the fair-speak taping. He called you by your maiden name, Shannon, but you rebuffed him."

"Because I'm married."

"I didn't put two and two together until it dawned on me that the Post-it note he'd stuck on his computer with the word *Get MEDS* and a heart symbol wasn't a reminder to pick up heart medication; it was your nickname, one he used during the taping. Nick also wrote a note to *Fix it*. I think he hoped to fix whatever had happened between you two. Why did you lose touch? The truth. Was it Sean's idea?"

Melody shook her head. "No, it was mine. Nick wanted a normal life. I craved celebrity and fame. I intended to be a world-renowned ceramics potter, like Carol Long or Annie Woodford. Sean understood that. Now, really, it's time for you to leave." She dismissed me with a flick of her hand.

"You went to see Nick on the afternoon he died, didn't you? Around four thirty. What did the two of you talk about? Did you admit who you were?"

"I didn't—"

"You took him a vase like the one you're holding. You also brought him tomatoes from Pepper's garden. Why the tomatoes?"

She looked at me, eyes wide, and suddenly exhaled as if she'd been holding her breath for a long time and desperately needed oxygen.

"Melody?" I asked softly.

"He loved tomatoes. When we were kids, he . . . he . . ." Tears trickled from her eyes. She wiped them away. "Yes, I saw him. It was intense. Insane. The chemistry . . ." She shook her head. "When we kissed, I knew I never wanted to leave him. But I had to."

"Did you tell him why? Did you tell him that Melody Shannon needed to remain buried because she killed a professor? That was when your dream of fame evaporated, wasn't it?"

"That's not true. You don't understand. It was an accident. Professor Loveland was . . ." She hugged the vase and bubble wrap like they were her lifeline. "He was always groping me. What could I do? He ran the art school. He made the ultimate decision which work was featured and which items were entered in competitions. I . . ." She licked her lips. "When I admitted what was happening to Sean, he suggested that I teach Loveland a lesson. He said I should knock him out using sleeping pills, and added that if he ever tried to paw me again, I should tell him what I'd done and threaten to do worse."

"Sleeping pills?"

"Yes. I thought it was a brilliant plan, so I arranged a lunch meeting with Loveland when his secretary was out. Of course, he assumed I would be throwing myself at him." Bitter memories flickered in her eyes. "Sean sneaked into the office with me, to give me courage. I dosed Loveland's tea—he fancied a cup after lunch—and entered his office. We ate sandwiches and drank tea. Before I had to stomach another unwanted kiss, he fell asleep."

Melody batted the air and continued. "He was alive when I left his office, Jenna. I swear it. But the next thing I knew, I heard on the radio that he was dead. I'm not sure how it happened. Maybe he was allergic to the sleeping pills." She swallowed hard. "I wanted to go to the police, but Sean said we had to run. No one would believe me. He quit his job and we fled that night."

"The professor didn't die from an allergic reaction, Melody. He was poisoned with arsenic."

"Are you kidding?" She gagged. "I had no clue. Sean forbade me to listen to the radio after that. He didn't want me to relive the horror. He . . ." She paused; her face brightened. "Wait. If Loveland died from arsenic, then that means I didn't kill him."

Maybe not, but I knew who did. All Sean would have had to do was a sleight-of-hand trick like Tito had with the magic funnel. "Melody, you said Sean was with you, to give you courage. Is it possible that he added arsenic to the tea while you weren't looking?"

"He wouldn't have. He—"

"Why did Sean change his name to Beaufort after the professor died?"

"He said if we changed our names and got married, no one would find me. Ever. I didn't know what to do. I was scared." She moaned and wrapped her arms around her body. "We drove to Reno and eloped."

"Melody"—I touched her shoulder—"after arguing with Sean about Nick, you went for a walk on the beach. Did anyone see you?"

She shook her head. "No one was there because the queen's procession was taking place on the Pier."

"Sean claims he went to the beach with you."

"He didn't, but he didn't go to Nick's, either, if that's what you're suggesting. Our car was parked at Pepper's when I came back. He must have taken a walk, too."

Tigger sprang from the steamer trunk with something in his mouth. A ribbon that was attached to a shredded blue scroll.

"Tigger, stop." I leaped toward him and took the document. As if to avoid a scolding, he dove back into the steamer trunk. "Melody, I'm sorry—"

She snatched the document from me and a moan surged from deep within her.

"What is it?" I asked.

"Poetry."

"From Nick?"

She nodded. "Sean was so angry when it was delivered. I'd wondered what he'd done with it."

"Jenna," Bailey hissed. "I see Sean. Coming this way. Let's go."

When I heard the spanking of shoes on the boardwalk, my heart began to pummel my rib cage. At the same time, a theory occurred to me. "Melody, Sean is a long-distance runner, isn't he?"

She bobbed her head.

I whispered, "He could have run to Baldini Vineyards and back in less than an hour."

# Chapter 24

Bailey *eek*ed gleefully. "Whew! The mayor waylaid Sean. Saved by the bell."

I held up a finger. "One more quick question. Melody, Pepper said your husband was wearing his blue-and-gold costume when she saw the two of you arguing. Was he wearing it when you came back from your walk?"

"Why would you care?"

"Because if he killed Nick . . ." I twirled a hand, encouraging her to figure it out.

"It would be bloody," she finished, the words catching in her throat.

"Do you know where it is?"

"No." Melody squeezed the sheet of bubble wrap so hard a bubble burst. The *pop* made us both jump.

Tigger leaped out of the steamer trunk, a glove hanging from his mouth. Not any glove—a gauntlet.

I bolted to him and said, "Drop it." He did. I noticed something that looked like dried blood on it. Was it Nick's or Crow's? I scooped Tigger into my arms and caught a glimpse of something dark blue with gold trim at the bottom of the trunk. It was wedged beneath layers of pale blue tablecloths.

I set Tigger on the floor and dug my cell phone from my purse. "Bailey, there's evidence in the trunk."

"Evidence?"

"I think it's Sean's costume."

Melody keened. Her skin turned ash white, her eyelids fluttered, and she swooned.

I threw an arm around her and walked-dragged her through the labyrinth of boxes and display tables to the pottery wheel stations. I settled her onto a stool and steadied her with a hand. "Bailey, call Cinnamon." I flipped my cell phone to her. "Her number is in my speed-dial list."

After a moment, Bailey said, "She isn't answering."

"Call the precinct. Have them track her down now!"

I did my best to minister to Melody, patting her cheeks and rubbing her shoulders. She was as limp as a wet noodle.

Bailey said, "Cinnamon and Bucky are at Mum's the Word having dinner with my mom and your dad."

"To announce their engagement. Find them."

"But—"

"Go. I can't leave Melody. When Sean shows up, I'll think of something. Promise."

Bailey dashed off.

"Melody, c'mon, wake up," I whispered. "We've got to leave."

Languidly, she roused. "Wh-where am I?"

"In your stall on the Pier. You fainted. Let's get you on your feet."

"Thirsty. Water." She smacked her lips. "Thermos. On the sales desk."

"Can you sit by yourself?"

"Think so."

I propped her against the table, fetched the thermos, and sped back. I whisked off the top and handed the thermos to her. She drank greedily.

"Okay, that's enough," I said. "On your feet. We—"

The sound of creaky wheels paused outside. Sean. He must have broken free of the mayor. In an instant, he rounded the edge of the tent with the dolly. He seared me with his gaze, and my insides snarled like Tigger's ribbon.

"What's going on, Jenna?" he asked. "Why are you here?"

Faster than you could spell *lie*, I said, "I brought Melody a replacement set of salt and pepper shakers." I pointed to the gift bag. "I think the sentiment made her faint." I stroked Melody's upper back. "Are you feeling better?"

Her eyes betrayed her; she was scared spitless.

Sean set the dolly near the stack of boxes by the sales desk, locked the wheels, and gazed at me like a raptor assessing its prey. Then he glanced at Melody. Her shoulders were trembling. "What did you tell her, honey?"

"N-nothing."

"The truth."

Melody stared at him as if mesmerized. "You lied to Jenna."

"About?"

"About your alibi for the night Nick was killed. You didn't go to the beach with me."

*Swell.* I'd hoped she was made of sturdier stuff and wouldn't crack.

I met Sean's cruel gaze and raised my chin. As far back as elementary school, my father had told me to face my adversaries with defiance. "You didn't believe she was going to the beach, did you, Sean? You were certain she'd sneaked off to see Nick. You were jealous, so you hightailed it up there."

"Me, jealous?"

"Like you were of Professor Loveland."

"Professor *Who*?"

"She knows," Melody rasped.

"Knows what?" His gaze swung to me.

"I know you used to be Sean Ballantyne," I said. "And Melody was born Melody Shannon."

He cut a harsh look at his wife. She bowed her head.

"I found evidence about the professor's death online," I went on. "I copied the links and sent them to the police." The moment the words spilled out of my mouth, I mentally kicked myself for not having done exactly that. *Next time,* I promised. If I lived to see a next time.

"But I'm getting ahead of myself," I said. "When you arrived at the vineyard, Hannah was there, so you waited until she left. Maybe, in the meantime, you scoped out the place, believing you might spy your wife holed up inside the house. Even though you didn't, you stole inside. You wanted to take on Nick. How dare he flirt with your wife and send her poetry? How dare he screw up your life? You entered through the utility room. You saw the vase your wife made as well as the tomatoes from Pepper's garden in the kitchen. If you hadn't lost it yet, that put you over the edge. Those items confirmed your suspicion. Melody *had* been there. Am I warm?"

Sean grunted. His eyes narrowed. His lips parted, like he wanted to say something. To confess or to brag?

Banking on the latter, I said, "You were worried that she had revealed your secret, so you hunted down Nick. Where was he?"

"On the verandah."

"What did you say?"

"I told him I'd fix him."

The word *fix* made me think of Nick's note: *Fix it.* Maybe I hadn't been the only person investigating the Beauforts. Maybe Nick had discovered everything I had and hoped to *fix* or *repair* Melody's past. If Cinnamon studied Nick's Internet history, would she find links to Melody and Sean and the professor?

I said, "Nick figured out the truth, didn't he, Sean?"

His eyes flickered with irritation. *Oh, yeah, I was right.*

"He linked you to Professor Loveland and his death and told you so. What happened next? Did he threaten to call the police? Is that when you raced to the utility room and grabbed the winepress he'd stowed there? Did you hope by killing him with it that you could implicate Hannah in his death? They'd fought. You were a key witness."

I glimpsed the bloody gauntlet lying beside the steamer trunk.

Sean caught me looking in that direction and seized it. He tossed it back inside and slammed the trunk's lid with such force that Melody shrieked. Then he dashed across the tent and grabbed the clay hammer and the mallet off the pottery tool table. "You think you're so smart." He moved toward the rear of the tent, his intent obvious — to disable me and reclaim Melody.

"C'mon." I hauled Melody to her feet and steered her around the pottery wheel stations, toppling stools as we passed to create an obstacle for her husband. "Your wife is leaving you, Sean. Whether today or a month or a year from now, she will leave. She never loved you. She only married you because you convinced her you could save her."

"I did save her."

"You let her believe she killed the professor."

As we neared the steamer trunk, Melody staggered. "Buck up," I urged.

One of the stacks of boxes as well as the cartons on the floor blocked our exit, but if we could squeeze between the trunk and the tent wall . . .

"Melody, stop!" Sean hurdled over the second stool and the third.

Melody banged her toe on the trunk's corner and winced.

"Melody, I'm ordering you," Sean bellowed as he clambered over the fourth stool.

I heard the scrabbling of claws right before Tigger darted beneath a pottery wheel station and attacked Sean's bare ankle.

"Off, cat!" Sean shook his leg.

Tigger tumbled sideways. Brave kitty, he didn't whimper.

"The professor had to be brought down a peg, Melody." Sean continued toward us. "You agreed with that."

"Murder is more than a peg," I said as I wedged my foot between the trunk and tent wall. I shoved; the trunk didn't budge an inch.

"He had to be taught a lesson, honey," Sean said. "He fawned over you. He told you what an amazing artist you were. I told you the same thing, but you didn't look at me like you looked at him."

"No, Sean. I didn't look at him. Ever. You're wr-wrong," Melody stammered. "I didn't. You're *wrong.*"

"I couldn't let him win your heart."

"How about Nick?" I goaded, realizing what kind of man Sean was at his core—a dominating egomaniac who inspired fear and resentment, not trust and respect. "Did he look at her with lust?"

"Don't, Jenna," Melody begged.

"Nick was a dead man the moment I saw him. He was a lout. A no-good." Sean bolted around the last pottery station and paused. Cartons blocked his path as they had ours.

"But he won her heart," I said as I tried again to move the steamer trunk. No luck. Melody and I were trapped. I whirled on Sean, arms raised, ready to defend us both.

He raised the claw hammer overhead.

"Did he undress her with his eyes?" I taunted.

"Yes."

"Did he make her blush?"

Sean uttered a guttural rumbling sound. "He wanted her in the shameless way men always want women. He didn't put her on a pedestal. He didn't adore her."

"She was ready to run off with him," I said.

"No," Sean rasped.

"No," Melody mewled, but her voice held no conviction.

Sean waved the hammer close to my face. "Release my wife and you won't get hurt."

"Gee, why don't I believe you?"

Tigger sprang on top of the stack of boxes closest to Sean and hissed. Sean jeered at him.

Thanks to the distraction, I maneuvered Melody to the left,

through a narrow slot between cartons. We wound up in the space between the display tables with no place to go, blocked yet again by more boxes.

"That's far enough," Sean said and hurled the clay hammer.

I ducked just in time—the hammer's head whizzed by my left ear—but I lost hold of Melody. She tried to grip the table for balance but missed and crumpled to the floor.

"I'm going to kill you, Jenna," Sean said, wielding the remaining weapon—the mallet. "I'm going to bash in your skull. All that will be left is a pile of mush."

Fear lodged in my throat. I tamped it down and rose to my full height. "Speaking of bashing, Sean, you destroyed Nick's cell phone to get rid of the record of his call to your wife, didn't you? Then you stole a hat off the coat rack to disguise yourself and fled through the vineyard. His brother Alan heard you. He'll verify it was you."

"He *heard* me?" Sean said, catching my misstep.

"Alan has face blindness," Melody said.

Sean sneered. "Then he can't prove a thing. You have nothing on me."

"We have enough," I said, "Alan identified you when you were in my shop earlier."

"Worthless in a court of law."

Sean kicked a carton out of the way and stumbled forward, the rear display table the only thing standing between him and me. He leaned forward and swung the mallet. It whooshed close to my chin. I dropped to my knees and considered scrambling toward the exit, but I couldn't leave Melody behind. I didn't think he would hurt her, but I wasn't certain.

Where were Bailey and Cinnamon? What was taking them so long?

"The police have a heel print," I said. The lie was brazen, but Sean didn't know that. "It will match the shoes you wore with your costume."

"Liar."

He knocked packing supplies to the floor, crawled over the rear table, and wailed at me with the mallet. The head connected with my shoulder. Pain radiated down my arm.

"Sean, stop!" Melody screamed.

"Hush, woman!" Petruchio couldn't have said it more forcefully. "Sit there and bite your tongue, or else . . ."

"Or else what?" To my surprise, she scrambled to her feet.

Her defiance didn't last long. He backhanded her and sent her reeling over a box. She landed in a heap by the worktable.

*So much for treating her like porcelain,* I mused, which gave me an idea. I reached overhead, seized a piece of navy blue pottery, and cracked its neck on the table's edge. The remaining piece wasn't long, but it was sharp.

With a forceful thrust, I jabbed and connected with Sean's bare calf. He howled and bent to take another swing at me. His thigh was a perfect target; I stabbed again.

At the same moment, Cinnamon raced into the tent. "Stand up, Mr. Beaufort. Hands behind your back." She aimed her gun. "Now."

Cursing me and my entire family, Sean rose to his full height.

"Sorry we're late," Bailey said as she rushed into the tent with Bucky on her heels. "They had left the diner. I caught them right as they were getting into their car."

"Jenna, fill me in," Cinnamon said as she handcuffed Sean. "What is going on?"

"This man's real name is Ballantyne, Chief. Sean Ballantyne, former professor at Ohio State. He's wanted in connection with the death of an art professor."

"That's a lie," Sean said. "Melody killed him."

"No, she didn't." As speedily as I could, I laid out the specifics for Cinnamon. When I finished, I added, "By the way, you'll find one of Sean's costumes in that trunk. I believe it will have Nick's blood on it. There's a gauntlet in the trunk, too. It belongs to Alan Baldini, but he reported it stolen. I think there's dried blood on it, and I would bet dollars to dimes it's not the crow's blood."

Needless to say, Cinnamon wasn't happy that I'd taken it upon myself to confront him even though I swore on my mother's grave — and Bailey backed me up — that I'd come to the Pier to question Melody and only Melody. The way Cinnamon said *We'll talk* let me know I was in for a long, not-so-friendly chat.

# Chapter 25

Three weeks later, Bailey's and Tito's families and friends celebrated their union on the verandah at Baldini Vineyards. The weather was near perfect: a gentle breeze, temperatures in the seventies, and blue skies with a hint of cloud cover that would make wedding photographs a snap.

The person presiding over the wedding was none other than Old Jake, who had obtained his certificate to officiate after realizing that one of his greatest joys in life was bringing two people together in matrimony. He concluded Tito's vows and addressed Bailey. Though typically gnarled and weathered from driving the tractor around on the beach, Jake, like the other male attendees, looked particularly distinguished in his tuxedo. What was it about tuxedos that upped a man's game?

"Bailey Bird"—Jake cleared his throat as he drew the wedding to its conclusion—"do you take this man to be your lawful husband, to have and to hold from this day forward, for better, for worse, for richer, for poorer, in sickness and in health, to love and to cherish, till death do you part?"

"I do," Bailey said, her voice catching ever so slightly.

I'd never seen her look more beautiful. Her skin was glowing. Her eye makeup matched the moss green tones of the décor; her lipstick was burgundy. The beading on the neckline of her ecru off-the-shoulder gown glimmered in the sunshine. Her bouquet was exactly as Nick had described—luscious yet subdued. He had made copious notes that the wedding planner—not Hannah; she wasn't ready to take the lead—had followed. We all felt Nick's presence at the ceremony. How could we not?

"I now pronounce you man and wife." Jake smiled at Tito. "Young man, you may kiss the bride."

As they exchanged a sweet kiss, the crowd applauded. The wedding photographer swooped in for a close-up. Alan, having decided that he'd prefer to be a guest at the wedding rather than serve as the wedding photographer, had hired a professional.

When they came up for air, a guitarist began to play and sing "Hermosa Cariño," which translates to *beautiful love*. It is one of Tito's favorite songs and was a surprise addition from Bailey. She elbowed him and he poked her in return. I was overjoyed to see them so happy.

Rhett slung an arm around me and said, "May I buy the maid of honor a drink?"

"You sure may. But, FYI, I'm matron of honor. I was once married." It was the first time in a long time that I'd mused about David without a pang of guilt wrenching my heart; I took it as a sign that I was healing.

I clutched Rhett's elbow and traipsed along the travertine tile, making sure I didn't trip in my high heels. Bailey had forbidden me to wear flip-flops. Even I had to admit that the knee-length, burgundy-toned scarf dress she'd chosen for me went better with heels. I particularly liked the dramatic drape of the bodice.

We made our way to the bar, where Cinnamon and Bucky were accepting glasses of white wine. When she caught sight of me, she couldn't help herself. She glowered.

"C'mon, let it go," I begged as I took two glasses of pinot noir and handed one to Rhett. "How long are you going to stay mad at me?"

When Cinnamon debriefed me, I shared everything that I'd discovered. I reminded her that I had left messages for her numerous times to bring her up to date. For some reason, that hadn't appeased her. She concluded that I was stupid to look into anything. The word *stupid* had stung, but I had been smart enough to keep my mouth shut.

"Please, Cinnamon," I tried again. "Mahatma Gandhi said, 'The weak can never forgive. Forgiveness is the attribute of the strong.'"

She straightened the seams of her body-hugging taupe sheath. "Did you memorize that to taunt me?"

"It happens to be one of my father's favorites. You know Dad's penchant for quotations."

A reluctant grin tugged at the corners of her mouth, but she didn't allow it to morph into an out-and-out smile. She is stubborn; I'll grant her that.

Rhett jumped in. "Bucky and Cinnamon, I don't think I've said congratulations yet. May you have a long and happy life together."

Bucky chortled. "Thanks, bro. If we can ever pick a venue, a date, and a set of wedding songs, we'll be as happy as—"

"Don't say it," Cinnamon warned. "We will. We're making headway."

"Finding you a dress is not making headway. It's—"

"I beg to differ," I cut in. "That's probably the most important thing to the bride."

Cinnamon shot me a finger. "See? Girlfriends know these things."

The fact that she referred to me as her *girlfriend* meant I was close to being on good terms with her. *Close.* We would mend bridges soon. We had to. We were nearly family.

"Speaking of happy couples," I said, "Alan has asked Hannah to marry him."

"Aren't they moving a little fast?" Rhett asked.

"Not really. He's been in love with her for years, and as it turns out, she's had her eye on him for about the same time."

"What about her grandmother?" Cinnamon asked.

"Alan agreed to sign any contract the woman wants to assure her that he, as the titular head of Baldini Vineyards, is not usurping water rights, nor will he or Hannah ever allow the vineyards to become one entity. If that doesn't win her over, he's vowed to stay engaged to Hannah until her grandmother kicks the bucket."

"So he's going to run the vineyard?" Rhett asked.

"Yep. He asked Frank to stay on as foreman. Frank is happy to do so. He has worked for Baldini Vineyards for decades. Alan will continue to do the books. He'll also become the spokesman for the product, which the executor for the trust supports."

"Happy endings for all," my father said, joining the conversation.

"Not necessarily all," Lola said as she swept the skirt of her chiffon dress to one side and accepted a glass of champagne from the bartender. "Tell them, Jenna." She took a sip of wine.

"With the revelation about Sean," I said, "Melody realized she'd never known him. She has filed for an annulment in Nevada, claiming he coerced her into marriage through fraud. Once that's completed, she intends to turn herself in to the authorities in Ohio and face the consequences. She would like to live life without fear."

"She'll be exonerated, won't she?" Rhett turned to Cinnamon for the answer.

Cinnamon shrugged. "It's tough to say. It depends on the evidence her attorney can drum up."

I raised a finger. "Melody has always been diligent about saving receipts. She's hoping her lawyer can find a paper trail proving that Sean purchased arsenic."

"What about Sean?" Rhett asked.

"He's facing charges here first," Cinnamon said. "By the way, Jenna, I don't think I told you, but he admitted to being the person sneaking around outside your cottage. He heard you asking Alan questions at Hannah's stall that day and was worried you might figure out he was the one who sneezed in the vineyard. Deputy Appleby's arrival scared him off. You don't have to worry about prowlers."

Even though I felt a huge surge of relief, ever since the incident I had been diligent about checking my doors and windows to make sure they were secure. I doubted I would give up the habit any time soon.

"Jenna, how's Dolly?" Lola asked.

"She's settling into L.A. nicely," I said. "Last week she texted that she met with the psychic Aunt Vera recommended. The woman sees nothing but positive events in her future."

A whoosh of orange streaked by our feet, followed by a streak of black. Tigger and Hershey—Bailey and Tito's cat—were chasing each other. Tito had been adamant that Hershey attend the wedding and that Tigger come as Hershey's guest. He'd even put beautiful bows on the cats' necks.

"Tigger," I cried. "Slow down, buddy."

Seconds later, Tigger whizzed by me again, followed by Hershey and another streak of orange.

"What the heck?" I said. "What was that?"

"A stray." Alan approached with Hannah, who looked absolutely stunning in a sleek charcoal-colored sheath.

"A stray?" I said. "She's not your cat, Alan?"

"Nope. Can't have cats around here with my birds of prey. Not to mention there are plenty of wild red-tailed hawks and great horned owls about."

I shivered at the notion.

"She showed up yesterday," he went on. "I think the aroma of tuna tartar enticed her. Bailey was adamant that we have mounds of the stuff."

"How do you know it's a *her*?" Rhett asked.

"Animal anatomy 101," Alan gibed. "I picked her up. Anybody want a cat? Jenna, I think Tigger likes her."

Tigger and the stray were going at it in a friendly way. As they tumbled, they blurred into one big ball of orange. Hershey sat nearby, stoically watching them with fascination.

Rhett elbowed me. "Love is definitely in the air."

I whacked his arm. "Stop."

"Speaking of which . . ." He pulled me close and set his mouth next to my ear.

The warmth of his breath set my insides reeling in a good way.

Cinnamon wagged a finger. "Uh-uh, no secrets. What did he say?"

"Nothing," I replied.

"No secrets," the others chimed in unison.

"Out with it," Cinnamon ordered.

I grinned at Rhett and said, "We'll talk."

"You'll talk?" Lola cried. "About what? C'mon. Are you two—" She wagged a finger between us. "Cary, make them talk." She nudged my father.

"Jenna?" he asked.

"For us to know," I said.

Rhett slung his arm around me and guided me away from the group. "You're a tease."

"Who's calling the kettle black?" I poked him in the ribs. "So, what were you going to say after 'Speaking of which'?"

He laughed out loud. "We'll talk."

# Recipes

## Meat on a Stick

From Jenna:

*You know me and how much I like easy recipes. Well, this one is easy! And the result is simple to eat, too. Sure, it's a little messy, but it's fun to lick your fingers. FYI, this is Lola's recipe. If you can't eat gluten, substitute the soy sauce with gluten-free tamari sauce.*

(Makes 8–12)

*For the sauce:*
3 tablespoons soy sauce
2 tablespoons rice vinegar
3 teaspoons sugar, divided
1 teaspoon grated fresh ginger
salt and pepper
Olive oil, for basting

*For the skewers:*
1 1/2 pounds boneless skinless chicken breasts, cut into 1-inch strips

*You will need bamboo skewers, pre-soaked in water for 3 hours.*

In a small bowl, whisk together soy sauce, rice vinegar, 1 teaspoon sugar, and grated ginger. Pour half of the mixture into another small bowl and set aside.

Onto soaked bamboo skewers, thread chicken strips. Sprinkle skewers with salt and pepper. Baste with olive oil.

Grill 8–10 minutes on medium high or until cooked through, brushing with sauce each time you turn.

To the reserved sauce, stir in 2 teaspoons sugar. Drizzle sauce over cooked skewers just before serving, if desired.

## Cornish Pasties

From Katie:

*The trick to pasties is making sure they cook all the way through. This is really stew in a closed pie shell. So delicious; so easy; so basic. Feel free to add spices that you like. A dash of cinnamon or cloves might be nice. A teaspoon of rosemary could taste wonderful. Be creative. If you'd like to make a vegetarian version, substitute chopped rutabaga for the meat.*

(Serves 6)

*For the pastry:*
2 1/8 cup all-purpose flour, more for dusting
1/4 teaspoon salt
1 teaspoon baking powder
1/2 cup butter, diced
1/2 cup water, more if necessary

*For the filling:*
2 small carrots, chopped and cooked as below
3/4 pound beef stew meat, cut into very small cubes (about 1 1/2 cups)
1/2 onion, chopped fine
1/2 russet potato, peeled and diced fine
1/2 teaspoon salt
1/2 teaspoon ground black pepper
2 tablespoons milk

In a medium bowl, mix flour, salt, and baking powder together. Add butter and mix until it is the consistency of coarse crumbs. Add in water. If dough is sticky, add more flour. If the dough is too dry, add more water. Divide dough into six portions and roll each into a small ball.

Sprinkle a piece of parchment paper with flour, set a ball of dough on the paper, and top with a second piece of parchment paper. Roll dough into a circle about 5 inches around and 1/4 inch thick. Peel off the paper. Fill with filling (see direction below). Repeat for the remaining balls of dough.

Preheat oven to 450 degrees F.

In a small saucepan, cover chopped carrots with water. Bring water to a boil and cook until tender, about 4–6 minutes. Pour off water. Let carrots cool.

In a large bowl, mix the cooked carrots, raw meat, onion, potatoes, salt, and pepper.

Scoop the meat filling (about 1/2 cup) onto the pastry base, leaving the edge free. Moisten the pastry edges with water (you can use your clean fingers), and then fold pastry over the filling. Press the edges together with your fingers and then impress with the tines of a fork.

Transfer uncooked pasties to a baking sheet lined with parchment paper. Brush the tops with milk and make a small slit in each top to allow steam to flow out.

Turn oven down to 350 degrees F and bake the pasties for 35–40 minutes or until they are a nice golden brown. Let cool slightly before serving.

*For a gluten-free version, substitute 2 1/8 cup gluten-free flour mixed with 1/2 teaspoon xanthan gum for the all-purpose flour. Note: the pastry will be less pliable. Do your best when it's time to bend and fold. Be forgiving if the pastry breaks. It will. You might need to add more water to this mixture. You also might want to dust each ball of dough with cornstarch before rolling out.*

## Ginger Cheesecake

From Katie:

*This is a fifteenth-century-style recipe that I discovered on a medieval cuisine site on the Internet. The recipe was translated from a book from the fifteenth century. We wanted to serve something authentic during the Renaissance Fair. I wasn't quite sure the measurements would work out, so I tweaked a bit, but I have to admit, this was a real find. It's a dense cake. It's packed with protein because of the egg whites. The ginger makes it so flavorful. I personally like my addition of graham crackers for the crust. And, get this, I made my own rosewater to spritz on the top. I share that recipe below, enjoy!*

(Serves 8–12)

*Cheesecake crust:*
4–6 graham crackers (regular or gluten-free), crushed
3 tablespoons butter, melted

*Cheesecake filling:*
18 ounces ricotta cheese
6 large egg whites
2 tablespoons powdered ginger
1/3 cup milk
3/4 cup sugar
3/4 cup butter, melted
2 tablespoons rosewater, see below
2 tablespoons white sugar

Preheat oven to 350 degrees F.

Prepare a spring-form pan by lining it with parchment paper. Prepare the cookie crust by mixing the crushed graham crackers and melted butter in a small bowl. Press the cookie mixture into the bottom of the spring-form pan.

In a large bowl, beat cheese and egg whites until smooth. Add ginger, milk, sugar, and melted butter to the egg and cheese mixture, and beat well so there are no lumps.

Pour the cheese mixture onto the crust and bake for 50–55 minutes. Turn off oven and let cake stand for 1 hour.

Remove from oven. Just after the cake comes out of the oven, sprinkle with rosewater and fine sugar. Let cool to room temperature or refrigerate before serving.

### *How to Make Your Own Rosewater*

From Katie:

*What is rosewater good for other than a simple spritz on a cheesecake? Check out the properties on the Internet. You'll see that rosewater helps maintain the skin's pH balance. It has anti-inflammatory properties that help reduce the redness of irritated skin. Its antioxidant properties can help strengthen skin cells. And so much more.*

Gather 5–7 roses that are free of pesticides. Remove petals from stems and run them under lukewarm water to remove any dust or pests from the garden.

Put the petals into a large pot and top with enough water to cover. Don't add any more water or you'll dilute your rosewater.

Over medium heat, bring the water to a boil. Reduce to simmer and let cook for 20 minutes. The petals will have lost their color and will turn pale pink.

Using a slotted spoon, remove the petals from the water. Discard the petals and store water in a glass jar. Refrigerate when cool. Makes 2–3 cups.

## Hawker's Mush

From Jenna:

*Hawker's Mush happens to be one of Rhett's and my favorite dishes at the fair. It's basic yet so delicious. Think of it like potato pancakes. If you can't eat garlic, leave it out. The onions add plenty of flavor on their own. Also, I have to admit that I had no idea how easy hollandaise sauce was to make. What a find!*

(Yield: 6–8 servings)

4 tablespoons or more butter
1 large onion, chopped (about 1 1/2 cups)
4 cups raw spinach, chopped (becomes about 2 cups)
1 tablespoon fresh thyme, chopped, or 1 teaspoon dried thyme
2 cloves garlic, crushed
2 tablespoons sherry
1/2 teaspoon salt
1/4 teaspoon ground black pepper
2 cups cooked brown rice and wild rice mix
3 eggs, beaten
Hollandaise sauce (recipe below)

In a medium-sized frying pan, melt butter over medium heat. Sauté onions until soft and beginning to turn golden brown, about 8–10 minutes. If the onions seem dry, add another tablespoon of butter. Then add raw chopped spinach.

Sauté until all the moisture from the spinach is absorbed, about 2 minutes. Turn heat down and add the thyme, crushed garlic, and sherry. Add salt and pepper. Simmer until all liquid is absorbed, about 2–4 minutes more. Cool 5 minutes.

In a large bowl combine the cooked brown rice and wild rice, the onion-spinach mixture, and the beaten eggs.

For this next step, you'll have to do it in batches: in a medium frying pan, melt 1 tablespoon butter. Add rice-onion-spinach mixture in 1/2-cup portions. Flatten each down so you have rounds about 1/2 inch thick. Cook over medium heat until set, about 2–3 minutes. Flip over and cook until golden.

Slide onto a plate and put in a warm oven. Repeat until entire mixture is cooked.

Keep warm. When ready, serve with hollandaise sauce.

### *Hollandaise Sauce*

(Yield: 3/4 cup)

3 egg yolks
1/4 teaspoon Dijon mustard
1 tablespoon lemon juice
1/4 teaspoon white pepper
1/2 cup butter (one stick)

In the blender, combine the egg yolks, mustard, lemon juice, and white pepper. Blend for about 5–10 seconds.

Put the butter into a microwave-safe bowl or measuring cup and melt completely, about 30–45 seconds.

Set the blender on high speed and add the melted butter to the egg mixture in a thin stream. It will thicken up fast.

*Neat trick: You can keep the sauce warm until serving by placing the blender itself in a pan of hot water.*

## Heathen "Cakes"

From Katie:

*This recipe is really rustic and a little time-intensive because of the "stew" that you make first, but it's hearty and the aromas are divine. Think of this as a meat pie or meat quiche, and you've got the idea. You can make a homemade piecrust, of course, but a store-bought crust will do in a pinch.*

(Serves 6–8)

1 piecrust
1 pound beef stew meat
1/2 small onion, peeled and chopped
1 carrot, peeled and chopped
1 stalk celery, chopped
water
3 teaspoons salt, divided
1 teaspoon basil
1 teaspoon oregano
6 slices center-cut bacon, cooked crisp and crumbled
1 large pippin apple, peeled and diced
1/2 teaspoon ground black pepper
6 large eggs

Preheat oven to 400 degrees F.

Set parchment paper in center of premade piecrust. Top with rice or beans. Bake piecrust 10–12 minutes. Remove from oven. Remove parchment and rice or beans. Set piecrust aside.

In a stockpot, combine stew meat, onion, carrot, celery, 2 teaspoons salt, basil, and oregano, and enough water to cover. Bring to a simmer and cook on medium low until meat is fork tender, about 30 minutes. Remove meat from stock with a slotted spoon and let cool. When cool, shred or cut into tiny bites. You may discard stock or keep. It's delicious!

In a skillet, cook bacon until crisp, about 6–8 minutes. Remove bacon and let drain on paper towel. Do *not* throw out bacon fat. When cool, crumble bacon.

Now, cook the apple in bacon fat until tender, about 6–8 minutes. Remove apples and drain on paper towel.

In a large bowl, whisk the eggs. Add shredded beef, apples, crumbled bacon, the remaining teaspoon of salt, and ground pepper. Mix gently. Turn the mixture into pre-baked piecrust. Press down mixture, if necessary.

Bake at 400 degrees F for 40–45 minutes, until the pie is set. Remove from oven and let cool slightly. Serve warm.

*Note: If you feel your piecrust is getting too brown, you can cover the edges with foil for the last 20 minutes of baking.*

## Scotch Eggs

From Katie:

*These are very savory and very salty. If you need to, remove the salt. No matter what, have fun when you make the sausage and wrap the eggs. It's like being a kid again and playing with clay.*

(Serves 4)

1 pound bulk pork sausage
1 teaspoon dried parsley
1 teaspoon salt
4 hard-boiled eggs, peeled
Flour or cornstarch (to make gluten-free, use cornstarch or rice flour)
1 egg, beaten
3/4 cup panko crispy breadcrumbs (if necessary, use gluten-free crumbs)

Heat oven to 400 degrees F.

In a large bowl, mix pork sausage, parsley, and salt. You'll need to use your hands. Shape mixture into 4 patties.

Roll each hard-boiled egg in flour (or cornstarch/rice flour) to coat.

Place egg on sausage patty and cover egg by wrapping sausage around it. Dip each hard-boiled/sausage egg into beaten egg. Coat with panko breadcrumbs to cover completely (you may use gluten-free panko crumbs).

Set on ungreased cookie sheet. Bake 35 minutes or until sausage is thoroughly cooked through and no longer pink near the egg.

## *How to Make the Perfect Hard-Boiled Egg*

In a medium saucepan, cover 4 eggs with water. Bring water to boil. This takes about 7 minutes. Reduce heat to simmer and cook for 13 minutes. Remove saucepan from heat and immediately pour off hot water. Add cold water to the saucepan.

Meanwhile, fetch a dozen or so ice cubes from your freezer. Pour off the water from the eggs, and add fresh cold water and ice cubes. Let sit for 20 minutes. Remove eggs from water. Store in refrigerator until using.

## Shepherd's Pie

From Katie:

*Shepherd's pie was originally called "cottage pie" because the poorer people of Britain, who lived in cottages, started using potatoes in their everyday diet. Nowadays, a dish made with beef is referred to as cottage pie, while a dish made with lamb is shepherd's pie. I have fun scoring the mashed potato topping. I hope you do, too.*

(Serves 6–9)

1 to 1 1/2 pounds potatoes (about 1–2 large brown potatoes), peeled and quartered
2 teaspoons salt, divided
8 tablespoons (1 stick) butter, divided (more, if necessary)
2 medium onions, chopped (about 2 cups)
1 cup diced carrots
1 1/2 pounds ground lamb
2 teaspoons ground black pepper, divided
2 teaspoons Worcestershire sauce
1 cup broth (more, if necessary; beef or chicken will do)
1 teaspoon rosemary
1 cup peas
2 tablespoons cream or milk (more, if desired)
Cheese, if desired

First, peel and quarter the potatoes. Then place the potatoes in a medium-sized stockpot and cover them with cold water. Add a teaspoon of salt. Bring the potatoes to a boil and reduce to simmer. Cook until tender, about 20 minutes; a fork should be able to easily pierce them. When done, drain the water, but leave the potatoes in the pot.

Next, melt 4 tablespoons of the butter in a large sauté pan over medium heat. Add the chopped onions and carrots and cook until tender, about 6–10 minutes.

Add the ground lamb to the pan with the onions. Break into small pieces with the side of a spoon. Cook the meat until no longer pink. Season with 1/2 teaspoon salt and 1/2 teaspoon pepper. Add the Worcestershire sauce, broth, and rosemary. Bring the broth to a simmer and reduce heat to low. Cook uncovered for 10 minutes, adding more broth, if necessary, to keep the meat from drying out. Add the peas, stir, and then remove meat mixture from heat.

Add the remaining 4 tablespoons of butter to the potatoes that you have reserved in the stockpot, plus add 2 tablespoons cream or milk. Mash with a fork or potato masher, and season with 1/2 teaspoon salt and 1/2 teaspoon pepper. (Add more butter, cream, or milk if necessary so potatoes are moist.)

Preheat oven to 400 degrees F.

Place the meat mixture in an 8 x 8 pan. Top with the mashed potatoes. Score the surface of the mashed potatoes with a fork so there are peaks that will get well browned. Be creative.

Place casserole in oven and cook until browned and bubbling, about 20–30 minutes. If necessary, broil for the last few minutes to help the surface of the mashed potatoes brown.

If desired, sprinkle grated cheddar cheese or Parmesan cheese over the top of the mashed potatoes before baking.

* For a 13 x 9 pan, double the recipe.

## Sin-in-a-Cup
### Frozen Cheesecake Bites

From Katie:

*These are easy but messier than all get-out to prepare. You'll want to lick your fingers a lot. Try not to or you will OD on chocolate. LOL. Also, don't be disappointed if the first few times you try to make them they don't turn out "pretty." Working with chocolate and ice cube trays isn't easy. But the result is divine. Remember, you'll want a square-shaped ice cube tray, not the rectangular kind. If you do use the rectangular kind, then forgo serving these little tasty treats in mini muffin cups.*

(Makes 12)

8–12 ounces semi-sweet chocolate chips (8 ounces is probably ample)
1 tablespoon coconut oil
8 ounces cream cheese, softened
2 tablespoons sour cream
1/3 cup powdered sugar
1 tablespoon liqueur (I like an orange-based liqueur like Grand Marnier)
pinch of kosher salt
12 raspberries

*You will need a 12-cube ice cube mold and, if desired, mini cupcake holders.*

In a medium bowl, microwave the chocolate chips and coconut oil for 30 seconds. Stir. Microwave longer, if necessary, until just melted, about 15–30 seconds more. It's okay on this round of microwaving if the mixture is not completely smooth. Don't overcook.

Pour a teaspoon of the melted chocolate into each ice cube mold. Using clean fingers, press the chocolate around the sides of the mold completely. Freeze the mold until the chocolate is solid, about 10 minutes. If you feel you didn't get enough chocolate around the mold, remove from freezer and add more chocolate and repeat the pressing and freezing action. You'd like a nice "crust" to form.

Meanwhile, in another medium bowl, combine cream cheese and sour cream. Beat with a hand mixer until smooth. Add powdered sugar, liqueur, and salt, and mix until fluffy and light.

Remove the ice cube mold from the freezer and fill 12 cubes about half full with the cream cheese mixture. Press a raspberry into the center of each cube. Fill the rest of the cube with the cream cheese mixture and top with melted chocolate. (You might need to remelt the chocolate. Again, don't overcook. Zap in 15-second intervals. Do not overcook. You do not want the chocolate to *seize*.)

Freeze the mold until the mixture is solid, about 90 minutes.

Invert the mold to release the cubes. If you need to, twist the mold to make the treats pop out, or loosen each treat with a knife. Serve in mini cupcake holders, if desired. Keep frozen whatever you don't eat.

# About the Author

Daryl Wood Gerber is the Agatha Award–winning, nationally bestselling author of the French Bistro Mysteries, featuring a bistro owner in Napa Valley, as well as the Cookbook Nook Mysteries, featuring an admitted foodie and owner of a cookbook store in Crystal Cove, California. Under the pen name Avery Aames, Daryl writes the Cheese Shop Mysteries, featuring a cheese shop owner in Providence, Ohio.

As a girl, Daryl considered becoming a writer, but she was dissuaded by a seventh-grade teacher. It wasn't until she was in her twenties that she had the temerity to try her hand at writing again . . . for TV and screen. Why? Because she was an actress in Hollywood. A fun tidbit for mystery buffs: Daryl co-starred on *Murder, She Wrote* as well as other TV shows. As a writer, she created the format for the popular sitcom *Out of This World*. When she moved across the country with her husband, she returned to writing what she loved to read: mysteries and thrillers.

Daryl is originally from the Bay Area and graduated from Stanford University. She loves to cook, read, golf, swim, and garden. She also likes adventure and has been known to jump out of a perfectly good airplane. Here are a few of Daryl's lifelong mottos: perseverance will out; believe you can; never give up. She hopes they will become yours, as well.

To learn more about Daryl and her books, visit her website at DarylWoodGerber.com.

Printed in the USA
CPSIA information can be obtained
at www.ICGtesting.com
LVHW042206131123
763865LV00039B/611